Night Attack

Mortar fragments whined overhead, gouged the ground and ripped into human flesh. Claude and Billy Two had rolled close to Lee, and Claude shouted, "Lee, can you be number two for both of us?"

Lee nodded and chambered a round in her FAL and pulled the Starlite goggles over her eyes. Together they unleashed furious volleys at the enemy perched in the craggy dark peaks above them. The noise was deafening, but when the mortar barrage ended, it didn't bring silence.

The doctor in Lee found it hard to bear the groans and whimpers of the wounded. She wanted to shove the ammo at Claude and Billy Two and pull out the medical kit. But she couldn't. The end of the mortar barrage meant only one thing: the Chinese infantry was coming.

SOLDIERS OF BARRABAS

SOLDIERS OF BARRABAS

THE BARRABAS HEIST

JACK HILD

A GOLD EAGLE BOOK FROM

WORLDWIDE ®

TORONTO · NEW YORK · LONDON · PARIS
AMSTERDAM · STOCKHOLM · HAMBURG
ATHENS · MILAN · TOKYO · SYDNEY

First edition May 1989

ISBN 0-373-61630-9

Special thanks and acknowledgment to
Roland Green for his contribution to this work.

1

Like giant fangs, the peaks of the Gangdise Mountains bit at the southern sky. Shadows were swallowing the eastern slopes as the sun sank toward the western horizon.

Here on the Tibetan plateau, even a spring night brought cold. It could bring wind or even snow. Regiment Commander Yao—he refused to use the counterrevolutionary rank of "Colonel"—decided that it was time to finish with this superstitious fool of a Tibetan pilgrim and move on. With luck, his column might still reach the next Chinese garrison by nightfall.

Yao told himself that he was only concerned for the men of the column. Any other concern was unworthy of a man who had commanded a battalion of the People's Liberation Army in battle against the Vietnamese running dogs of Soviet imperialism.

He told himself this, looked at the fanged peaks again and once again knew the truth. He was too far from his native Shanghai. He would be farther still before he ended his hunt for Prince Su's rubies.

Anger at things he dared not name roughened Yao's voice as he turned back to the Tibetan pilgrim. The man didn't even blink, although some of his comrades backed away a little. They would have backed farther if Yao hadn't signaled to Company Commander Zhou.

"We're not done with you!" Zhou snapped. The platoon behind him held their assault rifles across their chests, blocking the Tibetans' retreat. They halted. Yao was glad to finally see fear in more than one pair of Tibetan eyes.

"Now," he said to the huge Khampa interpreter. "Ask him again if he has ever seen the cave we described."

The exchange seemed to take much longer than it should have. Not for the first time, Yao thought it ironic that his request to hunt Prince Su's rubies had been granted so quickly. If it had taken the usual year or so, he would have been able to learn Tibetan himself. As it was, he knew only the names of a few Tibetan foods, none of them fit for a civilized stomach. For anything else, he was at the mercy of this brooding giant of a Khampa outlaw, Ragpa Dapon.

"He says no," the interpreter concluded.

Yao frowned and looked at Commander Zhou. As quickly as an actor in the Peking Opera, the younger commander picked up his cue.

"It's possible that the cave has been covered by a glacier or an avalanche," Zhou said. "It might not have been visible when this man passed it."

"True," Yao said. His dismay wasn't entirely an act. Glaciers and avalanches were one more injury these cursed mountains inflicted on civilized men, like their treacherous slopes and their thin air that clawed at ears and lungs.

"Well, then," Yao continued. "I cannot ask that you tell me about what you have not seen. But I can ask you to listen to other pilgrims and travellers. Ask them what they have seen, and tell me. Doubtless some of them will have passed by the cave when it was in plain sight."

The pilgrim's reply needed no translation. Even if he hadn't been human, it would still have been an obscene refusal. Then he took a deep breath and launched into a tirade of incomprehensible words. The Khampa was silent, but Yao noticed that he was sweating in spite of the rising wind.

"Translate, you fool!"

"He says the Lord Buddha did not give men eyes to see through ice or rock. He is grateful for this. He wishes you good fortune in searching every mountainside in the Gangdise—"

"Enough!" Everyone, including Zhou, flinched at Yao's tone.

Yao unslung his Type 68 rifle. It was a point of pride with him to carry a fighter's weapons himself. It also saved time when he needed a rifle, for fighting or anything else.

"Science did better than the Lord Buddha," Yao said. "It gave us machines that can do what our eyes cannot. We will take those machines into the Gangdise. One day you will hear that they have found the cave. But you will never again be able to go on pilgrimage to urge the Lord Buddha to stop us."

The Tibetan heard the menace in Yao's voice and turned to run. Ragpa Dapon's hands clamped down on his shoulders and lifted him into the air like a puppet. Then four soldiers grabbed the Tibetan and spread-eagled him. He began to scream as two more pulled down his trousers.

"Silence him!" Yao shouted. The fool must think he was about to be castrated. That was an idea to try on some other stubborn mountain barbarian. Zhou pushed a handful of footcloths into the Tibetan's mouth, and his screams died.

Yao raised the rifle high overhead and smashed the butt down precisely on the pilgrim's kneecaps, first the left, then the right. Even through the cloth, the man screamed.

Yao raised the rifle again. An extra blow or two would do no harm.

"Look out, Commander!"

Zhou's pistol leaped from its holster and the Khampa's sword rasped out of its scabbard. The 7.62 mm pistol bullet struck the charging Tibetan first, tearing into his mouth and out the back of his head. Blood, brains, and fragments of skull spattered the people behind him.

Then the Khampa's sword swung down, and the mangled head leaped from its shoulders. The Tibetan fell almost on top of the crippled friend he'd tried to avenge. A pool of blood spread around both of them.

Yao slung his rifle and looked at a point just over the heads of the other pilgrims. "If you want your friends, take them. With or without them, you have five minutes to be out of our sight."

Under the muzzles of leveled assault rifles, the Tibetans collected their dead and wounded. The man with the shat-

tered knees had fainted, so he didn't scream when a woman
pulled the footcloths out of his mouth. In a final gesture of
defiance, the woman threw the cloths at Yao's feet. Dapon silently picked them up and wiped his sword clean with
them.

He didn't sheathe the sword until the Tibetans were a
hundred meters away. Then he slammed it so hard into the
silver-mounted scabbard that the hilt rang against the sil-
ver.

"You think I am too harsh with your people?" Yao
asked.

"I have no people," the Khampa replied. "So what you
do is between you and them." He turned his back and
strode away toward his usual place in the center of the column. Even the squad carrying the column's two Type 74
light machine guns stepped out of his way.

Yao wondered whether he'd been treated with contempt
or merely told the truth. It would help if Dapon would say
more than ten words at a time, except when he was inter-
preting. Even trying to get him drunk had failed to change
that. Commander Zhou had used up two bottles of liquor
and made himself sick for a whole day without even making the Khampa fall asleep!

The man had to be more than a barbarian outlaw. Otherwise he wouldn't carry such a sword, let alone speak five
Tibetan tongues, Mandarin, some Cantonese, and even a
little English. How much more, was probably something
Regiment Commander Yao Feng Zhi of the People's Liberation Army wasn't going to learn.

It hardly mattered, either. In a battle of wills, the will of
a Chinese must prevail over that of a mountain barbarian.
The will of one instructed in scientific dialectical material-
ism must prevail over the will of a demon-worshipper. The
will of a trained soldier must prevail over the will of a man
who still fought with a sword.

Yao told himself these things as he ordered the column
to move out. He knew that he might even have believed
them if he'd been a thousand kilometers farther from these
mountains.

2

The chauffeured green Mercedes swept silently out of the Lion Rock Tunnel and began the descent into the New Territories of Hong Kong.

Next to Walker Jessup, Mr. Lo tried to turn in his seat. He was a muscular young Chinese in a beautifully-cut three-piece gray suit that didn't entirely hide his shoulder holster.

Lo couldn't quite finish his turn. Walker Jessup currently weighed in at three hundred and twenty pounds. He took up quite a bit more than his share of the spacious leather-upholstered back seat.

"If you will look behind us, you can see Waiting for Husband Rock," Lo said.

Jessup turned his head and saw a rock jutting from the mountainside above the mouth of the tunnel. It did look rather like a woman carrying a child.

"The legend is that the wife of a Sung Dynasty nobleman who had been killed by the Mongols waited there every night for her husband's return. Eventually the gods took pity on her, released her soul to join her husband, and turned her body to stone."

Jessup nodded. "Like the widows' walks on New England houses."

"Widows' walks?"

"Sailing ship voyages lasted so long that a captain's wife could never be sure whether she was a widow or not. So they built the old seaport houses with walkways on the roof. The women could stand there and watch for their husbands' ships."

"Ah," Lo said. "I fear I never traveled as far as New England when I was in the United States. Only to California, on family business, and once to Las Vegas."

Jessup nodded again. "Family business" was probably the truth. He'd still bet a week of banquets at the Regent Hotel that not all of Lo's "family" were blood kin. It was written all over him that he was a high-ranking field man for the Triads, the Chinese answer to the Mafia.

Walker Jessup had been known as "The Fixer" in American intelligence circles since the Vietnam War. When nobody else could solve a problem by covert or any other kind of action, Jessup somehow always managed to come up with a "fix."

A few of those fixes had meant getting help from the Triads or their friends. Jessup struck those bargains with his eyes open, knowing that he was running up quite a tab with the Triads.

Now the Triads were about to present the bill. They had the Chinese sense of the sacredness of a debt, which made a Mafia-backed loan shark look wimpy. Jessup had known that the bill was on its way ever since Mr. Lo called on him at the Regent three days ago. The only question left was how big the bill was going to be.

No, that wasn't quite the only question. There was another.

Would Jessup be able to pay it? And that led to a third question.

If he couldn't pay it and said so, would he come back through the Lion Tunnel alive?

Ten miles into the New Territories, the Mercedes turned off the main road. As twilight settled over the countryside, the vehicle began a zigzag course along back roads. The first miles took them through modern suburban villas and even a few apartment complexes built to relieve the crowding in Kowloon and Central.

Then the modern world gave way to traditional Chinese farming villages, each surrounded by fields of vegetables. The fertilizer used on those fields was traditional, too. For the rest of the trip, the reek of human excrement challenged the air-conditioning and the rich smell of the leather upholstery.

At last the Mercedes climbed another hill, the night-soil stink faded, and a large brightly lighted house appeared ahead. The tires crunched on fine gravel, then the driver pulled to a stop outside a large bronze gate.

Two more Chinese, larger and younger versions of Mr. Lo, trotted out of the shadows on either side of the gate. Jessup mentally labeled them "local muscle." Literally, too—he'd bet they had black belts in forms of unarmed combat most Westerners had never even heard of.

One of them opened the door on Jessup's side. The Mercedes rocked noticeably as the Texan shifted his weight, then bounced as he slid out.

"This way, Mr. Jessup," Lo said. The gate was opening already as he led the way toward it. The muscle fell in behind Jessup, closing the gate on a view of the Mercedes backing away down the driveway.

Inside the gate was not just one house but a whole compound of them. Jessup counted at least half a dozen, with an elaborate garden laid out in the middle. One of the houses was presumably the home of the man he'd been brought to meet. The others might be for blood relatives; they would certainly hold enough guards and weapons to fight a small war. Not to mention opium, heroin, pirated films and records, jewels, counterfeit money, stolen industrial secrets, or whatever else the Triads were currently dealing in.

They would be dealing efficiently, too. That was one reason Jessup felt reasonably comfortable about paying his debt to them. He didn't demand scruples from the people he worked with. After half a lifetime spent in intelligence work, he knew that they were worth a hell of a lot less than efficiency!

Jessup's escorts literally led him down the garden path, over a bridge with an archway at either end crowned by stone lions. The garden was deceptively small; the whole thing would fit in the backyard of the average suburban Texas house. But it was laid out so that every time you thought you'd seen the end of it, another little patch of flowers or a carefully pruned bush popped into view.

A lot like Chinese boxes, Jessup realized. Or like the men waiting for him inside. At least the spring flowers were in bloom, and they didn't fertilize this garden with night soil. Jessup inhaled the perfumed air as the party reached a teakwood door to find it already opening.

"This way, Mr. Jessup," Lo said again. "Dr. Weng is at leisure to see you at once."

"I am honored," Jessup replied. He would have said the same thing if Dr. Weng had been tied up for the next two hours. At least now he could say it sincerely.

Maybe he'd even be back in Kowloon in time for a late dinner at the Spring Deer Restaurant. His mouth watered at the thought of their Peking duck.

JESSUP'S HOST faced him across a table with an ivory-and-ebony chessboard inlaid in the middle. He matched the description in Jessup's files of the man who used the name "Weng." Whether he was really a doctor, the file didn't say. Compared to the Triads, the Mafia were a bunch of blabbermouths.

It did say something about Weng's position, the fact that he was meeting with Jessup alone. He had to be up toward the top to be allowed to handle negotiations like this solo.

Or could he be cutting a deal without his colleagues' knowledge? Jessup ran a finger around the inside of a collar suddenly soaked with fresh sweat. The Triads had only one reply to that sort of treachery. Their reply might not stop short of Jessup himself. It certainly wouldn't stop short of Jessup's people in Hong Kong.

The fat Texan decided to play this one by ear. Ideally he wanted both good relations with the Triads and an intact network in Hong Kong. Hong Kong was already too good a listening post for hearing what went on in China. With Peking scheduled to start moving in within a generation, it would get a lot better.

Jessup also knew how seldom intelligence work let anyone achieve anything like the ideal solution. That was why he played by ear, and he knew that particular part of his body was still in good shape. Fat didn't affect it.

"Mr. Jessup, it is a pleasure to see you so prosperous." Weng's English was fluent, with an upper-class accent. His handshake hinted that he'd kept himself in shape, although he didn't appear to be much less than sixty.

"I don't see you having to scrimp and save, either, Doctor." Jessup waved a hand around the room. Every part of the wall that wasn't covered with antique hangings was hidden by teakwood display cases of jade.

"Are you a lover of jade, then?"

"Not quite that, Doctor, though I did pick up a few pieces while I was in Vietnam, and helped evacuate some antiques."

"A wise step. Truly, the Communists have little appreciation of beauty. You and I are more civilized. Perhaps you would care to examine my modest collection?"

This was Chinese manners—delaying serious business as well as a demonstration of who was boss here. Jessup's stomach rumbled as his dreams of the Spring Deer's duck blew away.

At least he had one consolation. Good jade really was lovely stuff, and any museum in the world would spring five million dollars for Weng's "modest collection."

A second consolation followed the hour-long tour of the jade collection. Two hefty servants brought in a serving cart loaded with *dim sum*, the succulent little Chinese dumplings with a dozen different fillings, and a tray of bottles.

The servants had to reload the cart twice before Jessup stopped stuffing himself. They'd have had to do it a third time if it hadn't been a business occasion. Enough good food made Walker Jessup euphoric, the way drugs or liquor did other people. He couldn't afford that tonight, even if he did dream of another helping of the dumplings with the prawn and spring onion filling.

Not that he was in any physical danger tonight. He'd been Weng's guest; the man wouldn't violate the laws of hospitality that far. The danger was being so stuffed with *dim sum* that he couldn't think clearly!

"Your hospitality is beyond what I would have dared expect," Jessup said, as the last dumpling settled into the last free corner of his stomach.

"You do not do yourself justice, Mr. Jessup. My colleagues and I have much cause to be grateful to you. Not, perhaps, as much as you have to be grateful to us. But certainly enough to justify generosity to a guest, even if good manners did not require it."

"Gratitude is like the smell of the flowers in your garden," Jessup said, sipping the last of a glass of Wan Fu wine. "No one can deny its existence, yet to find a way of measuring it may elude the wisest of men."

Jessup's grin was intended to send a message—now that he'd eaten dinner, he could toss fancy phrases back and forth as long as his host, and ten minutes longer.

Weng read the message correctly. His own smile tightened. "Then perhaps you would care to discuss a small service you can render my colleagues and myself."

"No harm ever came of a discussion, Doctor. It cures ignorance, if nothing else."

"Certainly ignorance is deadlier than any disease. So I propose to dispel some of it. Have you ever heard of Prince Su's rubies?"

"I can't say that I have."

"They were property of the Imperial Chinese government, sent to safety with a provincial governor in the 1860s during the great Taiping Rebellion. Since the Imperial government had some difficulty reasserting its authority afterward, the rubies were never returned to the Imperial coffers.

"The great-grandson of the governor still had the rubies in his possession in the 1920s, during the time of the warlords. For safety he sent them into Tibet. Then he died fighting against the Japanese. He left behind some information about where the rubies were hidden, but not enough to justify our searching for them."

The two heavyweight servants returned. This time the cart carried tea, glazed fruits, and an expensive cassette recorder. Weng poured tea for both men, smiled at Jessup's refusal of any dessert, then waited until the servants left.

"However, the rest of the information seems to have been collected by one Colonel Yao, of the Chinese People's Liberation Army. It was brought to us by a defector, one Major Gui, who ran afoul of Colonel Yao's ambitions. The colonel, it appears, has a long memory for those who fail him so as to endanger his rise."

Jessup hoped Weng didn't notice how he'd jerked like a fish on a hook at the mention of the name "Yao." A captain—or "company commander"—of PLA Intelligence had advised the North Vietnamese so well that a couple of Jessup's fixes hadn't taken.

Jessup had a few debts to settle with Yao. So did a prematurely white-haired ex-Special Forces officer named Nile Barrabas, who'd helped Jessup out with more than a few of his fixes since they both left Vietnam on the last chopper from the American Embassy. *If* this was the same Yao.

Weng turned on the recorder. Jessup listened to a heavily-accented voice telling the story of Colonel Yao's obsession with finding the Su rubies. A coup like that would be worth a lot on his way to the top in Chinese military intelligence, and even beyond.

In the past few months, Colonel Yao had put together a complete description of the cave in the Gangdise Mountains of Tibet where the jewels were hidden. Now he was on his way to Tibet, with a free hand to go where he wanted and do what he pleased to find the rubies.

The voice faded into the hissing of the tape, and Weng turned off the recorder. "How long that free hand will last, of course, we cannot be sure. He is not without enemies. But it may last long enough for Yao to find the rubies."

"I suppose they're worth a good deal?" Jessup knew that the effort to keep his voice steady was worth making. He hoped it would be successful. This had to be the same Yao—and for damned sure he wasn't without enemies!

"If the descriptions we have are remotely accurate, they cannot be worth less than four hundred million dollars."

That was a pretty good chunk of the world's total supply of gem-quality rubies. Peking would slobber all over anybody who brought them that much hard currency.

The Triads would also have their uses for it. Jessup suspected those uses were connected with the impending transfer of Hong Kong from British to Chinese rule.

Four hundred million dollars could finance the evacuation of the Hong Kong Triads, letting them set up very comfortably elsewhere—Singapore, maybe, or even San Francisco. It could also be a nice fat bribe to Peking to let them continue business as usual in Hong Kong. That much money could corrupt angels, let alone politicians.

"You are doubtless curious as to what your connection with the Su rubies might be?" Weng asked. His smile didn't reach his eyes.

"I was curious, but I think I've got a hunch about the answer now. You'd like a little help getting the rubies out of Tibet ahead of Colonel Yao."

"I hope it will only be 'a little help,'" Weng said. "In the face of a man like Colonel Yao, however, more may be required."

I hope to kiss a pig it will be, Jessup thought while he cast a benign look at the good doctor. "If it is, how am I supposed to produce it? Remember, Doctor, I'm not a government official anymore."

"I am sure that some of your friends still in the intelligence services will be able to help. At the moment we have Major Gui under our protection. If we receive help from those who can give it, we will be happy to make the major available to our friends."

A major in PLA Intelligence might be a gold mine. A chance to pick his brains was certainly a king-size bribe. It was also one that would obviously be offered to somebody else if Jessup didn't take it.

He gulped tea and considered the best way of agreeing without ending the bargaining, which Weng was clearly enjoying. Spoiling his fun might screw up the whole deal, or at least get less favorable terms.

"As you said, facing Colonel Yao may require extensive resources. Not just intelligence, either. People on the ground in Tibet, preferably with guns in their hands."

"It is my understanding that your resources also include people in the, ah, 'mercenary' community. If your colleagues cannot be persuaded to use their resources, would you be prepared to use yours?"

The reward for this would be first crack at Major Gui. Jessup's people in Hong Kong or anywhere else the Triads operate would be left alone. And just to ice the cake, he'd have a chance to pay that bastard Yao everything he'd owed the man since Vietnam!

Now, he wondered, how to up the price a little more?

"Mercenaries are a mixed lot, Doctor," Jessup said judiciously, filling his teacup again. "The ones who come cheap couldn't execute this mission. The good ones might not be available."

"Would they be more available if we provided all the intelligence we had on the rubies?"

Point for Mrs. Jessup's little boy! "The good ones don't like suicide runs. I expect it would help a lot. Does your intelligence include anything besides what Major Gui brought over?"

"You will be agreeably surprised at how much we have to offer."

"Then I can promise to make the best effort I can, with all the resources I have available, to get the rubies out of Tibet." Jessup grinned over the rim of his teacup. "I think you will also be agreeably surprised at how much I can do."

Unless he already knows about Nile Barrabas and his team, in which case we are in deep shit. However, let's not spoil digesting a good dinner by worrying about what can't be helped.

"Out of Tibet, and into our hands," Weng said.

"Make sure that your hands are open and ready, then," Jessup said. "My best efforts have been pretty damned good, all things considered."

"If we did not know this, Mr. Jessup, we would hardly have asked you here tonight," Weng said. "May I offer you any further hospitality, or do you wish to return to your hotel?''

"I'd rather you whistled up the Mercedes," Jessup said, lurching to his feet. "If we're racing Colonel Yao, the faster out of the gate the better."

"I could hardly agree more," Weng replied.

THE MERCEDES GLIDED out of the Kowloon end of the Lion Tunnel. The mist had lifted, and the lights blazed from both sides of Victoria Harbor. It looked as if somebody had upended hundreds of giant boxes of jewels—not just rubies, but emeralds, diamonds, sapphires, in every imaginable shade.

It was spectacular, yet so fragile. How much of it would survive the heavy hand of Peking over the next half century?

Probably not much, Jessup thought. Five and a half million people could be actually weaker than Nile Barrabas and the five other SOBs who'd be going to Tibet.

It wasn't just that they were a bigger and slower target, either. How many of those five and a half million were most alive when they faced death? All six SOBs were like that, and it made them pretty damned hard to kill.

It didn't make them immortal. They'd lost comrades since Nile Barrabas put them together to help Walker Jessup with his fixes. All six had scars, and sooner or later there would be a mission they wouldn't come back from.

Was this the time? Maybe. But even if it was, Colonel Yao's life was about to get a lot more interesting—in the way the Chinese used the word in their traditional curse:

"May you live in interesting times."

3

Dr. Leona Hatton stared out of the floor-to-ceiling window of the Manhattan penthouse. The rain had stopped, and the lights of the city blazed in their hundred colors.

The lights rose to a climax in the twin towers of the World Trade Center. On the far side of one tower, Lee knew that there was a patched hole. She and her teammates of the Soldiers of Barrabas had made that hole with a TOW missile. That was only one of the weapons they'd used, fighting and beating an American general either so mad or so ambitious that he would kill thousands of Americans to win the power to "save" the rest.

Did it matter whether General Goetz had been mad or merely ambitious? When Lee Hatton was a new resident, she was sure such questions were vitally important. Now, with years of experience as a mercenary warrior added to her medical training, she wondered.

In the glass beside her, a reflection was outlined against the darkness of the night outside. Without turning, she smiled.

"Hi, Claude."

She saw Claude Hayes's reflection smile back. "Dollar for your thoughts, Lee."

"A dollar?"

"Well, you know what inflation has done to the penny. I figured you can't have a thought that cheap."

"You'd be surprised."

"Any thought about Geoff Bishop is worth a lot more."

The mention of her dead lover, the SOBs' teammate and pilot, made Lee whirl, halfway between anger and surprise. "Been learning mind reading from Billy Two?" Shocked somewhat by her emotional response, Lee paused, then continued. "Sorry, I didn't mean to snap your head off. Or joke about Billy."

"I was out of line anyway, Lee. But you're right. I don't know what really happened to that wild Indian. One of these days I'm going to find out, even if I have to go through the rituals myself."

"Let me go first, Claude. I'm a doctor. Maybe I'd learn more from the experience."

"Or survive it better. Billy once said that not everybody who looks on the face of Hawk Spirit is found worthy to use that wisdom. He kind of hinted that the unworthy don't always come back."

Billy Two was William Starfoot II, son of a wealthy Oklahoma family of Osage Indians. He'd rebelled against their comfortable life, and that rebellion had taken him into the Marines, then to join up with the SOBs. The other SOBs had followed pretty much the same path; living and dead, they were all square pegs who wouldn't be shoved into round holes.

Billy Two had gone farther. In the aftermath of a torture session in the USSR, where he'd been driven beyond human endurance, he'd explored the traditional shamanistic lore of his people, and reached their Hawk Spirit—or so he said. Whatever he'd reached, he now had the ability to do things that by normal standards seemed physiologically impossible.

"Want to blow this party, Claude?" Lee asked. "I've already had three propositions, one of them from the hostess."

"I've had four. No sweat. But there's somebody who just came in who asked if you were Lee Hatton. Said you were a med school classmate of his."

Lee's mind made an intuitive leap. It was the same kind of leap that made her so formidable in unarmed combat. It let her build a picture of her opponent's strengths and weaknesses from the first few passes. Now it started little warning bells chiming.

"What did he look like?"

"I'd say Eurasian. Western dress, but at a guess half-Chinese, half-Caucasian. Late thirties, about five nine, looks like he misses every other meal. Fluent English, with an American—"

"Did he give his name? No, never mind. I know who it is."

"He's on the level?"

"Absolutely." Giving in to another intuitive leap, Lee added, "But we'd better consider that we're back on the job. I trust Dr. Gonpo completely. But he may be here on some business, have people on his tail we don't want to meet."

"What kind of people? Would they stand out in Harlem?"

"Like a candle in a cave."

"Okay, Lee. You collect our Eurasian doctor and make our regrets to the hostess. I'll arrange wheels and make a couple of phone calls. Then we can split." From Hayes's tone and the way he now held his muscular six-foot frame, Lee could tell he'd gone to the same alert as she had.

She didn't waste time hoping the alert was unnecessary. The last letter she'd had from Chopel Richard Gonpo was two years ago, apologizing for being so long in writing, but adding:

"I fear that my travel is going to be limited to urgent matters for some time. I truly wish I had half the importance the Chinese ascribe to me, considering the number of men they had on my trail the last time I was in London."

That was Gonpo's usual modesty. Son of an American Air Force officer who had been a West Point classmate of Lee's father General Hatton, and a Tibetan woman, the doctor saw himself as a Tibetan. He had also dedicated himself to the struggle for his country's freedom from Communist Chinese rule. Few in the Dalai Lama's government-in-exile knew more about what was being done to bring that day closer.

Lee spared a moment to hope that she could get through the night without any *conspicuous* fighting. The New York authorities frowned on having large quantities of real estate demolished or littered with bodies.

FROM DOWNSTAIRS, Diana Ross doing "Touch Me in the Morning" faded away. Something by Marvin Gaye replaced it. Claude Hayes's trained ears told him that the dining room was closing down, with the rest of the action moving to the bar for the night.

Footsteps climbed the stairs. Bull Donovan loomed in the doorway of the private dining room. In spite of his Irish name, he was bigger and blacker than Hayes. His broad face with the nose broken in the Super Bowl a few years back showed through the glasses and bottle on the tray he was carrying.

"Thought you people might want a refill to celebrate being right."

Hayes's eyes met Lee Hatton's. She nodded. "How many?"

"Two. Don't know if they were Tong, Triad, Chicom, Taiwan, or Straits. We rolled them, so we got their IDs. They'll be fake, but you want me to check out what kind of fake?"

"Not worth it. They'll have cutouts all along the line. You'd just get them interested in you. You don't owe me that much, Bull."

"I got a wife and kids because of you, Claude baby. Don't go telling me what I don't owe you."

"Don't sweat it, Bull. Something tells me this won't be the last time I drop around. Dump our friends some place where they'll wake up in the morning. Between rat bites and loss of face, they'll be slow reporting to their boss. By then we should have things arranged so we can handle any reinforcements ourselves."

Donovan shrugged. "If you say so, brother."

"I do say so."

Hayes and Donovan exchanged palm slaps and the restaurant's owner headed back downstairs. Hayes turned back to his companions to discover Dr. Gonpo looking at him as if he was a particularly interesting patient.

"What's your diagnosis, Doc?"

"That you are someone who can help us."

"Fine. Now tell me what I can help you with. That's always useful at this stage."

"Mr. Hayes, I sought Lee Hatton out because I had heard she knew people of a certain profession. I begin to think the tales were true."

"What profession?"

"Mercenaries."

Hayes added ice to his drink. A closet teetotaler, he had a number of techniques for spinning out a single drink over a whole evening. A well-filled ice bucket was one of them.

"Supposing I was a merc, what would you want to hire me for?"

As the story unfolded, Claude Hayes had a strong feeling that Gonpo had come from Cloud-Cuckoo Land, not from Tibet. Not that the Tibetans weren't pretty weird, in Hayes's opinion, with their reincarnated Dalai Lama and everything that went with him.

Hayes stamped on the feeling. He'd come a long way from a respectable middle-class Detroit suburb. The way included black terrorism, a Southern chain gang, the Navy, several wars in Africa, and now the SOBs. He'd learned that *nothing* was too weird to be completely impossible.

"So you want to arrange for some mercs to pull these rubies out of Tibet before the Chinese get their hands on them," Hayes summarized.

"Yes, and the sooner the better. The man who seeks them is not an opponent to be despised."

"Glad you see it that way. Despising your opponent is the shortest way to losing before you start fighting. I got a couple of problems, though. First, why can't you let the Indians help?"

"Do you really not know, or are you merely testing my knowledge?"

Lee frowned at her classmate's tone, but Hayes grinned. "I guess I asked for that. Yeah, the Indians are too penetrated by Soviet intelligence to keep the secret. Besides, even if they didn't tip off Moscow, they'd probably want a cut themselves. Like about eight percent.

"We probably will have to give the Indians something to keep them out of our hair," Hayes went on. "And if we want to purchase weapons locally, it has to be more than a token. Same goes for the Nepalese."

Hayes didn't know what arrangements the Fixer might be able to make, but he thought they had better plan conservatively. That was always the best way, when planning was possible at all. Sometimes, of course, all you could do was shoot and pray, like the time the SOBs pulled a Soviet scientist out of the gulag.

"I do not imagine there will be a problem with paying anyone once the rubies are in our hands," Gonpo said. "But I have heard of mercenaries that you always want money in advance."

"You heard right."

"We are not without resources. Also, we will make available to you all the... intelligence... we have on the location of the rubies. I am sure you will wish to move as quickly as possible once you are in Tibet."

"Is the Pope a Catholic?" Hayes said. His feet and his guts were telling him to start moving fast right now, out the door and to a secure phone for a call to the Fixer. Every minute gave the bad guys more of a chance to bring up reinforcements. Bull's people were tough and street-smart, but would that be enough?

Probably not. But he had to play the hard-nosed freelance merc for a while longer, otherwise Dr. Gonpo might guess a little too much about the exact nature of Lee's contacts. He probably wouldn't object to working with American intelligence, but Hayes would very much object to his knowing even that much about the SOBs.

Rule One of SOB Security was, "God isn't on the need-to-know list."

"This is going to be expensive even before we start for Tibet," Hayes went on. "It's also going to be hairy. What about twenty-five thousand up front, the same each month, and fifty thousand for any KIA's next of kin or anybody who gets hit?''

"What about asking us to move Chomolungma to New York?'' the doctor said. "It would be as easy.''

"It might improve the scenery, too,'' Hayes said. The idea of Mount Everest squatting on Staten Island made him chuckle. He slipped another ice cube into his glass and looked at Lee.

"I think this is going to take a while. How about you run down and ask Bull for some of his private stock coffee? You might want to ring up Eli's Pharmacy too, just in case we need something stronger.''

Lee nodded. "Eli's Pharmacy'' was one of the current codes for a call to the Fixer's New York message drop. The Fixer didn't have quite the men and money he'd had a few years ago, but he had enough to make a difference.

Hayes watched Lee's slim figure disappear gracefully down the stairs and reflected once again what a damned lucky man Geoff Bishop had been. He'd had not only one hell of a good fighting partner like the rest of them, but one hell of a fine woman.

As for Dr. Gonpo, Hayes considered that the man was about to pay the first installment of the SOBs' fees. He had just been volunteered to be bait.

THE MAN WHO WAS POSTED on the corner looked like a street-fighting version of Bull Donovan. He didn't blink at the odd trio suddenly appearing out of the darkness.

"Anybody messing around with the car?'' Hayes scanned the pearl-gray Audi rented for the drive up to Harlem after several changes of taxi and subway.

"Not yours, there—'' the driver paused to point "—somebody parked that Chevy about half an hour ago. The driver was fiddling around under it for a couple minutes.'' The man pointed. "He split when I went and kind of loomed over him.''

Lee Hatton studied the Chevy. She couldn't see anything wrong with it, but its location triggered her intuition. They'd parked the Audi down a little cul-de-sac so that one guard could keep an eye on every approach to it.

Now they had a problem. They'd have to go right past that Chevy to reach the street, practically scrape the paint off it. Lee exchanged looks with Hayes.

Hayes reached into his attaché case and took out two small black plastic boxes. Separately the two boxes held nothing that would be out of the ordinary for an optical-goods salesman, his current cover identity.

Together they made one of the most sophisticated miniature night-vision scopes around.

Hayes took his turn at studying the Chevy, shook his head, then went to work on the rooftops. On the third building he stopped, adjusted the scope and looked again. Then he made an urgent hand signal.

They tried to look casual as they walked out of the cul-de-sac. When they'd rounded the corner and Lee had stopped mentally hunching her shoulders in anticipation of a bullet between them, she shot a questioning look at Hayes.

"Somebody on the roof, with line of sight to both our car and that Chevy."

"Lot of people go up on the roofs," the guard said. "Take a blanket and some foxy company—"

"It's been raining, and this guy's got a walkie-talkie and what looks like a rifle."

"Oh, shit," the guard said. "Guess I screwed up."

"Maybe not," Lee said. "Or maybe you can help us get things unscrewed again. Claude, what do you think we've got here? My guess is they want Chopel in one piece, or at least alive. So our friend's supposed to snipe any guards, then call in reinforcements. Probably the driver of that Chevy."

"And the Chevy?"

"Backup. Command-detonated bomb to take out the Audi if the sniping doesn't work. Sloppy but quick."

"Want to bet those two guys Bull's people coldcocked were the rest of the reinforcements?" Hayes said. "Now if

I know any of the organizations these people are likely to be working for, the driver's not going to skip out.

"But he's going to be one mighty nervous Chinaman. If he's in contact with his buddy on the roof, we've got *two* mighty nervous Chinamen. I think it's time we made Mr. Up on the Roof a little bit more nervous."

"Which of us goes up?" Lee asked. "I'm lighter."

"Yeah, but I'm black. That makes me just part of the scenery around here, baby. Besides, I spent a lot of time on this kind of roof, back when.

"Oh, yeah. You and Dr. Gonpo might want to switch clothes. You're about the same size. I figure Up on the Roof's going to go by size and maybe clothing. No way he can make out faces."

"Good luck, Claude."

"Wish Up on the Roof the luck, Lee. *He's* the mother who is going to need it."

Hayes sprang to the roof of an Oldsmobile parked under the bottom section of a fire escape. Another leap and he'd gripped the rungs. Rusty hinges screamed in protest as the section slammed down on the roof of the Oldsmobile, bashing it in, clear across.

Hayes looked at the damage. "Damned cheap imported parts." Then he was vanishing up the fire escape as swiftly and silently as a panther on the hunt.

Lee started unbuttoning her jacket, ignoring the guard. Gonpo frowned. "Turn your back, my friend," he told the guard.

"He can't do that without taking his eyes off the Audi and the roof," Lee said. She handed her jacket to the doctor and started unzipping her skirt.

Gonpo held the jacket at arm's length. "You are not as you were, Lee."

"If I was, I'd be dead. Modesty doesn't have a lot of survival value." The skirt followed the jacket, and the blouse joined it. The half slip was the last item, leaving Lee in bra, panty hose, and shoulder holster.

"Come on, Chopel, I won't look at you if you mind. But I'm darned if I'll stand around here in my underwear until I catch a cold!"

Gonpo managed a smile, then began unbuckling his belt.

HAYES CLIMBED the five stories to the roof in four minutes. He could have gone faster if he hadn't wanted to be quiet, but he was taking his own advice about not despising an opponent. The sniper could be right at home in the tar-paper-and-ducting world of New York's roofs.

From behind a chimney, Hayes studied the battleground. His opponent hadn't moved, but the rifle now looked like an M-16. There were worse sniper weapons. Also better ones, particularly if the guy used full rock and roll.

Hayes did a low crawl across the first roof, outflanked an air shaft to reach the second and came to a three-foot gap between the second and third. He peered down and got a fine view of a couple wearing out their mattress. The woman was on top and by any standards a lot more worth looking at than her partner. She also seemed to be having one hell of a good time.

Hayes allowed himself a whole five seconds to appreciate the scenery, then studied the alley walls for an alternative to jumping. At the street end another fire escape reached up to the next roof. Hayes crawled until he was opposite it, rolled over the edge and swung out until his feet hooked the railing of the escape. Seconds later he was on the next to last roof, drawing his gun.

Hayes was packing a Ruger Blackhawk .357 with a four-inch barrel and Pachmayr grips. Not a perfect weapon for this kind of work, but concealable on somebody of Hayes's size. Also, it was registered in the ID he was currently carrying, which might save just a little bit of trouble if the police showed up before any of the Fixer's more useful people.

In this kind of business, the police were good guys only when they and nobody else stood between the real bad guys and your personal private ass.

Now the real fun began. The roof sprouted TV antennas, ducts, chimneys, skylights and rotting pigeon coops. Every one of them looked to be in just the right place for bumping into and warning the sniper.

Hayes eased past them all. No way this sniper could be as alert as the Charlies, and Hayes had taken out VC and NVA sentries so regularly his buddies made bets on his nightly score. Pretty soon he'd be in range. Then one shot to take the guy down but not kill him. That kind of trick shooting Hayes normally left to movie cowboys, but tonight they wanted a prisoner.

A car bomb going off right behind a man's friends can spoil his appetite for breakfast. Being in the dark about who is chasing him can ruin lunch and dinner as well.

Hayes looked for a position where he could take his time aiming. He'd just spotted it when a car pulled up at the street end of the cul-de-sac.

The sniper rolled, bringing his rifle up. The guard from Wild Bull's sprinted onto the street, waving his arms. The car burned rubber backing up as the sniper let fly. Hayes and the sniper fired together; Hayes missed, the guard went down but rolled under cover. Hayes's suddenly announced presence kept the sniper from firing again.

Hot from ricocheting, the sniper's bullet punched into somebody's gas tank. Yellow light flooded the cul-de-sac. Hayes saw that the car had left behind two passengers. One looked like a billiard ball on legs, even in a fancy suit. The other was a head taller and half as wide, with close-cropped white hair.

Walker Jessup and Nile Barrabas had come, either instead of, or in addition to, the hired help.

"Down!" Hayes yelled. His next shot at least sent the radio skittering out of the sniper's reach. Jessup and Barrabas unlimbered Browning Hi-Powers with shoulder stocks and let fly. The only problem was, they thought Hayes was the sniper.

At least he was close enough to the real thing that the bullets kept both of them down. Except that the sniper didn't need to shoot back to finish his job. All he had to do was get to that goddamned radio and tell the bomb, "Okay, time to blow!"

Hayes couldn't get a clear shot at the sniper without exposing himself. He put another slug into the radio, then the sniper reached it, and Hayes again yelled "Down!" The bomb went off.

Flying fragments scoured the cul-de-sac. Hayes saw both men go down, Jessup on top. Behind him he heard windows tinkle and crash and the woman scream, half in ecstasy, half in fear.

The sniper was rolling back toward the roof edge, gripping his M-16. What Hayes intended as a head shot hit the sniper in the shoulder. The M-16 plunged over the edge of the roof.

"Freeze!" Hayes shouted. Just maybe they'd have a prisoner after all.

The man lurched to one side as his knees gave out. He struck the low edge of the roof, overbalanced and fell.

"Shit!" Hayes said.

Then he said it again as bullets went *spung* and *wheet* around him. "Applegate, Applegate!" he shouted, as he ducked.

The code name stopped the shooting. "Is that you, Claude?" Nile Barrabas said.

"Alive and breathing, no thanks to you. Here I go giving up a prisoner to save your asses and what happens? You damned near shoot mine off!"

"'Damned near' is good enough," Walker Jessup put in. "Now how about getting your ass down from that roof?"

"On the way," Hayes responded, and joined the others quickly to assess the situation.

Bull Drummond's man had a through-and-through shoulder wound. He was mad enough to have a stroke, but it wasn't going to kill him any other way. Lee Hatton had bandaged the shoulder and was examining Walker Jessup's wide back by the time Hayes reached the ground.

"Most of the fragments went over you," she told Jessup. "There's still enough so that either you go to a hospital—"

"No way!" Jessup snapped.

"—or we go someplace where I can give you an antibiotic and a good going over with forceps. Either way, you can plan on sleeping on your stomach for a few days."

"I've got a safehouse lined up for your Tibetan friend. That okay?"

"How safe?"

"Would you believe a complete medical kit? Also, an honest Mafia Don as landlord?"

"Honest?"

"When you buy him, he stays bought."

Hayes was kneeling, scribbling something in a notebook. Then he tore the page out, picked the trunk lock on the Oldsmobile with the dented roof and shoved the paper into the spare tire well.

"What was that all about?" Barrabas asked.

"A number where the guy can call in to get his roof fixed at my expense. I dinged it by accident."

"Claude, you are the last of the old-school gentlemen—" Lee began, pulling out a bottle of painkillers.

Distant sirens interrupted her. "Or the first of a new breed," Hayes said. Jessup's car pulled up and both left-side doors flew open.

Jessup flipped the cap off the bottle and popped a handful of painkillers into his mouth. "You'll be the next SOB to go to jail if we spend much more time jawing. Let's move it, people."

Getting everybody into the car made Lee think of an old-fashioned Volkswagen-stuffing contest. She found herself jammed up tight against the driver, so close that his right elbow jabbed her left breast every time he turned the wheel. She twisted, squirmed and finally resigned herself to reaching Staten Island with a few extra bruises.

The screech of tires drowned out the approaching sirens. The sirens finally faded as the driver took them through Harlem's maze of alleys and back streets, then west toward the George Washington Bridge. As they hit the bridge's approaches, Lee remembered the two tails Bull Donovan's guards had taken out.

"How long before we get a clue on who's after us this time?"

"Tonight," Jessup said.

"Our tails are going to talk that fast?"

"Not exactly. I—"

"What do you mean, 'not exactly'?" Barrabas asked. His light tone didn't hide his anger.

"Turns out the Chevy driver got to his friends before my people did. He shot Bull's guard, and all three of the heathen Chinese hauled ass."

"Great." Hayes put a world of disgust into the one word.

"Not quite. The guard's going to pull through, and I've got a few clues about who's after whom."

In silence, they rolled toward the east tower of the bridge.

4

Nile Barrabas pulled a bottle of Corona out of the six-pack and passed the rest around the circle of SOBs. They were all there in the library of the safehouse, except for Billy Two. With assessing eyes, Barrabas took stock of his crew again.

Liam O'Toole, ex-IRA, ex-Army, battered, boozy, and an explosives expert who could, if you asked him, wire a charge to sing "The Star Spangled Banner" as it went off.

Alex Nanos, ex-SEAL, ex-Coast Guard, equally good at diving, small-boat handling, and chasing women.

Claude Hayes, the gentleman. Another ex-SEAL and expert diver, as well as a veteran of both Southern chain gangs and African wars of liberation.

Lee Hatton, the lady. First-class doctor and first-class martial artist both.

William Starfoot II—Billy Two—was on his way to New York from a trip out west. "To survey the sacred lands of the Osage" was what he'd called it. Barrabas would have liked to know just how Starfoot—ex-Marine, martial-arts and guerrilla expert—was carrying out the survey. Was there an answer that didn't begin with believing in the Hawk Spirit?

Oh yes, himself. Concise summary of Nile Barrabas: ex-U.S. Army, Vietnam veteran—ex-Special Forces colonel, to be specific—jack of all the warrior's trades and master of quite a few, professional survivor.

In the middle of the circle of leather loungers, Walker Jessup. The Fixer, who'd saved Barrabas's life that night in Vietnam when a head wound turned his hair from dark to mostly white. The Fixer, one of the best brains in American intelligence, even if his body was weighted down with fat.

Jessup sat upright in another lounger. He was bare to the waist except for the bandages Lee Hatton had applied to the fragment wounds in his back. Below the waist he wore only a yellow sheet wrapped like a sarong. He reminded Barrabas of a poorly carved, battle-scarred temple Buddha.

Jessup lifted his head like a dog hearing a whistle too high-pitched for human ears. His hand tapped the arm of his chair three times. The door at the far end of the library slid open, and the driver of their getaway car staggered in with an armload of pizza boxes.

"Thanks, Gene," Jessup said. The Corona had reached him now. He pulled out the last two bottles. "Grab one for yourself. Anything except the anchovies. Then ice down some more beer and leave us be."

"Okay, chief."

Gene obviously knew Jessup's appetite. He tucked one pizza under his arm, then gave the huge Texan one-third of the rest. When the man was gone, Jessup looked up from opening a pizza and said, "Any questions?"

Hayes glared. "Yeah. How come two of my friend's people nearly got killed tonight? Not to mention my ballet act on that roof. You said you were going to give us a few clues."

Jessup's answer came out around a mouthful of anchovy-and-pepperoni pizza.

"It's pretty obvious what they were after. Dr. Gonpo as a hostage for the rubies. Somebody didn't want to simply rely on my reputation for paying my debts. They wanted to provide me with, ah, an incentive."

"You expect us to put the rubies in Weng's hands after that?" Hayes said. His tone lowered the temperature in the room about five degrees.

"The Triads don't always act together," Jessup said. "They do more often than not, when they're dealing with non-Chinese. But for something this big, I suspect they're going to be scrambling. If Dr. Weng had anything to do with tonight's nonsense, I'd be surprised.''

"I wouldn't be," Lee Hatton snapped. "It doesn't make any difference, either. You're asking us to repay your debt to the Hong Kong Triads by letting them turn the rubies into drugs, salaries for their hitmen, and God knows what else. *Tibetan* rubies."

"Chinese rubies, at least originally," Jessup corrected her. "Incidentally, you aren't the only one who objects to paying off the Triads with the rubies. The Senator thinks they ought to go to Taiwan."

"Seriously?" Barrabas asked.

"More of a preference. He's not going to push it."

"You can't believe how grateful we are," Hatton said, and Barrabas threw her a warning look.

The Senator had been chairman of the secret Congressional committee that gave Walker Jessup his original orders: Form a small team of elite veterans for covert operations in defense of American interests, a team likely to succeed but easy to repudiate if they failed.

That was a while ago. Now the Senator was no longer in the chain of command as much as he'd been. Unless he raised a stink, the SOBs could ignore him. They preferred to do that, since the Senator had once put out a termination order on them to cover his tracks. The SOBs hadn't been terminated, but they hadn't forgotten, either.

Where the chain of command led now, Nile Barrabas had some educated guesses. He kept them to himself. It didn't matter who proposed a mission, as long as he and the SOBs could turn it down. Besides, Barrabas had to admit that he almost trusted Walker Jessup, at least half the time.

It was beginning to look like one of the other times.

"I don't care if the Emperor of the Galaxy puts in a claim!" Hatton snapped. "The Tibetans *need* the rubies."

"Ah, the ideals of youth," Jessup bantered.

Lee made a classic obscene gesture they'd all picked up from Alex Nanos. "You talk as if ideals were a disability. Let me tell you something, Mr. Jessup. They're better than being three hundred pounds of pure sleaze like you!"

"Dr. Hatton, I was in this business when you were a dewy-eyed intern. There's not a goddamned thing you can teach me about sleaze, so don't waste your breath trying. And don't talk to me like that again. You want to be listed as a security risk?"

Barrabas bounced to his feet. "Jessup, one more threat and you don't have any SOBs."

"Okay. Then who's going to protect Dr. Gonpo? You think you can keep the Triads and everybody else off him by yourselves? Dr. Hatton, have you ever seen a woman worked over by a Triad interrogator?"

"Jessup—" Barrabas began.

"I'm not threatening. I'm stating facts. The Triads have dealt themselves into this game. We can't get out of it, so we're better off trying to take the pot. You people are a pretty good hand. At least you've been one in the past."

"You weren't trying to blackmail the whole team in the past, either," Barrabas said. He wanted to wrap his fingers around that fat neck and squeeze until the eyes popped.

With a corner of his awareness, Barrabas noted Lee Hatton staring at him. But it was Alex Nanos who broke the deadly silence.

He'd been holding an unopened bottle of Corona in one large hand. Now he opened the bottle with his teeth, then spat the cap into a wastebasket twenty feet away. When he saw he had everybody's undivided attention, he grinned.

"People, I think we're fighting over who gets the rabbit stew before we've caught the rabbit. Hell, I don't even know if we're going rabbit hunting or not.

"I also don't know if we're voting on this. But if we are, I'd vote for loading up and moving out. This is too goddamned big a rabbit to leave for the Chicoms. I don't know who's got a good claim, but theirs is *shit*."

"Alex, me boyo," O'Toole said, "I salute your perspicacity." He raised an empty bottle. "Now, all we need is a proper hunting horn."

"If Bull's people had got offed, I'd tell you where to put the rubies," Claude Hayes said slowly. "I'd settle the score myself. As it is, going after the rubies makes sense." He smiled for the first time that night. "Getting the Triads fighting each other over a pile of hot rocks is going to be fun."

"Lee?" Barrabas asked. She shot him another of those strange looks, then nodded.

"I can't speak for Billy, but he's not the sort to be a lone holdout," Barrabas said. He shrugged. "Okay, Fixer. I guess you've got yourself some SOBs. On three conditions."

Jessup grinned around a slice of onion-and-sausage pizza. "Half a million apiece?"

"That's the first. The second is, I can use some of my own contacts in Nepal for air transport. If they fall through, I'll let you know. But I want to try some people who will listen to me as well as you."

"You really are a trusting soul, aren't you Nile?"

"I'm a live mercenary. Any more questions, besides what's my third condition?"

Jessup looked positively smug. The urge to strangle the man very slowly returned for a moment, then vanished for good. What the hell, Alex was right about the rabbit, and Jessup was right about the Triads and Lee! Start ignoring who's right because they come on too strong, and you won't be a live mercenary or a live anything else for long.

"Third condition. You tell Weng that he uses his people to keep the rest of the Triads off Gonpo. No protection, no rubies."

"Weng's not the kind to take threats well."

"Who's threatening?" Barrabas said. "I'm just defining debts and obligations so Weng will understand them. He's an honorable man. I'm sure he wouldn't appreciate being left in the dark about an obligation, would he?"

The look on Jessup's face told Barrabas that he'd finally succeeded in getting through the fat Texan's thick hide.

LEE HATTON closed the door of Dr. Gonpo's room. As she locked it, Nile Barrabas came up behind her.

"Is that necessary?"

She turned to face him. "Chopel asked for it. I think the team makes him a little uneasy."

"If he's been a Tibetan freedom fighter as long as you say, he should be tougher than that."

"He's never been across the border with the guerrillas. He's always been a courier, when he wasn't a doctor in the refugee camps. Right now he feels like a sheep who's just been saved from one pack of wolves by another pack."

Barrabas flexed from the waist to ease the ache where Walker Jessup had fallen on him. Maybe that had saved his life, but couldn't the slob have found some other way of doing it?

"Your friend's going to have to learn to tell one wolf from another."

"Is there a difference with Jessup in our pack?"

"Fifth Amendment," Barrabas said, replying to Lee's frown with a grin. "How is he, by the way? Medically speaking, that is."

"I picked out five fragments. Nothing went in more than a few centimeters. No major vessels hit, no vital organs—"

"For that you'd need a recoilless rifle."

The joke fell flat. "—and there's no danger of infection. He's in shape for anything he's planning to do."

Barrabas twisted again. "Good. One of these days that fat bastard is going to do something that makes me forget he saved my life. It hasn't happened yet."

"Nile, were you hurt in the bomb blast? The way you keep twisting from the waist—"

"You try being protected from fragments by a 320-pound shield! It is not a figure of speech to say that Walker Jessup can be a pain in the ass."

"Want me to check it out?"

"Okay."

Barrabas thought he heard a slight hesitation, but decided it was the beer and imagination. Lee's professional manner wasn't something she put on and took off like clothes. It was grafted on to her, more like a second skin.

When they made it to the master bedroom, Barrabas lay facedown and stripped to the waist on the bed. He lay close to the edge, or Lee Hatton would have had to swing from a trapeze to examine him. The bed was large enough for three not particularly friendly people or five friendly ones. It also had a purple bedspread with a pattern of gold and green diamonds, maroon hangings, and a VCR and TV built into the headboard.

Barrabas decided it was too much to ask of the Fixer to buy a Mafia don with good taste as well as loyalty. He still hoped he wouldn't have to spend too many nights in this new safehouse. Besides, it didn't sit well with his moral sensibilities to have this kind of association, even if very secondhand.

Lee finished the last of her "Does this hurt?" probings, and Barrabas gave his final grunt. She stood up. He rolled over as she pulled a bottle out of her medical kit.

"A couple of pulled muscles at worst. Nothing serious, but they could nag at you if you're careless. Painkiller tonight, a hot bath every day for a few days, and try not to lift any heavy weights."

"No painkiller tonight, Lee. I have to be up early. We're in a race with a whole bunch of people who are both nasty *and* smart."

"All right. Just make sure that if we have to haul heavy weapons up a mountain, you let Billy do the lifting."

"And if we have to haul Billy down the mountain?"

"You take the feet. Let Alex take the head." This time there was no mistaking the hesitation. "If you don't want the painkiller, what about a massage? I can't do everything a Thai bath girl would—"

"I damned well hope not! I've already been squashed once tonight. You walk on my back, and I'll feel like a run-over cucumber!"

"Fine. Move over to the center of the bed and relax."

Lee straddled him and went to work. She didn't need her blinding speed for a massage, but the coordination and strength that made her so deadly in unarmed combat had other uses. Barrabas felt muscles he hadn't known he had, let alone thought were strained, relaxing under those supple fingers.

A drop of sweat hit him between the shoulder blades. He looked up to see Lee's forehead and arms glistening. The thought got as far as his mind: why didn't she strip, too? Fortunately it stopped before it reached his mouth.

It still reached Lee. The steady rhythm of her fingers broke for a moment, and she looked away.

Barrabas kept monitoring his thoughts. Well, they always said at West Point that defining the problem's the first step to solving it. So here we are. I can think of Lee as a woman now, and she knows it.

Not a damned thing to do about it, either. You can't get unaware of somebody. Particularly not somebody like Lee.

Can't push it, either. I owe too much to too many people. The rest of the team. The Fixer. Geoff Bishop's memory. And there's Erika...

So let's not push it, and nobody will have a problem. Besides, I've never seduced anybody I liked in such a shitty-looking bed!

Barrabas drifted off to sleep so gently that he never noticed when Lee stopped the massage, rested a hand briefly on his shoulder, then pulled the blankets over him and climbed off the bed.

5

The Fong Shou-2 biplane banked sharply to clear the ridge. As it swept low over the column, a green bundle plummeted from the rear door. The plane climbed away from the mountain while a parachute flowered above the bundle.

Company Commander Zhou watched the bundle swaying down toward the mountainside. As the biplane vanished behind a peak, he pointed to the spot where he judged it would land. A squad dropped their rifles and scrambled down the rocky slope.

Yao watched without interfering. One of Zhou's many gifts was an instinct for where parachuted loads would land. A valuable gift at anytime, it was more precious than ever now that the column was moving into rugged terrain beyond easy resupply from the Chinese garrisons.

Yao thought that the garrisons might have shown more of the proper spirit. Many of them were from Sinkiang or other mountainous provinces of China. If a Shanghai man such as himself could face these mountains undaunted, why not they?

At least they had provided him with men already acclimatized to the altitude or fit enough to become so quickly. He would remember this with gratitude when he returned with the rubies. Almost certainly the cave of the rubies lay at an altitude where an unacclimatized man could barely live, let alone fight.

Now it seemed that they had thought of his having to fight as well. Zhou's men had reached the bundle and were unwrapping it as he ran up. He raised his arms over his head, waved and shouted. His words came faintly up the slope to Yao.

"The grenades! They've sent the Type K's!"

Yao cupped his hands. "How many?"

"Four boxes!" Zhou called, and for the sake of the men farther away raised his hand four times. The soldiers were too well disciplined to cheer, but on the nearer faces Yao saw smiles.

The column's four launchers for antitank rocket-propelled grenades were the venerable Type 56. Now they had been rendered much more potent by a supply of the new Type K grenades. Instead of a shaped-charge warhead to defeat nonexistent tanks, the Type K had a fragmentation warhead. Hundreds of steel balls set in plastic and scattered by the explosive charge would scythe down unprotected men.

In these mountains, that meant death to guerrillas. The Type 56s could scour any mountainside, even reach those hiding behind rocks with their rifles. The grenades would burst overhead, and their load of steel balls seek out those safe from the machine guns.

Placing this still-new weapon in Yao's hands was a good sign. It meant that his friends were still strong—his friends, or at least those who preferred not to be his enemies. A time would come when it was important to tell the two apart, but not yet.

A long broad shadow fell across the stones at Yao's feet. He turned, forcing the anger he felt out of his voice. He had told Ragpa Dapon many times not to sneak up on him as silently as a thief. Either the Khampa did not know how uneasy it made Yao, or he did know and it was a subtle rebellion.

Yao turned to face Dapon. "What do you want?"

"To know where you wish to go from here, now that you have the new bombs."

"I have already told you. We go up through the Uluk Pass, then east."

"Better that we not go through the Uluk Pass. Better we go down now, then cross through Khib Pass."

Yao managed not to look outraged at the guide's boldness. He was proposing that the column lengthen its journey to the far side of the Gangdise Range by at least fifty kilometers.

From the pain-filled interrogation of enough Tibetans, Yao had added to his knowledge of the cave's location. It lay in the southern fringe of the Gangdise Range, on a mountain from which one could see two double peaks, one due north, one to the northeast.

The maps had told him somewhat more, but not enough to save taking the column out on the ground. Too many maps of this wretched land were still out of date or inadequate. This failure of the People's Liberation Army after thirty years of ruling Tibet shamed Yao.

It shamed him the more because the men under him were now doing work that should have been done by others who had instead sat in comfortable offices. Revolutionary will had abandoned too many in the PLA, and it would not return in time to save Yao and his men a long walk.

He had decided yesterday that the quickest way across the mountains lay over the five-thousand-meter Uluk Pass—high, but close at hand. Now this barbarian of a Khampa wanted to add fifty kilometers to the march!

Yao decided that either the guide would explain, or the column would move on without a guide. It would be better off with no guide than with one who seemed either a fool or a counterrevolutionary. There were ways around a lack of loyalty, but there was no way around a total lack of wisdom.

"Why?" Yao asked.

"Higher up we disturb the mountain spirits," Dapon said. "More than we have already disturbed them, I think."

"There are no mountain spirits. I have told you that before."

"I have heard. But will the spirits hear you? And if they hear, will they obey?"

"*You* had better obey, or no spirits will save you."

The Khampa's look almost made Yao reach for his pistol. The huge man's hands did not quite close on his sword hilt before they dropped to his side.

"I would not call on the spirits for that. They will come or not, as they choose. But the closer we go to their homes, the sooner they will come. The noise of that airplane must have already aroused them. They will be watching as we climb the pass. If we make more noise, surely they will come."

Yao felt relieved. Translated into the speech of civilized men, the Khampa was saying that the Uluk Pass was dangerous because of avalanches. He might even be right. It still wasn't worth an extra fifty kilometers of marching, not with the rubies so close.

"We will still climb the Uluk Pass. But we will be careful. I thank you for your warning."

"How to be careful against the spirits? Also, it is bad ground for a fight. The guerrillas can go where you cannot."

"The soldiers of the People's Liberation Army can go anywhere!" Yao snapped. "We also carry the new bombs. Any guerrillas who come too close will learn what they can do."

"They will make much noise, and disturb the—"

"I do not want to hear the word 'spirits' again. The new bombs will disturb nothing except men who mean us harm. If I decide you are one of them, we will let the gunners use you for target practice!"

The Khampa turned away without waiting for dismissal. That made Yao almost as angry as the talk of spirits, but left him with nothing to do if he did not want to run after the man. That would be undignified, and he had already lost enough dignity by having this quarrel within hearing range of his fighters.

Yao slung his rifle and beat his hands together for warmth. Many years ago, the Nepalese thought an earthquake had struck because the British Imperialists flew an airplane over their mountains, disturbing their spirits.

How many more years of Chinese rule would it take to change these mountain barbarians?

THE COLUMN MADE CAMP for the night at an altitude of 4,300 meters. A hundred meters higher and a kilometer farther, the Uluk Pass began.

Yao ordered camp made early. He feared no spirits, mountain or other, but avalanches were another matter. He did not wish to camp within the pass itself, and it was a full day's march to cross it.

They were closer to the mountains than they had been for some days. The snow-clad slopes shut out more of the sky than Yao cared for. Once more he had to fight the sense that the mountains were ready to fall upon intruders and crush them.

"Comrade Commander, I have brought your dinner." It was Zhou, holding out a bowl of rice mixed with canned pork.

"Have the men been fed?" It was a point of honor with Yao to eat last.

"They have been cleaning their bowls for the last ten minutes."

"Ah. It seems I have been standing here longer than I realized." He looked at the mountains again and realized that their lower slopes were already sinking into the shadows. Overhead, stars began to sparkle, and his stomach rumbled peevishly at the smell of the food.

Yao restrained his appetite before Zhou so that it was almost completely dark before he was finished eating. Wiping his bowl, he nodded toward the mountains.

"I was seeing if I could find any obvious positions for ambush in the mouth of the pass. Either there are none, or they are too subtle for the eyes of a lowlander." It was as close as Yao had come to admitting his unease in this mountain land.

Zhou smiled. "If the Comrade Commander will permit a suggestion—"

"If I did not, it would imply that I thought you incompetent for your post. Since I chose you with some care..."

"We should send patrols up the sides of the pass, on either flank of the column."

"That will slow the column if the patrols are not to fall behind."

"It will also force any guerrillas in ambush to either open fire on the patrols and reveal their position, or let us all pass. If we chose the strongest climbers for the patrols, we should not be slowed too much."

"What about 'the mountain spirits'?"

"Ah, our Khampa's ghosts. I think we should perhaps fire the mortar once or twice at the entrance to the pass. This should drive off any waiting spirits and trigger any lurking avalanches. I will order more mortar rounds sent with our first airdrop on the far side of the Uluk."

"Very good." Now, for one more test. "Are you satisfied with our guide?"

"I would be more satisfied if he were not so much in fear of those spirits. But I suppose we could not find a man who knew the mountains well who had more sense."

Zhou frowned, then continued. "His fear of the spirits concerns me less than his being only one man. If I could have anything I wished..."

"Yes, comrade?"

"I would have three guides, all from one family. One would be with the main column, one with each patrol. Each would be a hostage for the others, and obey us out of fear for his kin."

Yao's smile was sincere. "I am happier than ever that I chose you for this column." For a moment Zhou seemed awkward, as though he were a boy facing his father, unable to meet the older man's eyes or decide what to do with his hands and feet.

"Get some sleep, Comrade Zhou. I will take the first watch. If any of the spirits come, I will be sure to tell you what they said."

Zhou laughed and hurried back toward the camp. Yao watched him go. Indeed, if he had been the father of a son, he could hardly have wished for a better one than Zhou.

Every time Yao had tested the company commander, he had succeeded magnificently.

Not just the tests of skill at commanding an infantry company, either, although those were important. Those who actually led men into the enemy's positions bore a heavy burden. Zhou seemed well able to bear it.

He also seemed able to learn all the other things that Yao intended to teach him. Zhou would be grateful to his teacher, and support that teacher's rise.

When the teacher had risen high, he could surround himself with men like Zhou. Then let the enemies of the People's Republic and the revolutionary will of the People's Liberation Army be wary!

ZHOU STUDIED THE SLOPES with his binoculars as the 82 mm mortar crew set up behind him. When he had seen that both patrols seemed to be on safe ground, he raised a hand. The mortar loader held a round over the muzzle.

Zhou's hand dropped. The round plummeted into the barrel, then soared out with a reverberating *whamp*. Zhou counted, then at the right moment saw rock and snow fountain a kilometer ahead.

A second round followed, then a third. Zhou decided against firing a fourth. The column was on its way down the far side of Uluk. Unfortunately not even the patrols had good observation very far ahead. Time and ammunition spent here might be completely wasted, and needed later on.

Zhou was confident of the air force's ability to resupply the column. He also counted on the ability of the Tibetan guerrillas to choose the one moment the column was short of mortar ammunition to launch their attack.

In six years in the army, two as a fighter and four as a commander, Zhou had learned that real enemies never consulted your convenience when choosing the time to attack.

The mortar team was packing up their weapon. The lead platoon was moving out. Yao fell in behind them in his usual place. Zhou respected Yao's courage and determination to be quickly at the scene of any action.

He also wished the regiment commander would show a trifle less of it. What if the man was quickly at the scene of a Tibetan ambush? Zhou might soon be trying to apologize to senior commanders in Peking. Senior commanders seldom listened to a Company Commander's explanations of why he had allowed a Regiment Commander to be killed by Tibetan guerrillas.

Zhou turned toward the rear of the column. As the head of the second platoon passed him, he heard another *whamp*. It sounded so much like the mortar that he whirled, ready to punish the crew for firing a round without orders.

Instead he saw what seemed like half the left side of the pass on the move above the flanking patrol. Training kept him from crying out, and let him note the mixture of ice, snow and rock fragments in the avalanche. A cloud of snow rode above and ahead of the avalanche, and its sound was like some vast piece of machinery tearing itself to bits.

Zhou also saw that the patrol was not trying to outrun the avalanche. They were running across its path. The patrol's commander had remembered his training and given the right orders; his men had obeyed. Zhou swore to see the platoon commander honored, whether he lived to enjoy the honors or not.

The avalanche swept down across the rear of the patrol, and the snow cloud blotted it out of Zhou's vision. He drew his pistol and squeezed the butt until his knuckles turned white. He remembered to shout "Column, halt! Prepare for rescue operations!"

Yao reached him, grim-faced and silent. Zhou forced himself to speak. He was not sure he could be heard over the roar of the avalanche, or that Yao would care to listen. He still wanted to prove that he could command his tongue.

"Comrade Commander, I accept the responsibility for the loss of our men. The patrol was my—"

Yao raised a hand. "I approved your suggestions. I also ordered our crossing of the pass. Had I ordered otherwise, we would not have gone within reach of the avalanches."

Then Zhou really was speechless, and glad of the avalanche roar.

As the avalanche settled, Yao's first act was to study the pass ahead. Much of the avalanche seemed to have gone on sliding downhill toward the plateau. What remained was enough to make footing precarious, but the column was comprised of fit soldiers, moving by day. Those carrying heavy loads might need some help, but Yao would trust Zhou to see to that.

Indeed, he would trust Zhou with much more than that if necessary. The young commander had made a mistake, but one mistake was not enough to toss aside a competent and valuable ally.

Besides, Yao knew his share of the responsibility for the lost patrol. If he did not admit it now, he would be giving Zhou every reason to let others know about it. The only way to prevent that would be arranging an "accident" for Zhou.

There were men in the column Yao trusted to do that, if it became necessary or seemed wise. Now it was neither. Apart from Zhou's value, it would slow the search for the rubies if Yao had to do all the work of commanding the column himself.

The snow cloud faded, and Yao made out five specks on the slope beyond the avalanche. Through his binoculars he saw them making hand signals.

"One missing, one wounded," he called, loud enough to be heard by the column. The grimness of the men eased slightly as they hurried forward. They seemed ready to break into a run, if that would put this haunted pass behind them.

Yao found it difficult to resist the temptation himself. He succeeded, wishing to set an example that might prevent twisted ankles and broken toes. It was only when the head of the column reached clear ground that Yao headed up the slope toward the patrol.

He was so intent on covering ground that he was halfway up when he saw Ragpa Dapon and Zhou following him. He stopped and shouted, "Commander, return to the column." He'd have said the same to the Khampa if he'd thought the man would obey.

"Fighter Lin was carried away completely," the platoon commander reported. "Fighter Eng was swept into a crevice. He is still alive, but we have no way of reaching him."

"You did well to save most of your men," Yao said. "It will be remembered. Now, let us see about Eng."

Eng hung head-down fifteen meters below Yao's feet, still kicking feebly. From time to time he moaned. The smears of blood on the rock made it clear he'd been badly hurt in the avalanche, even before it thrust him into the crevice.

There was rope in the column, also some competent climbers. Eng could be hauled out. The price would almost certainly be to spend the night in the pass. What would Eng gain by this, other than dead comrades and his own last hours made more painful?

"He cannot live, and there is only one thing to be done for him," Yao said, drawing his pistol. The platoon commander stared at him. "Carry on with your patrol, Comrade."

"As you wish, Comrade Commander."

It took Yao a good five minutes to find a place that gave him a clear shot at Eng. Then he called, "Farewell, Fighter Eng. You did your duty," and fired three times.

The moans ceased. After a moment, so did the echoes. In their place came a high-pitched chanting. Yao stared at Ragpa Dapon, who stood by the crevice, his head thrown back and mouth open.

As the man caught his breath, Yao gripped his out-flung right arm. The Khampa stiffened the arm, nearly tossing Yao into the crevice. Yao raised his pistol.

"What are you doing? Tell me, or—"

"I sing for his spirit. Any sacrifice to the mountain spirits deserves the honor."

"Even a Chinese?" Yao blurted.

"Even a Chinese," the Khampa said, and began chanting again.

Yao endured the chanting for as long as he could. Then he practically ran down the slope. He was angry at the Khampa for continuing this nonsense of the mountain spirits.

He was also angry at himself. He knew if he spent much longer around that death chant, he would begin to believe in those spirits himself.

RAGPA DAPON LET YAO GO all the way back to his men before he finished his chanting. He had spoken part of the truth. He wished to honor the Chinese soldiers.

He also wished to hear what the mountain spirits said to him. If they spoke. They would not speak in the presence of so many men who did not believe in them.

Dapon stood on the lip of the crevice, listening to the subtle noises in the rock under his feet and the sky overhead. At last he turned away, satisfied that this day there would be nothing for him to hear.

Perhaps he himself had been judged unfit to hear the voice of the mountains. That was possible, and if so, he was the blind leading the blind. Then the worst blow he could give the Chinese was to go on pretending to be able to guide them. He could hardly do them more harm if he picked up one of their machine guns and turned it on them. In this land, the deaths men could deal were nothing compared to the deaths from the mountains.

As he approached the rear of the column, Dapon decided to remain with the Chinese. He would have decided otherwise, except for Commander Yao. There was a man who walked with the spirit world, though he did not know it. In Yao's presence, Dapon might learn more than he would alone.

6

Sunrise glowed on the ridge above the villa. Downhill, the shadows were fading. The lamps in the houses that trailed south from Kathmandu were going out, one by one.

On the veranda, Nile Barrabas saw a similarly colored glow as Randall Gordon lit a cigar. His son, Arthur Gordon, coughed politely.

"Dad, that's your third today, and we haven't even had breakfast yet!"

"Artie, a lot of things more dangerous than good cigars have been trying to kill your Dad for the last sixty-five years. None of them have succeeded. Why the hell should I start worrying now—just to keep you happy?"

Arthur Gordon threw a silently pleading look at Barrabas. Barrabas looked elsewhere. He wasn't going to be dragged into the family feud unless that was the only way to get the Gordons' help.

One thing for sure: the old man's definition of "good cigars" was a lot wider than it had been. He used to smoke good Havanas; then, decent leaf, hand-rolled by Cuban exiles. Now he was down to something that smelled as if it had been cured in yak piss. It made heavy going on an empty stomach.

"How about our having breakfast, then, to go with the cigars?" Barrabas suggested.

Randall snorted. "Getting old yourself, Colonel? Time was, my grandson said, you could go three days with nothing but water and snakes—"

"Dad!"

"Vietnam was awhile back," Barrabas said quietly. "I can still do anything I did then if I have to. But I have to rest a little more in between."

Although this "in between" was slated for five more days at most. That's when Jessup and the rest of the team were to fly in. By then, Barrabas wanted to have a line on a plane and weapons. Otherwise they were going to be completely at the mercy of the Fixer's connections.

"Sorry," Randall said. He almost sounded sincere. "I *am* getting too old to wheel and deal all night and all day, too."

"You'll still be skinning people alive when they're nailing you up in a box," Arthur said. "But I'm with Colonel Barrabas. Let's have breakfast and get down to business."

"That's two ayes and one nay," Randall said. "The nays have it." He waited just long enough for his son's face to turn red, then added, "But I'll concede the victory anyway. Tulbahadur!" he shouted toward the house. "Breakfast for three!"

Arthur Gordon handed his father his cane, and Barrabas helped him out of the chair. Once on his feet, though, the old man left both of the younger ones standing as he scurried into the house.

RANDALL GORDON was the last of the Gordon Highflyers, a barnstorming trio of the thirties. Randall, his older brother Ian, and Randall's wife Mary had looped and rolled biplanes all over the Midwest during the Depression.

Then World War Two turned them to new kinds of flying. Ian died in a B-24 over Ploesti, and Mary died when a B-17 she was ferrying ran into a thunderstorm over Kansas. By then she had given Randall a son, who was old enough in the 1950s to fly as his father's copilot, airdropping ammunition and reinforcements to Dien Bien Phu.

That was the end of Randall Gordon's combat flying, but not of Arthur's. Arthur went on to fly almost everywhere there was fighting and airplanes, particularly where there were mountains as well. That included quite a few places, from the Central Highlands of Vietnam through the Ogaden region of Somalia to Afghanistan.

Meanwhile his father went back to South Asia, where he'd flown the Hump to China before moving on to B-29s. In a few years the word was out that for anybody wanting something flown in South Asia the man to ask was Randall Gordon; he didn't fly it himself anymore, but he knew somebody who could, or at least could get a plane to do the job.

Nile Barrabas hoped to use both Randall's connections and Arthur's skill as a mountain pilot. He didn't expect to have much trouble getting the second, and maybe even the first. The Gordons had helped him before, and Arthur at least thought he still owed Nile Barrabas something.

Arthur's son Sean had gone into the Army in time to fly Hueys in Vietnam. The boy had the family touch; he could do things with helicopters that weren't in any manual. Manufacturers' representatives rode with Sean and turned green—not with envy, either.

That hadn't saved him, one rainy night in Vietnam. Nile Barrabas had brought the news to Sean's father, then led half a dozen of his Green Berets into the jungle to bring back Sean's body.

Sean had been the Gordons' hope. His mother had divorced Arthur before the war, returning to the United States with her daughter Kathleen. The last Barrabas heard, Kathleen was married to a drug pusher and draft evader, and even her mother had thrown her out.

Nile Barrabas had helped people in a lot of ways over the years. Some he'd helped to retire, others to get back into the fight, still others to get back their self-respect. This time, maybe he would help the Gordons get back their family pride.

Since Nile Barrabas was a mercenary, not a social worker, there'd be a price for that help. The Gordons would help *him* stay independent of the Fixer's Nepalese connections.

BARRABAS MOPPED UP the last of a powerfully seasoned chicken and rice stew with a *chapatti*. By itself, this South Asian flat bread looked and tasted like a panfried bath mat. Its real job was soaking up all the spices in the rest of a South Asian meal. It did that job pretty well.

An amusing thought occurred to Barrabas. Maybe they could take out the Fixer that way. Load him up on curries, then take away the *chapattis*.

Experience suggested otherwise. Walker Jessup could eat anything that didn't eat him first, and keep it down. He hadn't reached his present age and weight with a finicky stomach.

The smell of Randall Gordon's latest cigar jabbed at Barrabas's nostrils. A full stomach made the smell easier to endure, and being inside actually helped. The house's own ripe Asian odors diluted the cigar's odor just enough.

"So I suppose you're wanting something flown somewhere," Randall growled. "And Arthur to fly it, of course?"

Barrabas nodded and swigged the last of his tea. "I try to be predictable, at least for my friends. My enemies, I try to keep guessing. My insurance company requires it," he added deadpan.

"Well and good," Randall said. "Now, is it north you want to go? Or east?"

"North. Not quite to the Arctic Ocean, though. So you don't need to think about borrowing a 707 from Air India."

"Something smaller, that can get in and out of mountain strips with a payload."

"You got it."

"That let's out any kind of chopper, then. Unless you're only sneaking in a small payload?"

"Sneaking, yes," Barrabas said. "The lower and slower, the better. But small payload—no way it's going to be small going in. Coming out, the payload had better be enough to spare me and my friends a hell of a long walk. If we have to walk, we take the cost of the new boots and arch supports off your payment."

"You mean, this is worth *money*?" Randall said, letting his jaw drop open wide enough to display a full set of nicotine-yellowed teeth. "Why, I thought we were supposed to—"

"Dad . . ." Arthur said with a cough.

"If you save our asses by risking your assets, of course you get paid," Barrabas said. "But no helicopters." The lowest point of the mission, the landing on the Tibetan plateau, would be two and a half miles above sea level. At that altitude most helicopters *might* handle a payload consisting of Lee Hatton wearing a bikini and carrying a scalpel and a pistol with five rounds.

Even if they could get off the ground with more, they'd need refueling to complete a round-trip. Somehow Barrabas couldn't see the Chinese offering to fill up the SOBs' helicopter, check its oil, or even wash its windows. The SOBs' lives would be easier and longer if they had fixed-wing airlift.

"If it's worth it to you, I *think* we might get a Helio Courier," Randall added.

"It's not," Barrabas said. "Not unless you haven't got anything better. If you haven't got anything better, I'll look at the Courier and pay for your time. I won't promise anything more."

The single-engined, high-winged Helio Courier was a CIA favorite, going back to Vietnam and before. Barrabas knew they could land on a tennis court. They were also on the small side for hauling the whole team of SOBs and their gear deep into Tibet.

Barrabas saw Randall Gordon wince, then try to cover it with a coughing fit. Arthur pounded his father on the back and tried to look at both the major and Barrabas at once. Barrabas poured himself some more tea and wished he was back at the Eastern Star Hotel. It was Western enough to offer coffee, which had a better grade of caffeine.

"What about the Antonov-2?" Arthur put in. The reply from his father was a glare, but Barrabas nodded. Those big Russian biplanes looked like relics of an earlier era, but they were built to last. Their biplane configuration gave them natural STOL performance, and they were designed to haul a couple of tons of payload.

"What shape is it in?" Barrabas asked.

Under his son's steady gaze Randall Gordon shrugged. "Just finished a major overhaul on the engine and airframe," he said. "Even got a supercharger for it to boost performance at high altitude. I wouldn't bet money on the instruments, though."

"I'll check those myself, Dad," Arthur said. "Running into a mountain can ruin your whole day."

"So I've heard," Barrabas said. "I may be able to help with a fix, if my ass is going to be on the line, too."

A former SOB, Nate Beck, had the same talent with computers as Liam O'Toole had with explosives. One of Beck's private goodies for his old comrades was a plug-in computerized avionics suite, complete with a heads-up display. It could be installed in any plane with enough electrical power and give that plane's pilot a much easier job, particularly at low altitude.

Barrabas wanted Art Gordon to be able to take the An-2 into Tibet looking *up* at the tops of tall rocks. The An-2 was identical to its Chinese version, the Fong Shou-2, so it shouldn't make anyone too suspicious. Not being seen at all was even better.

"I don't suppose you'd be wanting some weapons," Randall Gordon went on. His voice was closer to a whine than Barrabas enjoyed hearing. "I've one or two friends who can manage just about anything you might want. I can even manage a Bren gun."

"In 7.62 mm NATO?"

"Of course. Chromed barrels, too."

"Depends on what else we're carrying. We may wind up deciding to take something that can use Chinese ammo."

"Well, then, some of those friends are Pakistani, and—"

"Right, Dad. But remember, they might not be too happy about the guns being used against the Chinese." Arthur Gordon stood up. "Colonel, is there anything more, besides making dates to see that Courier and the Antonov?''

There were quite a few things, but none of them worth spending more time with the Gordons today. Nile Barrabas had never run away from a battle in his life, but had to admit that now he wanted to run away from this whining, querulous wreck of a soldier and pilot who had once been Randall Gordon.

BARRABAS AND ARTHUR GORDON roughed out the agreement in the time it took them to walk to Barrabas's car.

"Don't be too angry with Dad," Arthur finished. "He's beginning to run down a lot faster than he was. Don't let on that I told you this, but he thinks Sean may be alive as a POW."

"Christ!" Barrabas exploded, loud enough to make Arthur look back toward the house. "Then who the hell did my people hump out of that jungle?"

"He says there never was a positive ID on the body."

"Bullshit!"

"You know that. I know that. He doesn't know it, or at least refuses to admit. Colonel, I know my son's dead and my daughter might as well be. But I'm strong enough to look the facts in the face and spit in their eye. Dad isn't. Not anymore."

Arthur opened the door for Barrabas. "Thing is, he wants to raise money, to finance an expedition to Vietnam. That's why he was so eager to deal on weapons. But he also wants to save our planes as much as possible. Half the time I have to remind him to fulfill our standing contracts!"

"Remind me never to live long enough to die in bed," Barrabas said. "Art, we're going to owe you one if this comes off. Any suggestions?"

"Give Dad something to think about besides seeing his family die out. You do that and I'll call it square."

"Art, I'm just retired Special Forces, not a miracle worker."

"Vietnam was a while back, as I said."

Barrabas rolled up the window and put the rented Nissan in gear. Art Gordon was still standing at the head of the driveway when Barrabas reached the road leading back to Kathmandu.

7

The meeting at the Gordons' villa bothered Nile Barrabas more than he wanted to admit. Seeing what waited for warriors who lived long enough to grow old was like ordering men out to die. No matter how often you did it, you never enjoyed it.

The meeting didn't affect Barrabas's alertness. In two minutes he'd noticed the gray Chevette apparently glued to his rearview mirror.

It was such an obvious job of tailing that Barrabas's first impulse was to assume coincidence. Why should he be the only man on his way into Kathmandu along this road this morning?

He also remembered friends whose first impulse to ignore a threat had been the last decision of their lives. He had better put whoever it was through the jumps.

Barrabas slowed down long enough to count four men in the Chevette. At least one of them, the man in the front passenger seat, looked neither Western nor Nepalese.

The Chevette slowed down, too, even though it was a good hundred yards behind Barrabas. Barrabas slowed further, waited until the Chevette started closing the gap, then stepped on the gas.

The Chevette's driver responded quickly. His car didn't. It nearly skidded as he accelerated, fishtailed through a puddle in a sheet of muddy spray, then settled down on Barrabas's tail. But he'd opened the gap by a good fifty yards, enough to make himself a harder target if he couldn't evade.

Neither compact had the suspension to handle the roads, or the acceleration to handle the slopes. That much became obvious the minute the chase turned uphill. Barrabas stopped thinking about back teeth knocked loose by the bumps and started looking for side roads. If he couldn't outrun the pursuers, that left evading or ambushing them.

Fortunately the Chevette was even more elephantine on the slopes than the Nissan. Barrabas had plenty of time to crank his car around the turns with one hand, while he pulled out his modified Browning Hi-Power and rolled down the driver's window with the other.

The Hi-Power was a specially modified version, with a folding shoulder stock, a 20-round magazine, full automatic fire, and sights to deliver the 9 mm bullets on target. By the time New York gunsmith Pat Lily was done, Walker Jessup had a bill that made him cringe, and the SOBs had a batch of the handiest, most easily concealable automatic weapons around.

The SOBs valued firepower. But firepower didn't help much if it was so conspicuous that it provoked the other side into shooting first. Weapons like the modified Brownings went a long way to solving that problem.

As the car chase wound its way up into the hills, Barrabas considered his chances of not having to shoot it out. He decided they'd already shrunk to the vanishing point.

The prospect annoyed Barrabas. Calling attention to yourself when you were in a strange country with nobody to guard your back had sent a good many agents and mercenaries home in boxes.

The Nepalese government was fighting in rearguard action to keep foreign criminals from shooting it out in Nepalese streets for control of the drug scene. Walker Jessup's connections would grease the way for the SOBs' weapons, but Barrabas didn't know if there was enough grease to smooth over wasting four Nepalese citizens.

The road wound and twisted, sometimes almost back on itself, as the slope steepened. Twice Barrabas caught a glimpse of someone a couple hundred yards behind the Chevette. It looked like a motorcycle. He wrote it off as the

Chevette's backup and messenger and kept looking for that side road.

Powhannnggg! Craaak! Wheeet! One bullet smacked into the Nissan's body, a second starred the back window and a third whistled past Barrabas's ear. Visibility to the rear suddenly shrank. Barrabas's hopes of evasion vanished completely.

He stopped looking for side roads and started looking for safe places to jump. "Safe" in this case meant safe for the Browning. He could survive landing on anything short of solid rock, at any speed the Nissan could manage on this slope. The Browning hadn't gone through jump school and Special Forces training; it was a bit more delicate.

A good jumping place and the next burst from the Chevette came together. Barrabas felt the Nissan slew as a back tire went. He looked at the slope to the right, picked a landing spot and hit the brakes. The car slewed almost sideways as Barrabas kicked open the passenger door, but it didn't go over the edge until he'd dived clear, rolling until he reached the cover of some scraggly rhododendrons. The slope was steeper than he'd guessed; he hit hard and the breath whooshed out of him. He got his wind back and checked his Browning as the Nissan rattled and crashed down the hill.

From just out of Barrabas's sight, a submachine gun rattled. The Nissan's gas tank spewed flame. Wrapped in an orange glow and a greasy black cloud, Barrabas's car rolled the rest of the way downhill.

He considered that it would be nice if they thought he was in it. Nice, but not too likely.

His pursuers might not be hard-core professionals, but they didn't need to be. They had numbers, firepower and the high ground. Barrabas had concealment and training—but he wouldn't be the first concealed professional to lose to a superior force of amateurs.

He remembered a long-dead instructor in Special Forces school: "If the other guy kills you first, I don't give a shit how much training you've got. He's better."

Sergeant Bosick had met the better man somewhere in Laos. So far, Nile Barrabas hadn't, and Bosick was one of the people he could thank for that. Since the next move was up to the bad guys, Barrabas settled back to let them make it.

He didn't have to wait long. Bullets clipped leaves and twigs over his head, showering him with debris. The bursts moved back and forth along the slope, feeling out each patch of concealment.

They were guarding against his being alive, even though they didn't know where he was. The bursts were covering fire to keep him from moving while one or two of them got down on the slope and started eyeballing each bush close up. There was an easy remedy for that: pick off the covering fire. What made that difficult to fulfill was that he had only two twenty-round magazines for the Browning. The way around that was find a place where he could hit the covering gunners with the first round, which was another bit of Bosick wisdom: "Always try for a first-round kill. You may need the second round."

Barrabas used all his skill at finding cover and concealment to make his way along the slope. Parts of it were so steep he had to hold on to roots and branches with one hand and the Browning with the other. Most of it was overgrown with rhododendrons, wild grass and scrub pine. In places he crushed patches of wild herbs, and pungent scents rose around him.

A flock of birds hurtled into the air. Some of them were better shots than the people up the hill. Barrabas ignored the bird droppings in his hair and kept crawling.

Somewhere about this point, he noticed that he had an audience. Half the far side of the valley was terraced into small fields of wheat and barley. Some of the farmers were leaning on their hoes, gaping at the firefight. Barrabas considered sending a couple of rounds their way to get them moving before the gunmen got any bright ideas about eliminating witnesses.

He decided that he'd better not. Likely enough, it would just convince the farmers that he was the bad guy. The birds were enough trouble. He ducked under a projecting root.

One the other side, he could see needles and leaves dancing from the muzzle-blasts of the SMGs. Beyond the bushes stood the Chevette. Barrabas put three rounds into the bushes to distract the SMG.

His real target was the Chevette. It got seven rounds, dumping the windshield onto the front seat, blowing front tires and taking out a headlight.

The muzzle-blasts died. Five seconds later, so did one of the gunmen, as he rose a little too far from cover. A head shot sent him catapulting over the bush and down the slope, taking his SMG with him.

A return burst told Barrabas he'd given the surviving SMG too good a notion of his location. One bullet creased the side of Barrabas's right knee. When he checked it out, his hand came away bloody, but it didn't feel like muscle or bone damage. Helpful, but with three enemies still alive, maybe not helpful enough.

From farther along the slope, another SMG fired two short bursts. At least one of the flankers was on the slope and on the move. He and the surviving gunner could now alternate covering and moving. If they had enough ammo, it might take very bad luck or very bad shooting to keep them from giving one Nile Barrabas, Lieutenant Colonel, U.S.A. (Ret.) a terminal headache.

More SMG fire, from another position on the slope. Correction: *both* flankers were on their way. Moving now had all kinds of risks. Staying put had only one—getting killed.

His mind whirled. Lucky the bad guys didn't put somebody behind me as well as ahead. Now, if the flankers will just rely on their upstairs cover for about two seconds—

Barrabas shot out of the bushes like a shell out of a mortar. Both he and the cover man had clear shots, but Barrabas shot first and straighter. Barrabas didn't wait for the man to stop screaming or thrashing around. He plunged up the slope, hit the level ground and rolled under the Chevette.

The two flankers took considerably more than two seconds to realize that they'd lost their cover. If they'd been twenty yards closer, Barrabas would have chanced a burst. As it was, all he could do was change magazines and swear as the men vanished under cover.

One thing he could do: cut off the rest of their retreat. The motorcycle, a red 500 cc Suzuki, was now clearly visible about seventy-five yards down the road.

The burst that wrecked the Suzuki brought both surviving gunmen out of cover. They were beyond comfortable range for Barrabas, but practically under the muzzle of a small figure in green who popped out of the streambed behind them.

The two gunmen dropped dead too fast to cry out. The green-clad figure vanished before the echoes did, then in what seemed like a matter of seconds, a polite voice broke the silence.

"Colonel Barrabas. Was it necessary to destroy my nephew's motorcycle? He was not happy about my borrowing it."

"How the hell do you know my name?"

"I am a friend of the Gordons. May I come up to discuss this privately?"

"Keep your hands in sight."

"As you wish."

The green-clad figure emerged from what Barrabas would have sworn was bare ground. In one hand was a Sterling SMG. The man slung the Sterling and began to climb the slope, hands open in front of him.

In five minutes Barrabas faced a short, wiry man of about fifty, with a fringe of gray hair around a scarred pate. His brown face split in an engagingly sinister grin as he held out a hand to Barrabas.

"Captain Ganparsing Thapa, formerly of the Second Gurkha Rifles."

"Nile Barrabas."

"It seems we are both friends of the Gordons. I—"

"How about you explaining what you were doing on my tail?"

"I was on the tail of our friends. Quite by coincidence, I assure you. I had an appointment with the Gordons and reached the villa just in time to see the Chevette drive off after you. I sent a message to Arthur Gordon and went in pursuit. They were better than I expected, to keep up with you."

Barrabas doubted the coincidence but not the intent of the Gurkha. "Are you the man with Bren guns for sale?"

"Are you buying some?"

"They're *heavy* mothers, you know."

"I carried one in Malaya, Colonel. There is not much I do not know about them. But you must know how reliable and sturdy they are. Also, the 7.62 mm NATO round is better for mountain warfare, at least in the hands of a marksman."

Barrabas decided that bouncing Captain Thapa off two or three nearby trees would not do any good. If the Gordons had blabbed, it wasn't the captain's fault for listening.

Besides, he wanted somebody to guard his back until the rest of the team flew in. Maybe Captain Thapa could be trusted. The question that emerged was whether it was worth loading up with Bren guns to get him on their side?

Maybe, Barrabas answered his own question silently. Brens in good shape were worth having. He could have Billy Two test them. Billy loved oddball small arms.

"Any deal for the Brens includes ammo and training. Okay?"

"Of course."

"Also, no deal until my small-arms expert tests it thoroughly."

"Understood. Now, Colonel, since you demolished my transportation—"

"If you're trying to get me to pay for the Suzuki—"

"Would I insult you by asking for something that I know your honor and generosity toward a fellow soldier will make you give?" Thapa's grin reminded Barrabas of the phrase "The smile on the face of the tiger."

"With friends like you, I don't need any more like those." Barrabas pointed downhill.

"You may have them whether you need them or not. Might I suggest a dignified retreat on foot, in case the enemy's reserves are on the way?"

Barrabas really couldn't argue with the suggestion. He'd had help in the shooting, but that could only mean that the police would take twice as long asking questions.

Satisfying the curiosity of the Kathmandu police could wait. Prince Su's rubies could not.

8

The Bren gun chattered. Bullets chopped into the gravel four hundred yards uphill in a tight group. Dust hid the white-painted boulder.

Nile Barrabas raised the Bren's muzzle. The second burst chewed bits of paint and rock from the boulder. The third knocked it loose and sent it rolling downhill.

The third also emptied the magazine. Barrabas's left arm snaked out. The hand closed on a curved magazine holding twenty-nine 7.62 mm NATO rounds. At the same time, the right hand was snapping the magazine release and popping out the empty magazine. The new magazine clicked into place as the old one hit the ground. Barrabas squeezed off another five-round burst, redistributing the paint chips. Then he looked over his shoulder.

Arthur Gordon pressed the button on his stopwatch and gave Barrabas a thumbs-up.

"I've seen a Bren reloaded slower with two men on it. A trained Gurkha crew, too. Glad you're on our side."

"I'm on my own side, Art. It happens to be your side, as well. Most of the time, anyway."

Barrabas stood up, brushing dust and gravel off his trousers, then retrieved his windbreaker. Both were civilian, indistinguishable from a thousand similar sets left by hikers and mountain climbers.

Nobody had moved against Barrabas since the hillside battle four days ago. He suspected that losing four men had made somebody do some heavy thinking. It was all right with Barrabas if they went on thinking for a few more days until the rest of the team flew in.

Meanwhile he didn't intend to stick out any more than he had to. That had been a good way to get killed in the Nam. Sometimes the world seemed just as big and bad a jungle as the Mekong Delta.

Barrabas hefted the Bren and practiced slinging it, then setting it up again. The Bren weighed a good twenty-three pounds, five to eight pounds more than most modern machine guns. It was magazine-fed instead of belt-fed, and generally looked like an antique.

It could also hold a man-sized group at a thousand yards—in the field, not just in the manual or the manufacturer's ads. Barrabas had never met a modern LMG that could do nearly as well. In mountain country, where you had to be able to hit something as soon as you saw it, the Brens would be lethal.

Art Gordon pulled out a pack of cigarettes and lit up. "I smell a deal," he said.

"Do you? I thought it was that yak dung you're smoking."

"How many do you need?"

"Two and a spare," Barrabas said. "All of them tested by my small-arms expert. How many magazines do you have available?"

Changing magazines in the middle of a firefight was no big deal. Reloading them could spoil your whole day, or at least keep you from spoiling the other guy's.

"Ten a gun."

"Fifteen."

"That's a lot of ammo to hump."

"We may have a lot of Chinese to shoot. And don't ask if we're going to be humping the ammo ourselves."

"I wouldn't dare," Gordon said.

"No, but you're thinking real loud."

A different kind of noise floated up the hill—a car in low gear. A battered Land Rover crawled out of the trees and stopped a hundred yards downhill. The driver hopped out, tucked a Sterling SMG under one arm and climbed toward Barrabas and Gordon.

"Hello, Captain," Barrabas said. "I don't remember inviting you. That's a statement of fact, not a complaint."

"Just as well. It is ungracious to complain about people who kill your enemies and bring you valuable intelligence."

"Nobody's ever rated me too high for good manners, Captain. I put more value on other things, like intelligence. You've found out who tried to kill us?"

"After a fashion. Two of the men were Nepalese and one an Indian. They were all petty criminals connected with the drug business, but for hire to anyone with enough rupees."

"That's three. Who was the fourth?"

"The apparent leader was a Malay from Singapore. The people who told me had records of some hard-currency transactions in his name. Enough to pay the three to cut their own fathers' throats, assuming they knew who their fathers were."

"Interesting."

That was a handy word when you wanted to be polite. Sometimes good manners really were useful, as when dealing with Gurkhas. Getting a Gurkha really mad at you was not smart, particularly when you might want to buy what the Gurkha was possibly thinking of selling.

"Very interesting," Captain Thapa said. "It tells us who they are, but not why they picked you as their target."

"They probably put two and two together and came up with five. They can't think beyond their ken. The assumption probably is that I'm a top gun imported to give some foreign boss a piece of the drug action. If they waste that top gun before he can shoot, maybe his boss will think again."

That wasn't even half a lie. The Triads pretty much stayed with ethnic Chinese for jobs like the Malay's. They would hire local talent, but it was always a Chinese doing the hiring. But no law said that Chinese couldn't get drunk in a bar and say one word too many. Certainly not in Singapore, which had a lot of bars and a lot of Chinese to get drunk in them. Not to mention a hell of a lot of Malays to overhear that extra word....

Four hundred million dollars in rubies was a pretty damned big rabbit. Barrabas didn't really blame anybody else for setting up to hunt it. He still didn't intend to stick around in a forest full of rabbit hunters all banging away at each other.

Barrabas narrowed his eyes musingly.

The faster we get north, the better. Once we square off with Colonel Yao, we'll at least be fighting one set of bad guys at a time.

Which is not going to help the Gordons a hell of a lot, if any of the other hunters think they know something.

"Art, I think I can smell a deal on the Brens, too, if my small-arms expert confirms my judgment. Twenty-five thousand?"

"Make it fifty, and I can manage a 3-inch mortar. Two hundred rounds, if you can hump that much."

"Got a recoilless instead? Handier and better for direct fire."

"How about a Carl Gustav Mark II?"

"I'll bite. And of course rifles, grenades, flares."

"Can do, Colonel. But no discount for a package deal."

"What makes you think I expect one? I didn't send your boy's body back to you and expect you to starve in gratitude."

Barrabas turned to Captain Thapa. "On the other hand, I also don't expect to see my friends wasted while I can't guard their backs."

"Are you asking me?" The Gurkha grinned.

Barrabas made a show of looking around the hillside. "Anybody else around who looks up to the job? I've never seen a sheep who could swing a *kukri* worth a damn."

The grin widened. "What is the job worth to you?"

"Why, I thought you might want to do it as a favor to the Gordons, who are friends of both of us."

Art Gordon rolled his eyes to heaven. "You can't pile it that deep on a hillside, Colonel. It'll flow down into the valleys."

"From what I've seen around here, most of the farms could use a little more fertilizer."

"That is quite true, Colonel Barrabas. My pension is wealth by Nepalese standards. Not so much wealth that it will buy many motorcycles, of course...."

"All right, all right," Barrabas growled. "You can cut the guilt trip. Besides, I wouldn't really want you to work for me out of the goodness of your heart. You might think I *owed* you something."

Barrabas was a long time forgetting the bargaining session that followed. If he'd closed his eyes, he might have thought he was dealing with a Yemeni bazaar merchant. Captain Thapa dotted every *i* and crossed every *t* and then double-checked the dots and the crosses!

At the end of the session, Thapa produced a flask of orange-scented rum. Barrabas thought it smelled more like perfume than booze, until he toasted the agreement with it. It was at least 120 proof. Barrabas made a mental note not to try outdrinking Captain Thapa.

As Art Gordon loaded the Bren and its ammunition into the Land Rover, the captain led Barrabas a few yards downhill.

"You want to up the price some more?" Barrabas asked. "I thought you Gurkhas soldiered for the love of it."

"The tales are true," Thapa said. "Anyone who serves the British has to love soldiering. He cannot love wealth!"

The grin faded. "I ask for as much as I do, not because I fear you would not pay the debt. The man who brought out Sean Gordon's body was not one to think like a merchant."

"You must have known the Gordons for a while."

"Not as long as I would have liked to. Is it true that Sean was trying to fly out a load of wounded VC prisoners when he was shot down?"

Barrabas nodded. "Yeah. He thought broadcasting it in clear would keep the VC from shooting. Maybe it did, with some. The rest—well, some of them probably just didn't get the word. VC communications were even more screwed up than ours.

"Maybe some thought they were saving their comrades from torture, or keeping them from talking. Sean didn't think of that, and I didn't stop him until it was too late. That's the big reason I went in after his body. In a way, it was my fault."

"As I said, you do not think like a merchant. Nor do I."

The grin returned as Captain Thapa added, "I asked what I did as the price of staying behind while you go to fight the Chinese. I still owe them a debt for some friends who did not return from Malaya. The Chinese have some virtues, but also the vice of turning up where they aren't wanted."

"HE WANTED *what*?" Walker Jessup bellowed. He sounded like a bull elephant giving his mating call.

"I told you," Barrabas said, as if speaking to a small child. "He would have liked to join us in Tibet. Instead he's going to stay and guard the Gordons and Dr. Gonpo."

"One man!"

"One Gurkha. There's a difference. Not to mention that he's probably got friends—"

"Who will know every goddamn detail of our mission here before we cross the border! Nile, I used to think you'd heard of security—"

"My turn to interrupt," Barrabas said, more calmly than he felt. He reflected that the Chinese weren't the only people with the vice of turning up where they weren't welcome. Right now Walker Jessup had that in spades.

Come to think of it, the rest of the team could just as well have been somewhere else too. It was nice to have them at his back, but this head-butting session with Jessup really didn't need an audience.

"Go ahead, Nile." Jessup heaved a whale-sized sigh and sat down.

"Captain Thapa's a thirty-year veteran of the Second Gurkhas. He's got one nephew serving and another joining up next year. Most of his friends are likely to be the same breed of cat. The problem's not going to be their keeping quiet. It's going to be counting the pieces of the bad guys after they try for the Gordons. Hell, a *kukri* might even get through *your* blubber!''

"Okay, so Captain Thapa's got all the Boy Scout virtues. But he doesn't have to talk, for somebody to get suspicious over all the hardware you've ordered from the Gordons.''

"At least one set of somebodies already suspects. There's no way to keep them from talking to their friends. The only thing to do is get over the mountains before the friends show up.''

"A bunch of Malay drug lords isn't Indian Army Intelligence.'' Jessup was at least going to go down fighting.

"No,'' put in Liam O'Toole. "Those Malays are lively lads. The Indians—I much doubt they could find the Himalayas if they weren't all along the northern horizon.''

"Right,'' Barrabas said. "Fixer, are you going back on our agreement to let me scare up our own transportation and hardware if I could? I always suspected that might save time. Now I'm sure. I'd be dealing with the Gordons and Thapa even if we didn't have that agreement.''

Jessup seemed to be too out of breath to sigh. He shrugged, a gesture that knocked a half-empty plate of mutton off the table beside him.

"I agreed, all right. And I'll be damned if I ever make such an agreement again.''

"Fine. Just as long as you keep this one. You back out now, and you'll have to find out just how many favors the Agency still owes you. If it's enough to get those guerrillas chasing Colonel Yao, I'll eat all three Brens!''

"I *said* I agreed, Nile. What do you want, my signature in blood?''

"Nope. It's got too much cholesterol to make good ink. Okay, people. We've got a few days before the Gordons and our Gurkha friends are ready. Let's go find a mountain to climb.''

NILE BARRABAS PULLED himself to the top of the ridge Now he could see something beyond the gray-streaked

brown rock a foot in front of his nose and concern himself
with more than the next handhold.

To the north, the giant peaks of Annapurna and Dhau-
lagiri loomed, flanking a pass that arrowed straight into
Tibet. For the twentieth time, Barrabas was grateful for
living in the air age. If the SOBs had been going into Tibet
on foot, they might just as well not have started. Colonel
Yao would have time to find the rubies, take them to Peking, decide to defect and use the rubies to set up a Swiss
bank account before the SOBs teamed up with the guerrillas. And for the twentieth time, Barrabas also understood
why the Gurkhas were what they were. Most of Nepal, except the southern lowlands, was built on a slant. Anybody
who grew up humping loads up and down those slopes was
either tough or dead by seventeen.

After five days of acclimatization, the SOBs were spruc-
ing up their mountain climbing on a more modest peak
than the twin giants. Jurungche barely topped nineteen
thousand feet, the reported altitude of the ruby cave.

Barrabas believed that report about as much as he did
any other intelligence. If there'd been time, he would have
found a second peak—say, around twenty-two thousand
feet.

Colonel Yao wasn't the kind of enemy to hand out free
gifts of time, though. Nothing else either, but time least of
all.

Below him on the rope, Billy Two was watching the tail-
ender, Lee Hatton. She moved with the grace of a ballet
dancer and the delicacy of a deer across a sixty-degree
slope, just above a thousand-foot drop. Farther down the
ridge, the second rope—Liam O'Toole, Alex Nanos, and
Claude Hayes—was creeping into sight.

Barrabas looked up at the sun. They had at least three
hours of daylight before they'd have to start looking for a
campsite. The push to the summit might have to wait until
morning, but no harm in that. They'd deliberately picked
the more demanding of the two routes up Jurungche. Taking the other one down, they'd be back at the airstrip in
twelve hours. A pretty stiff twelve hours, but—

The sound of boots scrabbling for purchase on stone alerted Barrabas, even before the rope started to tighten. Reflexes and muscles went to combat overload. He rolled up and over onto the crest, whipping the rope around himself as he did. He'd made himself into a firm anchor before the rope went taut.

From below came voices. First Lee Hatton's, sounding more disgusted with herself than frightened. "Sorry, people. I stepped off from one foothold before I was sure about my next one. Now I understand why that's a no-no."

Then Billy Two:

"Colonel, Lee's gone over the edge. So far she's hanging in there—"

"Mr. Starfoot," came Lee's voice. "Do you want to make lousy puns? Or do you want to wake up after the next time I treat you and find something vital missing?"

"As I was about to say, I don't want to leave her there too long. She pulled her rope across a sharp edge when she went over. It doesn't look too great."

"Right," Barrabas said. The word came out sounding nearly normal. He felt almost normal, too. He considered that he was reacting to the situation as a straightforward case of one of his people in danger and not as a man facing danger to his woman.

Pleasure at this knowledge seemed to double Barrabas's strength. The rope with Lee on the end of it became as easy to handle as a boy's kite in a March wind. He held it without sweating, as Billy Two uncoiled his second rope and threw one end up to Barrabas. Still without sweating, Barrabas crawled to a convenient outcrop and tied the rope around it.

Belayed in two places, Billy Two now slid backward down the slope until he was past the sharp edge. With both hands free, he gripped Lee's rope and pulled her in slowly, like a hundred-pound fish on a twelve-pound line.

Barrabas only held his breath when the top of Lee's head appeared above the overhang. He didn't breathe again until Billy had one huge hand locked on Lee's arm and another hooked into her belt. He was back to normal by the time Lee and Billy crawled up to join him on the crest.

"What some people will do for a better view," Barrabas said, shaking his head.

"Hey, don't knock it until you've tried it," Billy said. "Or would you rather take my word for it?"

"A good C.O. always knows when to trust his people," Barrabas said, sitting up. "This is one of the times. Lee, are you in one piece?"

"At least in the same number of pieces I was in before I went over," she said. There was blood on one knee and a raw patch on her left hand, but Barrabas decided to let her mention them first.

Lee prodded the scrapes, then felt in the bottom pocket of her pack. "Oh, damn. I think my first-aid kit took a dive."

"Here." Billy handed her an olive-drab pouch. Casually, Lee unlaced her boots and pulled off her trousers.

She didn't improve the scenery as much as usual. That was because the scenery was better, not because Lee was worse. Seeing the Himalayas from close up, Barrabas now understood what had drawn four generations of climbers to face death in their snows.

It occurred to him that if he ever wanted to give up fighting, but not meeting challenges, he should come to these mountains.

Meanwhile there was one hell of a fight shaping up beyond those peaks, and the SOBs would be going into it at full strength. Relief and the sun together made Barrabas want to bask like a lizard on a rock. He stopped at taking a drink of water.

By the time Barrabas recapped his canteen, Lee was pulling on her trousers.

"How is it?"

"Just skin, in both places. Anyway, I've got some to spare. Nate Beck once told me the definition of *zaftig*— 'extra skin in the right places.'"

Lee took the first turn as lookout, while they waited for the other rope to catch up. As she took her post fifty yards along the ridge, Billy Two caught Barrabas's eye.

"Okay, Mr. Starfoot. Spit it out. Or am I supposed to read your mind?"

"No, Colonel. It's just that I couldn't help noticing."

"Noticing *what*?" Barrabas's voice had a sharper edge than the rock.

"That what was bothering you doesn't seem to be doing it anymore."

The blazing blue sky overhead suddenly seemed a lot less friendly, and the sun less warm. "Mister, *have* you taken up mind reading?"

"No," Billy said, without a trace of smile. "Hawk Spirit didn't give me that power."

Barrabas refused to believe that the altitude was getting to him.

"Will he?"

"If and when he chooses. Certainly he won't let me do it for my own profit." Billy's grin suddenly returned. "Of course, I don't know if learning what's bugging my C.O. is for my own profit. Maybe it's just what I need to do a warrior's duty. I'm not going to try second-guessing Hawk Spirit. He doesn't like that a whole lot."

"No, I don't suppose he would," Barrabas said.

He was saved from having to say anything more by Lee's signaling that the second rope was on the ridge. Barrabas stood up.

"Okay, time to make like goats again." So that only Billy Two could hear, he added, "By the way, you guessed right."

9

Barrabas looked at the map of the SOBs' Area of Operation. A grisly display of contour lines looked back at him.

The whole team had acclimatized themselves to Himalayan altitudes in five days. Barrabas could feel his breath rasping and his legs growing heavy in anticipation of the climbing to come.

Claude Hayes stood in front of the map with a pointer. Barrabas was letting him take the briefing tonight. Hayes's experience in training African liberation fighters had made him as skilled a briefer as the West Point trained Barrabas.

"Art Gordon air-lands us here—" the pointer tapped the map "—to join up with a band of Tibetan guerrillas. They help hump the ammo and heavy weapons, and give us extra firepower. We give them a chance to kick some Chinese ass with more than small arms."

"Let's hope the lads aren't so eager for the ass-kicking that they'll forget to run when they should," Liam O'Toole put in. "If they think we're Superman come to save them, we'll have more Chinese than Colonel Yao askin' rude questions."

"These are experienced people," Hayes said. "They know their long-term survival depends on not provoking the Chinese to make a major push against them. The CIA has a man with them and keeps them supplied with Chinese weapons."

Walker Jessup grunted. It was a loud, eloquent grunt. Nile Barrabas had heard it before. It usually meant bad news. Claude Hayes looked at his chief.

"Okay, Fixer," Barrabas said. "Have you been holding out on us?"

"Cross my heart and hope to die—"

"Just stop right there," Alex Nanos said. "Last time Lee looked you over, you didn't have a heart. Just a stomach and a liver. So cut the comedy routine and tell us how you've put our tails in a crack this time."

Barrabas kept a straight face with difficulty. He really shouldn't let Alex jump on Jessup this way; that was part of the C.O.'s job. But Alex had said so nearly what Barrabas himself would have said that the colonel didn't have the heart to intervene.

Jessup grunted again. "Okay. Remember, the CIA backing for the Tibetan guerillas was phased out in 1971."

"Officially," Barrabas said. .

"Yeah, and quite a lot of it really was pulled. It wasn't just the new idea that the Chinese were nice guys, either. It was getting too hard to keep the Nepalese from arresting the Tibetans when they had to cross the border. The Nepalese were trying to keep their noses clean, and we couldn't really offer them any alternative. What the hell could we have done if the Chinese put them on the shit list along with the Indians?

"At least that was the way the higher-ups thought. That didn't keep them from lining up free lancers—mostly non-Americans who knew Tibet. Either they were greedy or they owed us something. But whichever, they could be repudiated if the Chinese did grab them."

"Sounds like a great way to get real sleazy people," Hayes said.

"Yeah, you might say that," Jessup replied. "Just look at yourself and your buddies."

Hayes was too dark to blush, but Barrabas thought he heard the sound of grinding teeth. Jessup had zinged him nicely. That was one reason for the SOBs' high price—they knew they would be repudiated if anybody ever made an official fuss about them.

That wasn't just words, either. Geoff Bishop had spent a while on the wanted list as an international terrorist because nobody would explain how he'd come to be involved in a bombing in Florida. He wouldn't be the last SOB to be in that particular bind, either.

Half a million a job wasn't really enough to pay for that kind of bother. But throw in the fact that working this way meant the SOBs could take out people nobody else could reach, people who if not taken out would kill anything from hundreds to millions and not give a damn—it changed the balance sheet.

At least it did for Nile Barrabas, and he doubted that any of the other SOBs would be here if they didn't think the same way.

Although come to think of it, Hayes did have a point. The kind of job the Company wanted done in Tibet was made to order for Karl Heiss or one of his gang.

If Barrabas had a nemesis, it was Heiss. An ex-CIA man with even fewer scruples than the Agency required, Heiss had been using his connections to grab a piece of the international crime scene since the closing days of the Vietnam War. His path had crossed Barrabas's at least a dozen times. Most of those times, Heiss had supposedly wound up dead. Except that he kept coming back, like a character in a TV sitcom but even less funny....

"I've got a problem with our CIA free lancer," Barrabas said. "It's named Karl Heiss."

"Heiss is *dead*, goddammit!" Jessup growled.

"Where have I heard that before?" Barrabas said. "Now, I'm not saying that we've been lied to about that unkillable little prick. Maybe the last four or five times he's turned up it's been a clone. But those clones have nearly killed some of *us*. As far as I'm concerned, if it shoots at you, it's the real thing."

"You got any suggestions, Nile, or are you just beating your gums?" Jessup said.

"A suggestion. We want those guerrillas willing to take orders from us. What's the best way?"

"Is this a quiz, or what?" Jessup muttered. "If it is, I'm going to call in sick."

"Fine," Barrabas said. "Then you won't want any dinner."

"Now just a minute—" Jessup sputtered, then grunted again. "Okay. Send them some ammo and heavy weapons, and you'll have them listening real good. At least as much as they listen to the Company's man."

"Right. And I'm sure that with your extensive connections you can fix lots of Chinese ammunition and maybe an MG and a mortar."

"It won't come cheap—"

"*Without* asking us to pay," Hayes put in.

Jessup glared, then he shrugged, making his chair sway and creak. "Let's look at the equipment list. You people already have enough to overload a Herky bird, let alone that piece of Russian junk."

If the SOBs had taken everything they thought they might need in Tibet, the Fixer would have been right. As it was, they'd stripped their list down five successive times, until it came out reading:

Three Bren guns.

Nine FN FALs, all with bipods, two with scope sights.

A 9 mm pistol and two knives for each SOB.

The Carl Gustav Mark II 84 mm recoilless rifle. They didn't expect to need it for tanks or heavy vehicles, but it would do nicely for blasting Chinese weapons positions.

Radios, Starlite night-vision goggles and scopes, a huge medical kit, Arctic-quality tents and sleeping bags, freeze-dried rations.

Lots of ammunition, including hand and rifle grenades, flares, and C-4 explosive.

No frills, no exotic weaponry or electronics, nothing but reliable, proven gear that professionals like the SOBs could make jump through hoops. Simple, rugged, reliable—those were the key words for this mission, even more than usual.

Not that there wouldn't be headaches. The ammunition was the biggest one. It weighed as much as everything else put together, including the SOBs. On the other hand, running out of ammunition in the middle of a firefight was frowned on by both tactics instructors and next of kin.

They gathered around the equipment list, working it over with hand calculators and checking equipment weights against the Antonov's payload. Things came out the same way three times in a row.

Alex Nanos finally put the conclusion into words. "No way we can squeeze in a decent load of Chicom hardware on top of our stuff. Think Art can make a second trip?"

"I'd feel a lot better if he didn't have to," Barrabas said. "A second landing means staying on the level ground. That's going to slow us down. It'll also give our Chinese friends a better shot at us."

The higher the SOBs climbed, the better their chances of using the ground for ambush or evasion. The longer they stayed on level ground, the more danger of the Chinese bringing up superior numbers and firepower, including air support.

"What makes you think you can't air-drop a second load?" Jessup asked. He had the look of a cat who's just put the canary up to broil.

"Have you seen that Antonov?" Barrabas snapped. "Have you figured out how many passes it would take to unload it?"

"Too many, I'm sure," Jessup said. Now he was grinning like a cat who's just heard the timer ring and was setting the table. "I, however, have seen a Fokker Troopship with a rear door."

"What were you drinking?" Barrabas said. "Or shouldn't I ask?"

"I was drinking some good bourbon with an officer in the Nepalese Air Force who owes me a few favors from my Company days," Jessup said. "It gave me a vision, of arranging to borrow the little Fokker for twenty-four hours. Long enough to load it with all kinds of good stuff, fly it into Tibet, air-drop a couple of tons and fly out again.

"Not to mention that the Chinese have got a few of the same birds in service. With a little quick-drying paint in the right places, nobody who sees it is going to suspect anything. Unless they see the actual drop, and I suppose I can trust you hairy-fisted merc types to prevent *that* as part of earning your inflated fees...."

"Jessup," Barrabas said. "I have to admit that at least two hundred pounds of you is still pure professional. I won't make bets on the rest, though."

"If that's your idea of praise, Lord help me if you ever want to insult me," Jessup said. "Do we have a deal?"

"You fix that Fokker," Barrabas said, "and we may even send flowers to your funeral."

"Your loyalty touches me," Jessup replied. He felt around his bloated torso. "Somewhere around here—no, that's my kidney—yeah, here." He patted his stomach just above the buckle of his size fifty-six belt.

"COMRADE COMMANDER! Comrade Commander Yao! Wake up!"

"Ah—ayahhh..."

"Comrade Yao! We have been attacked!"

"Attack...?" The word sounded as strange to Yao as if it had been in Tibetan. He knew that strangeness might hold danger, but did not want to believe it.

If there was danger, he would have to put aside his dream of being in his apartment in Shanghai, wake up and *do something*.

Shame flooded Yao at this weakness, shame so hot and painful that he knew sleep and dreams were done for now. He wrestled his way out of his sleeping bag, buttoned up his tunic and stared into the pale face of Company Commander Zhou.

"What is it now? If it is that Khampa barbarian whining about the mountain spirits—"

"A Khampa does not whine," came a voice from behind Yao. By sheer reflex he whirled, nearly drawing his pistol.

Ragpa Dapon said nothing, only loomed in the starlight like an outcropping of his native mountains. His usual reek of rancid yak butter and sweaty fleeces seemed stronger than ever.

"Anyone who believes in the mountain spirits..." Zhou began. Then he bit down on his anger. The Khampa would believe as he pleased. The only way to drive the mountain spirits out of that shaggy head would be to drive everything else out as well, with a carefully placed bullet. The time for that had not come.

Meanwhile Yao's ears were searching the darkened camp for the sounds of the attack. Hearing nothing, he turned back to Zhou.

"What kind of attack?" Yao would not humiliate Zhou before the Khampa by suggesting that the young commander had imagined things.

"Two sentries are missing," Zhou replied. "The northern two. We heard no shots or cries. I have replaced them, doubled the men at the other posts and loaded the mortar with flares. I can organize a search party if the column commander wishes."

Yao looked at his watch. Two hours until there was enough light for a soldier to see his hand in front of his face, or a cliff in front of his feet. He shook his head.

"I will wager a good dinner that the men only wandered off to relieve themselves and lost their way. Better that they stay where they are than try to return and lose themselves even more thoroughly."

"They should still be disciplined severely," Zhou said.

"I am sure I can leave that to you," Yao said.

"It is in other hands than ours, to punish those men," Ragpa Dapon interrupted.

"You are the interpreter, not I," Yao said, with more patience than he felt. "It is your duty to answer riddles, not ask them."

At least the fool had not mentioned the mountain spirits! Perhaps he was actually about to say something worth hearing, although Yao would not have wagered more than a single bowl of rice on that possibility.

"There is no riddle in the fate of the men," the Khampa said. "I heard the call of the *miqu*, as clearly as I hear you now."

"The what?" Yao wanted to believe that he had not heard what he thought he'd heard.

"The *miqu*," Zhou said helpfully. "The legendary manlike snow creature of the high Himalayas. The imperialists call it 'the Abominable Snowman,'" he added with a positive enthusiasm for sharing knowledge.

Yao wished he could feel some of that same enthusiasm. The Khampa had passed from mountain spirits to mountain apes, from one fairy tale to another!

"There is no such thing as the *miqu*," Yao snapped. "Perhaps there is some unknown species of ape in these mountains. If there is, perhaps we can bring back one for the Peking Zoo. It cannot be dangerous to a fighter of the People's Liberation Army. The morning will prove that."

"As you wish," Ragpa Dapon said. His tone implied that the wishes of a mere Chinese regiment commander made little difference to either him or the *miqus*.

Under his breath, Yao cursed the Khampa's retreating back until he noticed that Zhou was trying hard not to listen.

"You have done well, Comrade Zhou. Keep the sentries doubled and the flares in the mortar. Prepare a squad to reinforce any post that calls for help. Do not hesitate to wake me again if anything suspicious happens."

"Or if our strayed sheep return?"

"*When* they returned, Zhou. Surely you do not fear for their safety?"

"I—no, they are properly trained fighters of the PLA. Indeed, there is nothing we need fear except guerrillas, and there has been no sign of those. Sleep well, Comrade Commander."

Yao crawled back into his sleeping bag and let its warmth envelop him. Sleep was slow to come, however. When it did, he kept dreaming of hearing strange grunting noises outside his apartment window, and seeing a giant, hairy paw scrabbling at the shutters.

LEE HATTON SET her cup down. Dr. Gonpo looked at the gently steaming brass tea urn.

"More?"

She shook her head. "You still make a fine cup of butter tea. But I'd better get to bed. Tonight's my last chance to sleep in late."

Gonpo nodded and dipped up more of the thick Tibetan brew in his own cup, then pushed a plate of barley cakes at Lee. "Is there any point in my asking once more if I can go with you?"

"There's a point in *not* asking that again, Chopel. Do it again and I'll wonder if you're trying to protect me!"

The doctor raised his hands in mock horror. "Buddha grant me the wisdom to avoid *that* folly. Even if I did not know you, I have seen how the others treat you."

"Then why do you keep asking?" Lee wasn't quite sure she wanted to know. The world seemed to hold too many bleak, ugly truths since Geoff Bishop's death. If this was another one—

If this was another one, she would have to face it, and all the others like it. Hiding her head in the sand was a good way to get her other end blown off—if the SOBs didn't notice what she was doing and pack her off to safety.

That would hurt them more than it would her, and not just because they'd need to replace their combat medic. She was the one with the deepest roots in the sunlit normal world, thanks to her profession. The rest were natives of the shadow world of covert operations, mercenaries and organized—or improvised—mayhem.

The SOBs were a family, and her leaving after the losses they'd suffered in various ways would be one more step toward breaking it up. *Not* a step to be taken lightly, if she wanted to sleep at night.

"Why?" Gonpo said. "It is because I have no other hope of ever seeing my mother's homeland again. Once more before I pass to my next incarnation, I want to stand on Tibetan soil. I have done too much work for the underground, to go safely on one of our diplomatic missions. The Chinese would seize me, and my comrades would face a terrible choice—abandon me, or share my fate. So I must go secretly or not at all."

"Better not go at all, then," Lee said. She laid her hand on his. "How will we know where to send the rubies once we've found them, without your help?"

"I could—no, I could not change your mind by telling you the names. Your Walker Jessup probably already knows them. Also, you are your father's daughter. He also was one hard to turn aside from his chosen path. The Buddha guided his footsteps. May you be as fortunate."

Gonpo raised his teacup in salute, then emptied it and walked over to the corner of the tiny room. In a moment he was in lotus position, in another moment filling the room with "Om mani padme hum..."

"Hail, Jewel in the Lotus Flower," Lee translated under her breath.

She blinked stinging eyes and walked to the door, more than ready to change places with her classmate. He had faced as many grisly truths as she had, without losing a serenity that she'd never possessed to begin with.

Lee even suspected that Gonpo's serenity would survive the SOBs handing the rubies over to the Triads. She wished she could say the same about her loyalty to the team.

The Fixer was pushing her closer to her limit than ever before. That was one grisly truth she'd found remarkably easy to face. So easy, in fact, that she was tempted to lay it out for Nile.

The temptation passed quickly. He didn't deserve the extra headache—not until the moment when she actually had to act.

Not to mention that he probably had guessed already. Nile Barrabas might have problems understanding women. He had no problem understanding battle comrades.

10

Company Commander Zhou was the first to spot one of the missing sentries. The man lay on the edge of a hundred-meter drop. The body was oddly misshapen, and the rock around it smeared with blood. Zhou's last hope that the men would be found unharmed vanished.

His self-control nearly followed, after his first clear look at the man. One arm was missing—torn or, so it seemed, twisted out of its socket. Both legs were broken, and one seemed to have been gnawed on.

The head was the worst. A blow from—a stone? a club? a fist?—had crushed in one side, from the ear around to the nose. The remaining eye stared at the hard blue sky, while the mouth was twisted up into a ghastly half-smile.

Zhou was glad that he had led the search party out of the camp without eating breakfast. If he could just keep his hands and voice steady, Commander Yao would have no reason to doubt him.

"You and you!" he shouted, pointing at the two nearest fighters and then at the body. "Make a litter of your capes. The rest of you, lock and load." He drew his pistol and obeyed his own order. "Anyone who fires without orders will wish he'd been sent to a labor gang by the time I finish with him!"

"Shouldn't we send a message back to the Commander?" the deputy platoon commander asked.

"What would we say?" Zhou snapped. "That we've found one sentry and are looking for the other? Remember the commander's rule. 'To send incomplete information is to fail in a fighter's first duty.'"

"I have not forgotten, Comrade Zhou. But—"

"If you are going to be insubordinate, speak like a man instead of squealing like a pig."

"Are we not perhaps pigs trailing a tiger?"

"No tiger touched that fighter!"

"That is as certain as anything can be, Comrade Commander. I would not fear that a tiger could sweep us all out of existence before we gave a warning."

"Two men are not twenty," Zhou said. He knew that his authority was fraying, but he had no ideas except stating the obvious. Also, his mouth was too dry for long speeches.

"We know our own strength, to be sure," the deputy platoon commander said. "Do we know the strength of whatever killed the sentries?"

"We do not. But by daylight, we know the strength of our rifles. Nothing of flesh and blood can stand against them. What we can see, we can fight."

Zhou glared at the other man, daring him to ask about what might happen after dark. The junior commander opened his mouth, seemed ready to cross the line between advice and defeatism, then nodded and turned away.

They could have found the second body faster if Zhou had been willing to leave the first one. He refused to leave either the body or a small party to guard it. Whatever roamed these mountains, Zhou swore, would have no more easy victims. The platoon would stay together until it returned to camp.

Two kilometers to the west, the leader of the first squad saw birds wheeling above a crack in the rock. Zhou hurried forward, holstering his pistol as the ground steepened. He covered the last few meters on hands and knees, with the birds shrieking in protest above and the black hole in the rock yawning ahead.

Zhou approached the hole with a grenade tucked into the top of his boot. A quick pull on the pin, and a throw while he was rolling to one side, should finish any welcoming party without much risk to him.

What lay inside the hole didn't need a grenade or any other weapon. The body had all its limbs, but its head was twisted completely around so that it stared backward. From throat to groin, the body cavity gaped open, and fragments of half-eaten organs plastered the blood-smeared rock.

Zhou backed down to level ground, then remained on hands and knees until he was sure he could stand. The deputy platoon commander offered him a hand, but Zhou twisted away from the gesture and rose unaided.

"We have complete intelligence for Commander Yao," he said, "Fighter Beng is in there."

"Like the other one?"

"Worse. We shall have to leave him." Maybe Beng wasn't wedged too firmly to be pulled free. But Zhou wasn't going to order any of his fighters to do what he couldn't bring himself to do—wrestling that ghastly cadaver out of its grave in the rock.

Let these cursed mountains be Fighter Beng's tomb. Company Commander Zhou had his duty to the living!

Two new bearers took the load of the other body. The platoon began retracing its steps toward the camp.

THE SCREEN DOOR OF THE HUT banged as Arthur Gordon stuck his head inside. Ganparsing Thapa hid his surprise by turning slowly in his seat. None of the SOBs as much as moved, except for Nile Barrabas himself. He unfolded his fatigue-clad six foot four and ran a hand through his singular white hair, then looked a question at the pilot.

"Ready?"

Arthur nodded. "It's as clear as it's going to get, people. Ceiling's about fifteen thousand. That means using a different route, with a wider pass. I hate flying too close to stuffed rocks."

"Any other problems?" Barrabas asked.

"Well, we'll be deviating from our filed route a lot sooner. If somebody suspicious is monitoring the radar, he'll smell a rat as soon as we pass Tingjegaon."

"The Nepalese Air Force doesn't have anything that can intercept us," Barrabas said. "Right, Captain?"

The Gurkha nodded. "Embarrassing to a Nepalese, yes, but convenient for you."

"Very," Arthur said. "Even if word does reach the Chinese in time, we'll be right down in the rocks. I don't think a full-sized AWACS could plot a course from what they'll be able to pick up!"

"I can live with that," Barrabas said. "Okay, people. Let's move it."

Thapa was first out of the door and first to the edge of the haze-shrouded landing strip. Arthur Gordon came next, doing his final walk-around of the vast, clumsy-looking Russian biplane. As he climbed into the cockpit, the SOBs filed out of the hut.

Thapa climbed onto the roof of the Ashok Leyland five-ton truck, unslung his Sterling, and watched the SOBs boarding the plane.

The Greek, Alex Nanos, as strong as two men.

The hard-drinking Irishman, Liam O'Toole.

The American Indian, William Starfoot, who moved like a prowling tiger even when carrying a Bren gun and its ammunition.

Claude Hayes, the black American who seemed to see every side of an issue without ever doubting what his own side should be.

Lee Hatton, a woman, but clearly treated by the others as both doctor and battle comrade.

White-haired Nile Barrabas, the leader who wove all of them into a single seamless fabric.

Barrabas sat in the pilot's chair while Arthur Gordon jumped down again and swung the big propeller. Three times the starter whined without the engine catching. On the fourth try the engine banged like a charge of dynamite, making the whole plane shake. Through the window, Thapa saw Nanos frowning and saying something to the Indian, who smiled and shook his head.

Afraid? No. It was not in any of these people to fear dying. Only to fear failing in their mission—or even worse, failing their comrades.

Every one of them would have made a good Gurkha.

Arthur scrambled back into the plane; his head appeared in the cockpit window again. Randall Gordon snatched the chocks away from the wheels, moving with the briskness of a man thirty years younger. Thapa said a prayer of thanks to the SOBs, Prince Su, and even Colonel Yao and Walker Jessup.

Among them, they had brought the Gordons back to life. It hardly mattered where the rubies ended up. Father and son now had plan and purpose, instead of spinning out one year after another as they had done since Sean Gordon's death.

The second chock flew clear, and Randall waved both arms over his head. The throttle opened, and the big radial engine swelled from a rattle to a roar. Playing with rudder and brakes, Arthur swung the plane a hundred and eighty degrees, until its nose pointed straight down the runway.

The engine roar swelled further, and the plane crept forward as the engine overcame the brakes. Flaps wiggled in a final test. Then the plane surged forward as Arthur released the brake. It rolled down the steadily shrinking grass runway until suddenly there was air beneath the wheels.

Those wheels nearly clipped a stand of oak. Birds exploded from the plane's path in a rainbow spray. Thapa prayed again that none of the birds were large enough to break the propeller.

The plane climbed unharmed through the birds and through plumes of mist above the trees. It climbed steadily toward the face of Himal Chulj until Thapa began to wonder if the mission would end almost before it began.

At last the Antonov banked almost imperceptibly, swinging right to clear the south spur of the mountain. Then just as delicately it banked the other way and vanished behind the bulk of the central peak.

"Boy's still got it all," Randall Gordon said, looking up. He was kneeling beside the strip, plucking handfuls of wildflowers and dropping them into a damp canvas bag. "You don't swing wide around one mountain when there's another waiting for you on the other side of the valley. You sneak around them both."

Thapa nodded silently. Wrestling middle-aged airplanes through the Himalayas was an art he would gladly leave to others. He slung his Sterling and scrambled down from the roof of the truck.

"Climb in, Mr. Gordon. I have some friends I'd like to ask for help."

"If they aren't Gurkhas—"

"Do I look like a fool?" Captain Thapa threw the door open. "Climb in."

"Walker Jessup still won't like your breaking security that much. Colonel Barrabas won't mind, but he's not the one you'll be dealing with."

"May a camel tread on Walker Jessup's pubic hairs." Thapa waited until Randall was seated, then started the truck. "Let it also be known that it would not matter whether the Fixer colonel protested or not. I have eaten your salt, yours and your son's. I have promised to keep you safe from the Chinese, a large task for one man even when he is a Gurkha.

"So you and Dr. Gonpo will be protected by my friends whether you wish it or not. If Mr. Jessup's agreement with Dr. Weng makes this unnecessary, no harm will be done. But we will watch even Dr. Weng's men very closely."

Randall started to look indignant, then the truck hit a rut hard enough to bang his bald head against the roof. By the time he'd stopped rubbing the bump, he'd started to laugh.

"I guess the only way to stop you and your friends would be to shoot you ourselves. Right?"

"It would be risky, but certainly nothing else would work."

"That's what I figured. Okay, Ganparsing. Whistle up the whole damned brigade of Gurkhas if you want. I'll try to square things with the Fixer."

COMMANDER YAO SAW what was delaying Zhou's platoon when Zhou was still several hundred meters away. The time it took for the platoon to cover that distance did not improve Yao's temper.

"Comrade Yao," he said, with a restraint he did not feel. "You could have sent a messenger. I would have brought the column forward to join the search. From where you found the bodies, we could have marched quickly to the Khib Pass. As it is, we must retrace our steps. If we do not, there is danger of the guerrillas reaching the area of the caves before we do."

Zhou made a noise rather like a pot of rice boiling over and looked at the sky as if seeking assistance in keeping his temper. Then he replied, while looking everywhere except at Yao.

"Comrade Commander, I am aware of the menace from the guerrillas. But I ask you to examine the body we have brought back. You may then understand why I was reluctant to let men leave the platoon."

Yao frowned at Zhou's tone but decided that the younger man would not be asking him to examine a hallucination. He followed Zhou downhill toward the shrouded body.

Halfway down the slope, Ragpa Dapon joined the two officers. Yao could have done without the man's company.

Yao had a moment's satisfaction when Zhou unwrapped the body. The Khampa said something in his own tongue and stepped back a full meter. His massive hands seemed to shake—or perhaps he was performing some superstitious ritual.

Certainly the fighter was a memorably hideous corpse. "We left Beng up there," Zhou added. "He had been jammed into a crack in the rock. We could not pull him out."

"The guerrillas must be closer than the 115th Regiment's outpost believed," Yao said meditatively. "Perhaps also in strength. Otherwise they would not have taken the time to mutilate—yes, Comrade Zhou? Or are you going to deny that you were about to say something?"

Zhou had been under Yao's command long enough to know that the truth was the only acceptable answer to such questions. "I was merely thinking that there are possible explanations for the deaths of our fighters other than Tibetan guerrillas."

"Are there?"

If Yao had put into his voice all the sarcasm he felt, it would have humiliated Zhou in front of the Khampa. So he had restrained himself.

"I admit that guerrillas are the most probable cause. But some of the mutilations—they look more like an animal's work."

The Khampa seemed about to speak. In the shadow of the hood of his *chupa*, the man's mouth was working silently. Yao was tempted to ask what the man was saying, then considered what would happen if the Khampa refused to answer.

"Perhaps there is some animal yet unseen by science in these mountains," Yao said briskly. "In that case we have a chance to give the Peking Zoo the first specimen. All the imperialist mountain climbers will gnash their teeth.

"However, that will be only an extra victory for the People's Liberation Army. The victory we must win is over the guerrillas. They are beyond the Khib Pass, so we must begin retracing your steps at once. Is the platoon fit to take the lead?"

"Give me five minutes to pick the freshest men," Zhou said sturdily. "Then the platoon will be fit to lead anyone anywhere!"

"Thank you, Comrade Zhou. The wisest officer is one who asks of his men a little more than he thinks they can give. Thus are made the hardiest fighters, those of the People's Liberation Army."

Zhou hurried off. Turning, Yao saw that the Khampa had left sometime during the little lecture. Dignity would not let Yao shout after the man.

Besides, what was there to say? Yao was not in a mood to listen to more tales of *miqus* and other creations of minds diseased by superstitions. It was true that the column would now have to cross the last of the Khib Pass by dark, but that was Zhou's fault. He should have sent a message back and saved everyone hours of marching.

That great filthy barbarian was *not* to know that a commander in the People's Liberation Army officer had made a mistake!

11

Through the Antonov's cabin window, Lee Hatton saw the dusty-gray Tibetan plateau sliding up toward them. In the late afternoon sun the ground had a purplish tinge.

"Lock and load," Barrabas said.

The dice-box rattle of chambered rounds and snapped safeties was lost in the roar of the Antonov's engine. Lee's last glimpse of the ground was a shallow stream with dark shapes crouched by the bank. Then all she could see was sky as the pilot flared the plane for landing.

Wheels hit, bounced, hit again and stayed on the ground. Every rock and rut seemed to jar Lee's spine all the way up to her teeth. Once, the plane tilted sickeningly, and she heard the squeal of metal as a wingtip grazed something solid. She wedged her FAL between her knees and locked her hands on the edge of her seat.

The sense of rattling around like a pea in a thimble faded as the plane slowed. There was a final lurch as Arthur Gordon swung the plane into position for takeoff, then a finishing slaughtered-pig squeal of brakes.

A box of ammunition broke loose and bounced merrily down the cabin. It fetched up against Alex Nanos's foot. He said something, probably in Greek and certainly impolite, then unstrapped.

"If God had meant us to fly, he'd have given us more padding," Nanos added.

"Speak for yourself, Alex," Lee said. "I've never had any complaints."

"About airplanes or your padding?" Nanos said, with an amiable leer.

"When you come right down to it—"

"Anytime, Doctor."

"When all is said and done—no, don't touch that one either. Let's say I haven't heard any complaints about either."

"You won't, either," Barrabas said. "But Mr. Nanos just might, if he doesn't move it. Only a minuscule percentage of his inflated fee is being paid for comedy routines."

"Yassuh, Colonel," Nanos said. Claude Hayes rolled his eyes and pantomimed throwing Nanos out of the plane. The Greek ended the argument by swinging out of the door and dropping to the ground. The offending ammunition box went with him, tucked under one thick arm.

Quickly the team dropped to the ground and ran clear of the prop wash, crouching and blinking against the dust and pebbles blasting past them. Lee and Barrabas were the last out, the colonel with a Bren gun and Lee with a crate of Bren magazines in addition to their personal weapons and gear.

At the door, Barrabas looked back. "Thanks, Art. We owe you and your Dad for this one."

"You don't owe me a friggin' thing until I come back and get you. It's not my ass on the line!"

"Even flying home through the mountains by dark?"

"No sweat, thanks to your friend Nate Beck. He ever think of patenting these things?" Arthur slapped the control panel, where displays never dreamed of by the Antonov's designers glowed discreetly.

"We'll suggest it next time we get in touch with him," Barrabas said. "Good luck."

He dropped to the ground, then held out a hand to Lee. They sprinted away from the plane as the engine revved up. By the time they'd joined the rest of the team, the Antonov was bumping down the field. It bounced a little higher at each bump, until finally it bounced up and didn't come down. For a painfully long time it skimmed the ground, then suddenly pulled up into a climbing turn and shrank into the sky.

Lee started to unsling her rifle, then counted the shaggy figures who seemed to be sprouting from the ground all along the stream. She decided that maybe drawing a weapon on these people wouldn't be the wisest thing to do.

And it certainly wouldn't help if the hundred-odd Tibetans were led by someone working for Karl Heiss.

AT ONE END of the teak table stood a large plaster Buddha. Behind it hung a yellow prayer flag. At the other end of the table rose a tea urn. The two Tibetan lamas at the table made Walker Jessup think of two more Buddhas, or maybe two of the three wise monkeys.

The senior lama frowned, which was the most expression Jessup had seen him show since the meeting started an hour earlier. Then he shook his head, as his face returned to its former blankness.

"Mind translating that?" Jessup said. He was two hours overdue for dinner, and his last meal had barely deserved the name. Two scrawny chickens and a triple portion of *chapattis* were just enough to keep him from turning into a cannibal.

"Our answer to your request for guards has to be no," the junior lama replied. His senior glowered at him, as if speaking plainly had been bad manners.

Jessup grunted. If these characters wanted to play games, he couldn't do a hell of a lot about it. But he'd be damned if he was going to let them go without asking why!

"The Chinese won't even hear about it, putting guards around my—our—supplies for a few days. Once the stuff's hauled off to Tibet, your people can go home."

In fact, any Tibetan guards had damned well better go home once the second load of ammo was air-dropped to the SOBs. The fewer armed Tibetans around when Jessup handed the rubies over to Weng's people, the better. If the SOBs decided they didn't agree with the fate of the rubies Jessup wouldn't put it completely past them to try hijacking the cache, but he wasn't going to worry much about it. They didn't like him a lot, but they'd been covering his ass and he'd been covering theirs for too long.

It would be a different business, though, if Lee Hatton dropped a word in Dr. Gonpo's ear and that word reached the Tibetan Youth Congress. If a bunch of Tibetan muscle suddenly showed up and said, "Your rubies or your ass," Walker Jessup had a feeling they might get the rubies and to hell with the Triads—until the bastards found out.

The only thing that would save the ass and other parts of Mrs. Jessup's boy was the Triads being able to figure out whom to shoot first. By the time they did, Jessup might be able to explain that it wasn't his fault, and they might be willing to listen.

"We are aware of this," said the senior lama. "It does not protect us from the Indians. Our experience suggests they might learn within hours."

Walker Jessup grunted again at being told something he already knew. Why had he resisted recruiting Gurkhas for this job? Half the little bastards would be talking to the Indians, the other half to the Brits. There wasn't room in this pie for all the fingers that were already stuck into it! The last thing he wanted to do was issue engraved invitations to more.

"I can appeal your decision to the Dalai Lama," Jessup said. "You wouldn't go against him!"

"We would not, if his decision was in your favor. Yet would you trouble him with such a worldly matter? And if he deigned to render a decision, would it come in time? You seem to be in some haste."

Remind me never to play poker with these guys, Jessup thought. They have a nasty way of reading a man's cards right out of his hand.

Needing the people fast was Jessup's big weakness. Any delay was almost the same as a no-go. And he used to think it was just Company bureaucracy that slowed things up, when he needed warm bodies or cold guns ASAP!

"This matter is very close to my heart. So is the freedom of the Tibetan people," Jessup said.

"Is it?" the younger lama said. The shrewdness in the brown eyes and the skepticism in the low voice made Jessup start. The movement made his chair squeak and sway ominously, even though it was handcrafted teak. Designed for Indians and Tibetans, it was stressed to the limit by Jessup.

Have these two old priests guessed where the rubies are really supposed to go? Having to fight off Tibetans is going to be all kinds of fun, not to mention what the SOBS will say!

Since he had to say something, Jessup managed to get out, "How can you doubt me?"

"We do not doubt your good intentions," the senior lama said. "Yet we permit ourselves to doubt that working with the guerrillas is the only solution. Indeed, it might affect delicate negotiations about which we cannot speak."

Jessup was tempted to get a bit of his own back by describing the "delicate negotiations" with the Chinese in detail. The Chinese had been holding out hopes of a negotiated settlement with the Tibetans for several years. From what Jessup knew, all they really wanted was to get the Dalai Lama back to Lhasa, so they could use him as a puppet to prop up their occupation.

The Dalai Lama had both brains and balls. He wasn't going to screw his people that way. Some of the people around him were more like these two lamas, men who'd been middle-aged when they fled Tibet around 1960. Now they were old. If they didn't get home in another five years, they probably wouldn't get home at all.

"I wish such negotiations well. But I confess I have little faith in them. The Chinese will not go unless they are forced out. Such is the belief of many of your fellow Tibetans."

"I forbid you to approach the Tibetan Youth Congress!" the junior man practically shouted. It was his senior's turn to start, while Jessup tried not to grin. It never did any harm to get your opponents arguing in public, even if you didn't have any intention of doing what they wanted to prevent!

"I would not care to set Tibetan against Tibetan," Jessup said, doing his best imitation of a pious politician. "I merely remind you that the cause of the guerrillas is very close to the heart of many Tibetans. I certainly will not drive them from my door if they come to me."

The senior lama nodded. "No one will ask you to do that," he said, in a tone that practically dared his colleague to open his mouth. "I would hope that we can part, if not as friends, at least without danger of becoming enemies."

"I will never be an enemy of the Tibetan people or any opponent of their freedom," Jessup said, thinking it nice to be able to tell the truth for once.

"Then let us drink to our friendship," the junior lama said. "I believe the tea is ready."

Jessup's stomach rumbled in protest at the thought of more butter tea, then twitched as he poured it down. He wasn't quite ready to convert to Communism if the Chinese would outlaw butter tea, but he would be a lot happier if his next job took him to some civilized coffee-drinking place like Brazil or Turkey!

In fact, he was almost ready to contemplate turning in his operative's suit and settling down with a taco stand in Dallas. Almost. Jessup knew he might stand it for as much as six months—hardly worth the trouble of even trying in the first place.

Besides, he'd go crazy with nothing to eat but tacos!

Had the SOBs ever guessed that what drove the Fixer was the same thing that drove them? The knowledge that life was only worth living if you lived in danger of death every moment?

Good question—and not likely to help him with these lamas, even if he found the answer.

Jessup pretended eagerness for another cup of tea and actually managed to get it down. "Would you care to stay for dinner?" the junior lama asked.

"I am honored by your offer, but I have a plane to catch," Jessup replied, shading the truth only a bit. Dining with the Tibetans wouldn't guarantee his meeting anyone worth talking to. It would guarantee everybody and their cousin knowing about the fat American's presence.

Sooner or later, that knowledge would be passed on to somebody who would pass it on to Karl Heiss or the Chinese. Jessup honestly didn't know which he feared more. Heiss was only one man, which meant he could move faster than any government.

Of course he could also be killed more easily, but Walker Jessup no longer took bets on being able to kill Karl Heiss. He and the SOBs just went on trying to do it every time they had a chance.

THE NEAREST MOUNTAIN was a black silhouette against a mist of stars when the guerrillas made camp. They did this as efficiently and quietly as they'd done everything else since the SOBs joined them.

Lee Hatton, watching the Tibetans, realized that she hadn't seen a clean man or a dirty rifle in the whole band. The first, given the circumstances, didn't surprise her. The second did, considering how much work it must take.

The rifles themselves were a mixture of Chinese models, some Type 68 assault rifles but more bolt-action Type 56s, some of them so old they were probably Russian-made. A few hand grenades. They had only one battered LMG with three magazines, and they looked as if they'd never heard of RPGs or mortars.

"In the country of the rifleman, the machine gunner is king." Lee mentally rewrote the old saying for their circumstances and began checking her bandolier to see how her FAL ammo had survived the day's marching.

The CIA man came up, shielding a lighted cigarette with one hand. He gave his name as McPherson, and he was tall and rangy, with a dirty-blond beard and an accent Lee Hatton couldn't quite place. He wore a dirt-stiffened Tibetan leather *chupa*, baggy Chinese uniform trousers, and fur-lined boots as ragged as his followers'. He carried a Type 68 with a fixed bayonet and a holstered pistol.

"Hope your pilot's good or lucky," McPherson said.

"We know he's good," Lee said politely.

"Geoff Bishop would be," McPherson said.

The SOBs were professionals; nobody blew their cool by even as much as a raised eyebrow. Lee's eyes stung from more than the mountain air, but her voice betrayed nothing as she replied.

"Captain Bishop never relies on luck," she said. "That's why we trust him."

"Good move," McPherson said. Whatever reply he'd expected, he hadn't heard it. Crushing his cigarette underfoot, he turned away.

Lee Hatton let out a long breath and mentally cursed McPherson, since she couldn't plant a boot in his groin. Was McPherson just another Company prick, showing off his knowledge? Or was he hoping to draw the SOBs out and learn something he could pass on to—better not call it Heiss?

Either way, he seemed to be relying on the SOBs needing him more than he needed them. He was right, too. He had a hundred people against six, and looked as if he knew his business.

Well, Nile Barrabas would sort this one out if anybody could. If he wanted advice, he'd ask for it. Lee checked her ammo until the urge to use some of it on McPherson faded.

Another thought wouldn't fade. *I really didn't tell a lie. A dead man can't be lucky or unlucky. He's just—dead.*

A lot different from Nate Beck, who was sitting on his tail in Connecticut and piling up money putting together his software, somebody else's hardware, and input from people like Geoff Bishop. There wasn't any justice!

Anger at Nate Beck rose in Lee, then receded. The little guy had put his neck on the line often enough, before he pulled the plug on fieldwork. It was just luck that it was Geoff Bishop who was gone instead of Nate Beck.

This kept her from being mad at Beck most of the time, but never quite kept her from missing Geoff.

Lee decided there was something to be said for the notion of the bullet with your name on it. At least it let you sleep easier with the memory of your dead, and right now a good night's sleep was something she badly needed.

A PEBBLE SHIFTED under Ragpa Dapon's left foot. He froze, silently cursed the pebble and waited to hear it rolling freely, alerting the Chinese.

The blessing of the spirits was still with him. The pebble made only a tiny click that no Chinese could have heard. Dapon went down on all fours and crept the last few paces, then peered around the boulder at the Chinese sentry post.

Four men, not two. Commander Yao did not completely lack caution. Dapon frowned. Indeed it was fortunate that his approach had been silent. Against four Chinese soldiers, even a Khampa needed surprise. Dapon prayed that he would at least not be reincarnated as a Chinese, then drew his sword.

He meant to draw it silently, but the blade rasped faintly on the lip of the scabbard. Some trick of the night wind carried the sound to Chinese ears. The two standing sentries peered into the darkness, raising their rifles. The two seated sentries sprang to their feet.

Dapon gripped two stones the size of pigeon eggs in his free hand. One he threw as far to the left as he could. It clattered on the rocks, sounding as loud as an exploding grenade. All four Chinese turned to look toward the sound.

They were still looking without seeing when the second stone leaped out of the night. It smashed into the outpost leader's left temple, just above his ear. He went down as if trampled by a yak.

As he fell, he dropped his rifle and sent a comrade sprawling. Dapon leaped over both fallen men, not bothering with the rifle. He needed swift and silent weapons.

The other two Chinese turned. Dapon's sword slashed down, laying open one soldier's forehead and beating down the barrel of his rifle. He reeled and Dapon seized him, whirled him around and held him as a shield.

The lunging bayonet of the last Chinese plunged deep between his comrade's ribs. Silence ended as the bayoneted man gave a gasping cry and sprayed blood. The fourth Chinese stared appalled at his mistake. He was still staring when a Khampa sword sliced his head from his shoulders. More blood thickened the smell hanging in the night air.

Dapon ended the fight and the fourth Chinese by stamping on the man's ribs until they crunched under his boots like a basket. As he stepped back, he sensed a new smell joining the reek of blood. It was an animal smell— harsh, pungent, yet vital.

Then Dapon heard the soft click of claws on the ground behind him. He knelt and laid his sword on the ground, then held his arms spread wide with hands open.

Adopting the posture of submission did its work. The *miqu* snuffled and snorted, then padded past the four corpses and the kneeling man. Dapon dared to raise his head long enough to see a shape, half again as tall and twice as wide as a man, outlined against the stars. Then it vanished down the other side of the ridge.

"May your steps be sure and your path uncrossed by more Chinese, brother," Dapon said softly. "Even the weak and the cowardly can be dangerous if there are enough of them."

Still kneeling, the Khampa examined the fallen rifles, picking the best two and gathering all the magazines and grenades from the four men. His hands and clothes were smeared with blood by the time he was done. He could only hope there were no snow leopards on the path to the guerrillas. Submission would not turn the leopards aside. They would have to be killed.

To kill such fine creatures would not earn him favor in this life, let alone the next. It was still better than remaining to serve Commander Yao. Marching straight into the face of the *miqus* was crossing the border between courage and madness. Yao and his men would pay for that crossing. So would anyone who remained with them.

If Dapon did not flee and warn Yao's enemies, he could never again enter the mountains untroubled by their spirits. He would be doomed to struggle for existence in the valleys, something more than an animal but surely less than a man.

Sorrow was in the Khampa for the understanding that some of the Chinese who were wiser than Yao would suffer for their leader's folly. Commander Zhou was one who would hardly live to use that greater wisdom. But they had made the error of following Yao, an error upon which the mountains could have no mercy.

12

"Hey, Colonel, wake up!"

Barrabas's first reply was an inspiring example of command presence. He said, "Ukkh."

"Colonel, I think we got trouble."

Alex Nanos's voice erased the effects of sleeping on hard cold ground. Barrabas popped out of his sleeping bag and started limbering up. He needed the blood circulating to fight the chill of twilight already turning into night. It had been a long day's march, and Barrabas was planning on taking the first watch tonight.

"You need the exercise, Colonel, or are you learning how to fly? We need aerial recon, I admit, but—"

"What kind of trouble?" Barrabas said.

"A deserter from the Chinese came in. Not a Chinese, a Khampa."

"I thought that was Tibetan barley flour."

"That's *tsampa*," Lee Hatton said. "The Khampas are the nomads from eastern Tibet. They're less peaceful and less Buddhist than the other Tibetans."

"I don't care if they sacrifice virgins by the light of the full moon," Barrabas said. "I want to talk to him."

"McPherson's holding out on us," Nanos said. "He says we'll know anything he learns, but the guy's *his* prisoner. Says his Tibetans want to shoot the guy on the spot, but he'll head that off if we cooperate."

Barrabas's look made Nanos walk over to Liam O'Toole, sluglike in his sleeping bag, and start poking him awake. O'Toole protested the reveille.

"Alex, my friend, the next time you keep me from my beauty sleep—"

"What beauty? You could sleep for the next month and it would still be the same old ugly puss."

"I'd rather lay the question before Dr. Hatton. For sure, she'd be a better judge of male beauty than you."

"I'll plead the Fifth Amendment," Lee said. "But sleeping when the colonel wants you awake will uglify you out of all recognition."

That got O'Toole out of his sleeping bag fast enough. Barrabas waited until Billy Two and Claude Hayes came in from their sentry posts, then gathered the team into a circle so tight he could whisper and still be heard.

"Okay, Alex. What was this Khampa doing with the Chinese?"

"Guide and interpreter."

"Any particular kind of Chinese?"

"A company-strength patrol, according to Mc-Pherson."

"That sounds like more than a patrol."

"Maybe not, Colonel," Billy said. "In guerrilla territory, anything less would be meat on the table to the Tibetans."

"We'll see, once we've sat in on the interrogation. Billy, Lee. You're the diplomats. You back me up. The rest of you play it very cool. I smell something, but shooting's likely to be the worst way to clean it up."

Everyone nodded. They were all professionals; they knew you didn't start a fight with people whose help you needed. But if those people were holding out on you with intelligence you must have, it helped to convince them about their mistake.

Barrabas would be quite happy if the convincing didn't need the Bren guns. But one of them would be trained on McPherson before he opened his mouth. If the wrong words came out of that mouth, they would be Mc-Pherson's last words.

SOMETHING HIT WALKER JESSUP on the back of the neck. He jumped, making a sizeable splash in the puddle at his feet. He would have pointed his Sterling if he'd seen anything to point it at.

After a moment he felt water trickling down inside the collar of his bush jacket. He reached back and felt nothing but a damp spot in the fabric. Just an extra-big drop of water!

Jessup stopped and studied the darkness downhill from the shed where the second load of ammunition was piling up. Nothing moved, not even a bush. The air held the damp stillness of a Nepalese night between monsoon rains. Jessup hoped this would continue. The shed now harbored nearly two tons of ammunition and weapons, with containers and parachutes for dropping them to the SOBs.

The combined resources of Walker Jessup, Ganparsing Thapa and the Gordons had produced a fine arsenal. The SOBs and Tibetans would have to make do with their existing heavy weapons, but they'd have a lot more Chinese small arms and ammunition for everything. They'd even have some mortar rounds if they captured a Chinese mortar. The 81 mm NATO rounds would go in a Chinese 82 mm mortar; the other way around didn't work.

What they hadn't produced was reliable security for the supplies. Dr. Gonpo might have better luck. He had connections with the Tibetan Youth Congress and through them to some of the ex-guerrillas. Those old lamas in India couldn't stop him talking to his old buddies, or those old buddies from helping.

But Tibetans in the bush couldn't guard ammunition in the hand, or in the shed. Warm bodies were needed pronto, on the spot. Translated, that meant the Gordons—when they could take time off from working on the Fokker Troopship—Captain Thapa and Walker Jessup.

Jessup rounded the corner of the shed and suppressed a groan. The next stretch of the sentry's round was a fifty-foot uphill slog. His weight was hard enough to maneuver on the level, or even downhill. Uphill was a pain in a lot of places.

Not to mention that at this corner was the largest puddle anywhere around the shed. No way to get around it, either, without swinging so close to the trees that he'd be easy meat. Jessup tried to slosh quietly through the muddy water, and felt some of it creeping into his crepe-soled boots.

As he hit ground that wasn't actually underwater, he coined a new motto for the free-lance intelligence operative:

"Slop 'til you drop."

He was going to drop, too, and sooner rather than later. He was too old and too fat to be slogging through mud with an SMG slung over his bush jacket. It had taken Thapa awhile to find a bush jacket and a sling that would fit Jessup.

But what else could he do? The others were just as old if a lot leaner. The Gordons needed most of their time for the Troopship. The Gurkhas Jessup had reluctantly allowed Thapa to recruit hadn't shown up. Weng might be keeping his agreement to chase off the other Triads, but how to prove it?

As for Captain Thapa, he was like any Gurkha, a host in himself, but one man could only be a small host except in comic books. This wasn't a comic book. Jessup wasn't entirely sure what Nepal was, other than a place where he couldn't get a decent meal, but a comic book it wasn't.

No, it was one other thing. It was the place where he had a job to do until the ammo was in the hands of Nile Barrabas and his team. Walker Jessup owed the SOBs for more than his ability to buy gourmet dinners. He owed them most of his clout in the intelligence community, and on a couple of occasions he'd owed them his life.

That added up to debts he wouldn't even consider not paying. Particularly when the SOBs were swallowing their own objections to the Triads and helping Jessup pay his to the Chinese.

One cautious step at a time, Jessup slogged uphill. As far as moving silently, his caution was wasted. His only consolation was that at least he didn't slip. Maybe if he took off another fifty pounds, he might even be quiet.

No way, Walker, he told himself. Your days of being a mean lean Rambo-type are ancient history. There was no way back the day you discovered French cooking. And Mexican, and German, and Middle Eastern...

Jessup damned his mouth, which was watering, his stomach, which was rumbling, and the Tibetans, who could have spared him this by providing even four people who knew which end of a gun to hold and which to point.

As he turned the corner of the shed, he realized that he'd finally learned the difference between working for the Company and working free-lance. Working for the Company, it took three months to find out that something was impossible. Working for himself, he found out immediately.

That insight took Jessup halfway back down the north side of the hut. At that point a faint noise that wasn't the night floated past him from uphill. He stopped and studied the trees. They were second-growth pine with a little bamboo mixed in, too small to be cut up for building huts or even firewood, but thick enough to hide friends or enemies.

Also thick enough to deflect bullets, Jessup realized as he unslung his Sterling and quietly chambered a round. He'd have preferred a Uzi, lighter and more accurate, if he was going to be doing sentry duty, but he could hit with either SMG. In Korea, Jessup had been rated "Expert" with the Colt .45, the M-1 Garand, the M-2 carbine, the M-3 "grease gun" and the BAR. In Nepal his waist was thicker, but his eye was still good and his grip, too.

Jessup's night vision hadn't deteriorated, either. As the forest slowly turned into distinct shapes, he recognized one of them. A man was standing by a bush, taking a leak. A man with an assault rifle or SMG.

Jessup lowered himself to the ground, hoping he would only sink up to his elbows and not disappear completely. When he thought he was in a stable position, he snapped off the Sterling's safety and called:

"Halt! Who goes there!"

The figure spun around, frantically trying to lift his rifle and close his pants at the same time. Then from somewhere deeper in the underbrush came a wordless shout.

A burst of firing answered the shout, with at least four weapons pumping bullets at Walker Jessup. Splinters flew from the side of the hut and stung the back of his neck above his soggy collar.

Then an SMG came to life closer to Jessup. The Texan stared into the darkness. The man taking a leak had vanished, but it had to be him firing. Not at the shed, either. At the other visitors, or so it sounded from their new shouting.

Who was trying to do what to whom around here, anyway?

LEE HATTON WATCHED Nile Barrabas and McPherson each trying to read the other man's thoughts without giving away any of their own. It had a certain intellectual interest, and Lee wouldn't have minded having a videotape of it. It also involved a more immediate and practical problem—McPherson's refusal to let the SOBs know word one of what the Khampa defector might say until he was good and ready.

Lee Hatton didn't know when that would be and didn't need to know. It was enough to realize that if a Chinese company was really in the area, any delay in passing on the intelligence would be dangerous. If McPherson wasn't good and ready five minutes after he'd finished with the Khampa, there wasn't a whole lot the SOBs could do about it. Not without turning McPherson from a reluctant ally into an enemy with a hundred more or less loyal Tibetans ready to shoot anyone he told them to shoot.

If things got that out of hand, the SOBs' death certificates, when and if somebody made them out, ought to read "Suicide."

Not for the first time, Lee Hatton realized that she was experiencing a particular sort of frustration medicine hadn't prepared her for. Not that you didn't see a lot of human folly as a doctor, but at least you could apply your skills to patching up its victims without bureaucracy or kibitzers.

Beside her, Billy Two stirred and put a hand on her shoulder. "Relax, Lee," he whispered. "This turkey hasn't got the balls to refuse the colonel. So he's just showing off what little he does have."

Lee considered that maybe bringing Billy along as a diplomat hadn't been quite the best decision. Since she couldn't have said for half Prince Su's rubies what the best decision would have been, she turned her attention to the Khampa.

He wore a padded Chinese uniform with an elaborately tooled leather belt, a sheepskin cloak and one of those Tibetan hats that looked like a furry flowerpot turned upside down. He also wore a blooming collection of bruises. Lee would have liked a chance to look at them. The Khampa's captors had not been gentle with him, and he might have cracked bones or internal injuries.

Under the reeking clothing and the bruises was still an impressive physical specimen. He looked as wide as Billy Two, no more than an inch shorter and just as tough. Bound and battered as he was, it was hard to tell how he would move, but Lee decided to take no chances. If she ever had to go hand to hand with the man, she'd worry about her own neck first and his intelligence value second.

For the first time, Barrabas raised his voice enough to draw Lee's attention back to him.

"McPherson, you're really pissing into the wind, trying to screw around with intelligence this way."

"My people at the Company might not agree, Mr. Barrabas. Or is it Colonel Barrabas? Either way, they wouldn't want me pissing away Company assets to people who aren't Company."

"What makes you think we aren't Company?"

"What makes you think you have any way of convincing me you are?" McPherson replied. "Barrabas, if you were Company I'd have been told. I wasn't told. It follows that you aren't Company." He shrugged.

As a peaceful gesture it didn't seem to impress Barrabas whose long tanned face was still as hard as the rocks of the mountains on the horizon. Lee knew he was holding on to the ragged edges of his temper when he spoke.

"Look, McPherson. Who's working for whom doesn't matter a damn out here. In the Puzzle Palace they can play all the games they want. They don't have Chinese soldiers over the next mountain."

"What makes you think we do, Barrabas? You seem to assume this Khampa is telling the truth. I'm not. When I know which one of us is right, I'll tell you."

"How long will that be?"

McPherson shrugged again. "Your guess is as good as mine. The guy's tough, but my Tibetans are fairly good with prisoners. Most of them have lost friends or family to the Chinese. They won't like somebody who's kissed their little yellow asses. Even the other Khampas will be happy to stomp all over a traitor."

It was the longest speech McPherson had made, and it got its message across. If the Khampa didn't "die under interrogation," he would wind up being "shot while trying to escape."

Either way, the SOBs would have access to any intelligence he brought only at McPherson's whim, which began to look like no access at all.

The sense of helplessness swept Lee again. What McPherson needed was a discretion or maybe ethics transplant, and neither the doctor nor the warrior could provide that.

"We at least have to know if Colonel Yao's anywhere around," Barrabas said. He sounded like a man digging in for a long battle. "If he is, we ought to be heading east. If he isn't, a PLA company can still ruin the neighborhood."

"For people who can't blend in with the population, it can," McPherson replied with an unpleasant grin. "My people have done that before. We can do it again."

Barrabas raised both hands. From the look on his face, he might have been ready to either pray or strangle McPherson.

McPherson concluded that it was the second. He signaled to the dozen Tibetans behind him and started to draw his pistol. Lee got ready to drop, roll and fire. She didn't know how many of the guerrillas she would take with her, but she suspected quite a few.

She knew that it wouldn't be enough. The SOBs were about to end their career in the stupidest way possible. McPherson would be ending his along with them, but a fat lot of consolation—

A sound, felt rather than heard, made Lee turn. What she saw made her step back a couple of feet. She'd never quite been able to stand close to Billy Two when he was like this.

His wide dark eyes were unfocused, maybe not unseeing, but looking at something no one else could see. His body was as motionless as a tree, but not rigid. He seemed to have stopped breathing. It was as if he now shared his body with another presence.

Hawk Spirit was with Billy.

Then the massive chest heaved in a great hissing intake of breath. Billy's mouth opened, and he spoke softly but with a tone of authority impossible to ignore.

"The man the mountain spirits guided here is telling the truth. He is telling the truth about the Chinese, and about Colonel Yao leading them. All who honor the spirits and fight those who do not must be friends."

Beyond Billy, Lee saw the Khampa start, then nod as vigorously as his bindings and bruises allowed. Was McPherson holding out about his speaking English? Or were Billy and the Khampa communicating through Hawk Spirit?

Some of the Tibetans certainly spoke English, and Billy was definitely communicating with them. At the words "Colonel Yao" several of them started. By the time Billy was finished, most of the Tibetans had lowered their rifles.

McPherson didn't lower his pistol, but Lee doubted if he could have hit anything with it if he had fired. He was trying to watch Barrabas, Billy, Lee and the Khampa all at once. He wound up not watching any of them.

Barrabas spoke, matching Billy's tone as closely as he could. "We are not enemies to anyone who honors the spirits. I see that the men who follow you do so. What about you, McPherson?"

McPherson managed to get control of his mouth enough to make sounds, but not words. "What about you, Mc-Pherson?" Barrabas repeated.

"I'll be goddamned if I fall for this mumbo jumbo act!" were McPherson's first coherent words. They were also his last for a little while.

Behind him, several of the Tibetans raised their rifles again. This time they were pointed at McPherson. He saw the movement, turned, saw the rifles and went as pale as grease, dirt and windburn would let him.

His hands had a life of their own, though. They raised the pistol, sighting on Barrabas.

Before McPherson could shoot, Billy Two stepped between his C.O. and the CIA man. One gigantic hand closed on the pistol. Like a boy plucking a strawberry, he pulled it out of McPherson's grip.

"He is a warrior, but unworthy of this weapon," Billy said, handing the pistol to Barrabas while lifting Mc-Pherson with the other hand. Lee saw that the hand was tightening on McPherson's collar.

It tightened some more. The man's eyes bulged, his face turned red and the veins in his neck stood out like ridges.

"Billy, for God's sake—" Barrabas began.

"He will live or die by the will of Hawk Spirit," Billy said. His tone made Lee shiver more than the brisk mountain wind. There wasn't much of William Starfoot II around for the moment, except for his body. Everything else had been pushed aside by Hawk Spirit.

Just before his grip on McPherson's collar cut the man's breath off entirely, Billy relented. The huge hand opened. McPherson dropped to the ground, then fell to his hands and knees, gasping for breath. Some of his Tibetans ran to his side. He groped for their hands and let them pull him to his feet.

A proud man, Lee realized. One who won't accept that he's been the victim of something beyond normal knowledge. We've humiliated him in the eyes of his people is how he's going to see it. Hawk Spirit, you may know a lot of things, but you don't know people like Mr. McPherson.

Barrabas seemed to pick up Lee's thoughts. He reversed McPherson's pistol and handed it back to the CIA man. McPherson managed not to drop it.

He took a few more deep breaths and found the strength to speak. "Barrabas, I'm even more sure now that you aren't Company. We don't hire wackos like that."

"Mr. McPherson, let's not argue the merits of our employers or Mr. Starfoot's religion. Let's stick to the facts. Mr. Starfoot thinks the Khampa is telling the truth. If he is, that PLA company is even more dangerous than we thought. I get the feeling that your people have heard of Colonel Yao, too."

Several Tibetans nodded vigorously.

"Right. So I don't think they'll go along with assuming the Khampa's lying. You may not be popular if you try to lean on them."

McPherson nodded jerkily.

"Right again. So let's deal. You interrogate the Khampa. You know the language and the territory. But you share anything he tells you immediately. Also, you leave him in shape to be flown out and interrogated."

"You expect me to believe what your nut case says Eagle Shit or whatever it was told him?"

"No. I just expect you to leave the Khampa alive, so we can find out for sure."

"That's going to be risking my men if the Khampa is a Chinese plant."

"We'll take responsibility for that, McPherson."

McPherson looked from Barrabas to Billy Two to his men, then back to Barrabas. This time his nod was sharp and clear. He was holstering his pistol as he turned away.

Barrabas signaled to Lee. She stepped up to Billy Two and took his hand.

"Come on, Billy."

He stumbled as she led him away. Hawk Spirit had left him. It was now fatigue clouding his eyes. Fatigue, and what looked like rage at the things McPherson had said about his god.

13

Walker Jessup would have opened fire if he'd had any real targets. Just blazing away into a darkness that might hide friends as well as enemies wasn't his idea of smart.

He pulled out the other two magazines for the Sterling and checked to see they hadn't collected enough mud to jam. Then he set them on the driest piece of ground handy. Ninety-odd rounds was okay to start a firefight. It wasn't enough to finish it without a lot of luck or a lot of help.

Somewhere up the slope, a Sterling hammered. One of the weapons replying was a Czech Skorpion machine pistol. The sound of the others was too distorted by damp air and heavy foliage to let Jessup identify them.

A Skorpion could be in almost anybody's hands these days. The little machine pistols had traveled a long way from their roots as a Czech tanker's sidearm. Hearing one told Jessup a bit about the enemy's firepower and not a thing about who he was.

Jessup decided it couldn't hurt to shout again.

"Halt! This is a restricted area! Who goes there? Advance and be—"

He changed his mind as bullets sprayed the wall behind and above him and the mud to one side. All he'd done was give the bad guys a slightly better idea of where he was.

Jessup decided that for the time being he was in the traditional grunt's position. He not only didn't know the big picture, a man could get killed trying to find out!

In the silence that followed the firing, Jessup thought he heard footsteps on the far side of the shed. Then he knew for sure he heard someone scrambling up the far wall and onto the roof.

Like a mired hippopotamus, Jessup rolled over so that he could see the edge of the roof. The bastards probably wouldn't risk a grenade when they were sitting on top of an ammunition dump. They'd have to stick their heads over the edge of the roof. The sky was lighter than the ground; he could see them better than they'd see him.

It wouldn't save him for long. Just long enough to take one or two with him. Wouldn't the SOBs get a kick out of the Fixer going out doing brass-balls grunt work? The Senator would laugh so long and loud he'd probably have a heart attack.

Jessup was quite willing to be laughed at by the Senator if it would be the Senator's last laugh. Jessup had loyalties—although he'd have been the first to admit they were a bit frayed around the edges. The Senator didn't give a damn about anything except dying in office.

In the next moment, a whole bunch of people interrupted Jessup's philosophizing. Concussion grenades sailed out of the underbrush. One of them exploded against the wall of the shed, smashing and splitting planks. Another exploded on the roof, a third ten feet from Jessup. A fragmentation grenade would have punctured him in fifty places. The concussion grenade only sprayed him with mud.

He was wiping mud out of mouth and eyes when an SMG opened up from the roof. Through the ringing in his ears, Jessup recognized another Sterling. Was the man on the roof—alive and well in spite of the grenade—one of the good guys?

Jessup looked back to his front, just in time to see a man topple out of the bushes and writhe. The Sterling on the roof slammed a burst into him. His face and chest dissolved into a red mess the same consistency as the mud. He writhed a little more, then lay still.

The Texan had one loyal friend at least. A dark-shifted arm crept out from under the bushes, gripping the dead man's ankle. The roof gunner was a little too eager. He sent a burst at the arm, kicking up mud.

The arm vanished into the bushes. Not fast enough or far enough for Jessup. An old infantryman's eye told him where that arm was likely to join a body. He pointed the Sterling and held down the trigger until a second bullet-shredded body toppled out of the bushes. The man's arm was still trying to reach the friend, or maybe the friend's Skorpion. Neither Jessup nor the roof gunner gave him a chance. Two bursts of 9 mm cut the arm off at the elbow.

Jessup's hope that the Skorpion just taken out was the only one lasted all of ten seconds. The high-pitched note of another one sounded uphill, answered by a third Sterling.

The gunfire drowned out the sound of cracking bushes; the man with the backpack seemed to sprout from the mud in front of Jessup. He held a pistol, and even fired wildly. The range was so short that Jessup felt a bullet gouge an ear.

The man with the backpack felt a good deal more, as two Sterlings filled him and the air around him with lead. Bullets splashed close enough to Jessup to kick mud into his eyes. He ducked his head, just as a last bullet found the man's backpack.

Light flooded the hillside. Jessup's half-blinded eyes saw drops of water standing out like jewels on every leaf. Then leaves vanished as the blast tore them from their branches and hammered at Jessup's ears until he thought he'd go deaf.

The glare and thunder faded. Jessup felt wetness pattering down on him and felt for the rain. His hand came back red. Not rain, but the remains of the man with the backpack. The explosive charge he'd planned to use on the ammunition had done an equally thorough job on him.

Twenty feet farther, and the ammunition would have gone off from the concussion. Pieces of Walker Jessup would have been coming down in the same rain.

That would have made it a much heavier rain, Jessup realized. He laughed briefly, glad to learn that he could stop.

He was also glad not to be dead. Since he wasn't dead, the next thing to do was find out what the hell was going on.

Part of the answer came down the hill a minute later— Captain Thapa and a younger Gurkha, both carrying Sterlings. Jessup changed magazines and stood up.

"Howdy." He looked hard at Thapa. "How about telling me, the next time you have help lined up?"

"I'm sorry, Mr. Jessup. But I thought secrecy would make it easier to lay a trap. Are you complaining about the results?" The Gurkha's grin made him look anything but sorry.

"I would if I could but I can't. I'll just remind you that it could be all our asses if anybody talks to the wrong people."

The younger Gurkha understood enough English to look dangerously offended. Jessup hastily added, "Now, I trust any Gurkha's loyalty. I just don't know if everybody who'll know what the Gurkhas are doing is the same way."

"That is a danger I decided to face," Thapa said. "Since the ammunition is going to be on its way soon, I knew anyone who heard what they should not would have little time to act. They would act more quickly if they thought the defenses were weak.

"Of those who already knew and acted tonight, I believe there are no survivors. A pity that there are no prisoners."

From the shed roof, a low voice said something in what Jessup assumed was Nepalese. Thapa replied in the same language, then spoke angrily to his companion. Slowly the man nodded.

Captain Thapa spent the next two minutes delivering a royal ass-chewing. Jessup didn't understand a word of it, but he could hear tones and read facial expressions. He suspected that a couple of his old sergeants in Korea would have liked to study Thapa's technique.

When the younger Gurkha looked properly chewed out, Thapa switched back into English. "Bajbir says that there was another man uphill. Gaje let him get away, but Bajbir saw him and thinks he hit him. We should search the area."

Jessup was trying to find a polite way of saying his ass was dragging too much to go beating the bushes, when Thapa grinned again. "I think we had also better leave someone behind in case our friend is not too badly wounded to make one last attempt on the ammunition. Mr. Jessup, would you care to be the guard?"

Jessup managed not to cheer. He also managed not to start when the third Gurkha launched himself from the roof, landed with only a slight flexing of his knees and saluted. Thapa returned the salute, and the three men faded into the darkness.

Jessup had lost all sense of time, and his watch was clogged with mud. So much for the man who'd sold it to him as dustproof, waterproof and radiation proof! He didn't know if it was ten minutes or an hour before the three Gurkhas returned from beating the bushes.

"Bajbir did hit someone," Thapa said. "There's a blood trail downhill. We followed it to where the man either fell off a cliff or hid in bush too thick to let us follow him. Let us hope it was the second."

"Oh, I don't suppose it will be all bad if one of the bad guys got away," Jessup said. "He'll tell his friends that the ammo's guarded like the crown jewels. If they're planning a second try, they'll have to take a few days extra to beef it up. We could use those days."

Jessup slogged over to the two nearest bodies. Bullet-chewed as they were, they looked more Chinese than anything else. A quick search found as much ID as Jessup had expected: none. Fortunately his microcamera had survived the mud better than his watch. He snapped both faces and tucked the camera away.

"We'll get rid of the bodies but drop the pix in the hands of the local Company station chief. Time he earned a little of that cut he's getting." Jessup slung his Sterling. "Captain, how many more friends you got where these came from?"

"One. Any more, and people *will* talk."

"Four Gurkhas is enough. You're probably right. We don't want to outnumber the bad guys so much they just crawl into their holes and shiver. We want 'em to come out where they can be zapped.''

All three Gurkhas grinned, and Gaje said something in Nepalese. Thapa laughed.

"Gaje says you are like the SOBs, so he is no longer surprised that they follow you. You too would make a good Gurkha—if you lost about a hundred and fifty pounds.''

Right then, Walker Jessup felt that he would do best as a footstool. It wouldn't involve walking, standing, or even sitting up. He wouldn't even insist on a good dinner first!

"While the bad guys are making up their so-called minds, we're going to get the ammo on its way to the people who need it. There's an alternate drop point we can use two days early. This means moving the stuff closer to the airstrip in the next twenty-four hours.''

Thapa frowned. "I'd hoped to arrange for some Stingers—''

Jessup held up a muddy hand. "A good weapon when it's needed is better than a perfect weapon two days late. A hell of a lot better than a weapon that gets blown up before it's delivered. Besides, my people and the Tibetans have got to do more sneaking than shooting. If the PLAAF deals itself in, their best bet is to execute the classic military maneuver known as 'getting the hell out of there.' ''

"As you wish, Mr. Jessup,'' Thapa said. He saluted. "At dawn?''

Jessup groaned. He would have killed for the pleasure of being able to say "At sunset.''

Instead he said, "Dawn.''

Goddammit, how much more playing grunt was he going to have to do? If this went on, he'd have to seriously contemplate going on a diet. He might rather be dead, but he *would* be dead if he went on being too slow and too big a target.

AS THE SUN SET behind the twenty-thousand-foot peaks of the Gangdise Range, Nile Barrabas faced the shadowy eastern horizon.

Far off in the twilight, something moved. Probably a herd of wild horses or yaks. Some of them still survived, in places where the Chinese hadn't scoured the land clean of wildlife.

For two thousand years the Tibetans' reverence for life had let nature flourish. Then the Chinese came stamping in, and the wildlife vanished in a generation.

The more Barrabas learned about the history of Tibet, the more he respected the Tibetans. He also felt more and more that the history of their relations with the Chinese was a classic case of "Nice guys finish last."

Not everywhere, of course. Those guerrillas looked able to give anything short of a PLA battalion a crashing headache if it tried to walk over them. But then they were a long way from being nice guys, by any standard.

The shape the Khampa was in proved that. McPherson had almost kept his promise about leaving the Khampa in shape to be flown out for further interrogation. The man could move and speak. Lee Hatton said he had no internal injuries or broken bones. But he walked like an old man and talked with difficulty. His bruises had bruises. If he hadn't been as tough as Alex and Billy put together, he probably wouldn't be conscious.

As it was, he was sitting quietly outside the circle of the team. He was as motionless as a statue of Buddha, but looked more like the image of a god of war. He'd accepted the handcuffs the SOBs had snapped on him as if they were no more than a change in the weather. Barrabas would still have kept a close eye on him, even if he hadn't promised McPherson.

Barrabas turned back to the team.

"Okay, people. I'm not sure McPherson isn't going to try to get his own back. But if we keep our Khampa friend out of trouble, McPherson won't have a good excuse. What's more, he'll have to break a promise he made in the hearing of his Tibetans. How much would that count against him, Lee?"

"Probably more than he could afford," Lee said.

"Probably means—?"

"Better than an even chance," Lee said. "Of course, if McPherson isn't thinking clearly, that might not bother him. We'd better guard our Khampa from McPherson, as well as everybody from our Khampa."

Barrabas nodded. He'd pretty much concluded the same thing himself, but a second opinion never hurt.

The SOBs weren't a committee. Nile Barrabas was the C.O., the Old Man, the leader, the first in and the last out. He was also smart enough to know that every one of the others knew something he didn't. They'd proved it, too. There wasn't a single SOB, past or present, living or dead, who hadn't saved the team at least once.

When Nile Barrabas gave orders, he was obeyed. When his people talked, he listened. There was proof that this arrangement worked: they won and they survived.

"Yeah, Alex?" The Greek was looking fidgety.

"Anybody know if our Khampa speaks English?"

Billy nodded. "Does that mean you know, or that he does?" Barrabas asked.

Billy gathered his wits and chose his words with care. "I know that he understood much of what was said in your argument with McPherson. Hawk Spirit told me so. Whether it was because he knew English or because Hawk Spirit passed my understanding on to him...."

"Right," Barrabas said. "So we don't give our Khampa friend any more intelligence than he needs to survive. At least not until he's cooperated for a few days. Lee and Alex will take the first watch. Everyone else—weapons check, rack out, but be ready to come up shooting. Any questions?"

Nobody said anything then, but as Barrabas was field stripping his Hi-Power he sensed Lee Hatton standing behind him.

"Got a minute, Nile?"

"More than that if you need it. But before I get to what I really want to ask you, answer me about something that's puzzling me."

"Shoot." She sat down—no, flowed down into what was damned near the lotus position, in spite of her boots and camies.

"Lee, was Billy on the level this time about Hawk Spirit?"

"Medical opinion or fellow soldier's?"

"Both, if they're different."

"You've already heard part of my medical opinion. We simply don't know enough about psychic phenomena to make a firm judgment.

"But I'd give you both a doctor's and a soldier's opinion on another point. Billy is incapable of lying or joking about Hawk Spirit when the team's involved. I'm sure he's put on outsiders quite a few times. He wouldn't put on any of us.

"He believes that what happened came through Hawk Spirit. I'm not going to argue with him. Are you?"

"The head wound only turned my hair white, it didn't make me crazy or dumb."

"Fine. What did you want to ask me about?"

Barrabas realized that he'd completely forgotten. He tried to dredge it up, failed, then thought of making small talk. He decided against that, because it would be taking Lee away from her weapons check just for the pleasure of her company. Rank Hath Its Privileges, but that wasn't one of them.

"Would you insist on examining me if I said I'd completely forgotten?"

"No. I'd say you need some sleep, but you already know that." Lee rose as gracefully as she'd sat down. "See you at midnight, Nile."

THE RADIO OPERATOR looked up from his set and signaled to Company Commander Zhou. Zhou squatted as the operator scribbled the incoming message on his knee pad.

"Ah," Zhou said. "The scouts have done their work well. Send that with the acknowledgment."

"At once, Comrade Commander."

The operator spoke quickly, while tearing off the message pad with his free hand. Zhou folded it carefully to hide his excitement.

For the first time in weeks, Column Yao faced an enemy it could find—had found, indeed—fight and even destroy. Five hours' march would bring the Tibetans and their imperialist advisers to battle. An hour more and they would be broken, the survivors fleeing for their lives. Now that the column knew where the rubies were, this victory would remove the last obstacle to finding them.

Zhou was briefly surprised to realize how much he had come to share Yao's obsession with the rubies. But it was not foolish to do so. The column commander was a man who could convince everyone around him that his goals were the most important in the world.

Such a man could rise high. Those who followed him would be rewarded, and one of those rewards could be a chance to do the same.

If Yao ever wanted more from Zhou than the loyalty of a junior commander to a senior one, he could have it.

Right now, what Yao would get was the scout's report on the strength and position of the Tibetans. Zhou thrust the folded message into his tunic pocket and hurried uphill.

He had to shake Yao only twice before the colonel sat up, apparently wide awake. Using a hooded flashlight, Yao read the message, then unfolded and studied his map.

"Not more than five hours' march, even with the mortar."

"Comrade Commander, the RPGs might be as effective."

"They lack the range. Also, when you arranged the next resupply of ammunition, did you ask for more grenades?"

"No. We have used mortar rounds, but no grenades."

"If we took the RPGs, we might fire off all the Type K grenades. We might not have more by the time we reached the jeweled mountain. Then our best weapon against the cave's defenders might be useless.

"Also, the guerrillas now have imperialist 'advisers.' If these have brought night-vision devices, the RPG crews might be detected and neutralized. The mortar can out-range such devices.''

"Forgive me, Comrade Commander. I did not think clearly.''

"You thought very clearly, as far as you went. That you did not go farther only means you are not perfect. No man is, save Comrade Mao. We can only hope to learn as much as we can.''

Zhou relaxed. Yao would not have invoked the memory of Mao Tse-Tung if he had been seriously offended.

"Then shall I prepare the attack force? It seems to me that two platoons, the mortar and two machine guns will be enough. Extra ammunition, of course, and full canteens.''

"That seems adequate, Comrade Zhou.'' Yao lay down again. "Call me when the men are ready to leave. You will lead them, but I wish to address them before they go.''

"As you wish, Comrade Commander.''

14

The Tibetan who approached Nile Barrabas and Liam
O'Toole knew how to approach armed men at night. He
stopped in plain sight at a safe distance, then raised empty
hands and called softly:

"Colonel Barrabas?"

O'Toole drew his Hi-Power. At this range it was handier
and quieter than his FAL.

"Who goes there?"

"Gendun Tsering."

"Advance and be recognized."

Tsering advanced and was recognized. He wore a Chinese
tunic under his *chupa*, with Western-style work pants. His
rifle was a Type 68, and he also carried an old German P-
38 stuck in his belt and a long knife on the other side.
O'Toole counted only two spare magazines for the rifle and
none for the pistol, but noted that both weapons were clean
and well-kept.

"How can I help you?" Barrabas asked.

"You think Khampa speak truth about Colonel Yao?"

Barrabas nodded. "We think so. Certainly we hope so,
because we came to Tibet to fight him." O'Toole noted that
Barrabas didn't say *why* he believed the Khampa. The Tibetans had a lot of mysticism of their own, but they'd never
heard of Hawk Spirit.

"Good. Yao—strong fighter, bad man. He kill two
cousins and brother's wife. Brother's wife, he burn alive.
Brother go to India but die there. Coughing sickness."

O'Toole remembered that a lot of Tibetan exiles had died of lung disease from the heat and dust of India. "A real charmer, Colonel Yao," he said under his breath.

"I save bullet for Colonel Yao," Tsering went on. "Others, they do the same. They say to McPherson Colonel Yao maybe coming. Watch for him."

"And what did McPherson say?" O'Toole could hear Barrabas's desire to make a deal, fighting with the need for caution.

"McPherson not wise as he was. He say no Yao. He say—we not believe him, we get no more guns and ammunition from…Company. Then we have to go fight for guns. That be bad. We take one gun from Chinese, lose one man in fight."

That kind of score could use you up pretty fast. You could wind up with a lot of guns and nobody to use them.

Barrabas shrugged. "Once we too thought McPherson wise. Now it seems he thinks he knows everything. That is foolish in a warrior." Tsering nodded eagerly.

"We have guns and ammunition you can use," Barrabas went on. "Only one load first, and that mostly for us. But if McPherson stops your supplies, we will send more. We do work for those who can send what you need, though McPherson thinks we lie."

"I not think you lie, Colonel," Tsering said. He did an enthusiastic imitation of a Western-style salute. "I think now you wiser than McPherson."

"Let's hope not," Barrabas said. "My people and I have to go back to America when our mission here is done. McPherson will go on leading you."

"If he is not wise, he will not—" Tsering began.

The sentence ended in the whistle of an incoming mortar shell.

COMMANDER ZHOU lay beside the first machine gun and studied the Tibetan camp. The rebels had chosen good ground, with clear fields of fire and as much natural cover as one could expect on the plateau.

Cover from rifles and machine guns, at any rate. They had not found cover from mortars, and perhaps could not have. They would pay for that.

Zhou continued his examination. In the dim moonlight it was impossible to pick out the advisers, or see if they had any heavy weapons. If the imperialists had brought none, the Tibetans would be at a serious disadvantage.

It would have been more serious if the Chinese had enough ammunition for both Type 74s. One fool of a bearer had dropped a thousand rounds into a stream. He was paying for that mistake by staying behind to find them and would pay more after the battle.

The ammunition was still lost to the battle. Zhou had compromised, putting one machine gun forward to support the infantry and giving it most of the ammunition. The second Type 74 lay back in reserve, to defend the mortar team with only two hundred rounds.

Battles had been won in spite of worse mistakes, and Zhou did not believe in omens. He wished he could say the same for all of his fighters. The loss of the ammunition as well as the fate of the sentries four days ago had too many of them fearing their own shadows and footsteps.

There was a cure for that. Once they saw the Tibetans before them, they would look nowhere else. His men might not fight well against mountain ghosts. Against human barbarians, they would prove themselves masters of war. Zhou rose to his knees and aimed his hooded flashlight at the mortar post three hundred meters to his rear. With his hand over the lens, he gave the "Open fire" signal.

Two flashes acknowledged the order. The mortar crew must have been holding the first round over the muzzle, because the mortar fired before the crew finished signaling.

Zhou listened to the round whistling overhead, then the crash as it exploded among the Tibetans. It was a high-explosive round. The next five would be the same.

The manuals said to start a mortar barrage with flares to illuminate. But a flare did no harm, and could show both sides instead of just one. Better to strike the Tibetans with death from the darkness. When the barbarians were fleeing, *then* illuminate them for the machine gun and rifles!

The second round whistled overhead, but no explosion came. Zhou cursed briefly until he heard the third round explode and the fourth round fire.

LEE HATTON POPPED OUT of her sleeping bag, fully awake before her hands struck the cold ground. She didn't jump up to look around. That was too good a way of getting killed in a firefight. She stayed on hands and knees until the second explosion, then went flat.

Mortar fragments whined overhead, gouged the ground and ripped into human flesh. She heard curses, screams and prayers, the sounds of thrashing bodies, and close by, a sucking chest wound.

Claude Hayes and Billy Two rolled close to Lee, each holding one of the Bren guns. Swathed in cloth for concealment, the two guns looked like a couple of throw rugs. Hayes unwrapped his, Billy simply ripped the cloth off. Both slammed the curved magazines into their guns.

"Lee, can you be number two to both of us?" Hayes shouted.

Lee nodded and held out her arms for the extra magazines. The Bren was heavier than the average modern LMG and Lee was the lightest of the SOBs by a good fifty pounds. She reeled in the magazines as more mortar shells exploded among the Tibetans.

Stones and dust joined the mortar fragments. The screams went on, but Lee heard more curses and the click of rounds being chambered. She chambered a round in her own FAL and pulled the Starlite goggles over her eyes.

Before sunset the SOBs had taken accurate ranges to every landmark within a thousand yards of the camp. That wouldn't help if you couldn't see which landmark the Chinese were near.

The Starlites didn't turn night into day. They did turn darkness that could hide a regiment into a sort of translucent murk where anything that gave off heat would show up.

"Alex!" Hayes shouted.

"Yo!" came Nanos's voice.

"The colonel and Liam, they've got the other Bren. Here's a bandolier of magazines. Make an express delivery when the mortars stop coming in."

"Can do."

Nanos caught the tossed ammo and tucked them under his massive torso. A final mortar shell whistled in and ended its flight with a *thuck* instead of a *whoomp*.

"Nice to know the bad guys get duds, too," Claude said. Billy Two just nodded. For the first time, Lee noticed that the big Osage wore only his undershorts. The chill Tibetan night didn't seem to bother him. The smooth tanned skin didn't even show any goose pimples.

Lee used unladylike language, but to herself. One of these days, Billy was going to think Hawk Spirit was with him when the god was nowhere around. That would be Billy's last fight—although even without spiritual aid, he was going to give the other side's Graves Registration a lot of business.

The end of the mortar barrage didn't mean silence. Most of the screams had died away, but Lee found the groans and whimpers even harder to bear. The doctor in her said she ought to shove the ammo at Claude and Billy and pull out the medical kit.

The veteran warrior said that the end of the mortar barrage meant only one thing. The Chinese infantry was coming. The Brens would give them a nasty surprise, and the more ammo they had the nastier it would be.

It was Lee's job to handle the ammo. Also, to handle any Chinese kibitzers who might want to complain about how Claude and Billy were handling the Brens. Finally, to keep an eye on the Khampa.

The warrior was on duty tonight, not the doctor.

Lee braced her FAL in the prone fire position and scanned the ground in front of her. Every rock and fold of the ground large enough to hide a Chinese midget got a thorough going over.

Outside her field of vision, a scrape and rattle said that Alex Nanos was starting his delivery run. Memories of McPherson's face opened Lee's mouth.

"Alex, don't turn your back on McPherson."

"Lee, I'll be careful. Think of all the women who'll miss a good time if I don't come back."

She heard his first steps and looked back to see the Khampa sitting quietly in lotus position. Then a bugle and whistles sent the Chinese infantry forward.

COMPANY COMMANDER ZHOU listened carefully to the cries of the Tibetan wounded, trying to estimate their number.

Too few and he would call for the mortars again; too many and the platoon would rush forward. If the Tibetans had nothing left to do but abandon their wounded comrades and flee into the night, they would do so swiftly. Pursuit must be even swifter. Otherwise there would be vengeful Tibetans on the column's flank, like flies buzzing over a man's rice bowl.

Zhou's trained ears fed his trained mind; an estimate formed. The Tibetans had been hit hard enough that they would fall to the infantry, not so hard that they would simply flee.

Zhou's signal passed along the line of waiting infantry, and the trumpeter blew. The whistles joined him. Zhou jumped to his feet, drew his pistol and waved the first platoon forward. He let it pass, then waved the machine-gun team forward and fell in behind them.

If the first platoon broke through the Tibetans, the machine gun could shift left or right to pin down any not engaged at once. If the first platoon was stopped, the machine gun could keep the Tibetans from counterattacking while the second platoon came up.

Simple and straightforward. Against the Tibetans, nothing more was needed. Even imperialist advisers—

The *wheeet* of a rifle bullet passing his ear startled Zhou. The next bullet went *spunnnggg* off the machine gun.

The third went in under the machine gunner's right ear and came out through his left temple. The top of his head vanished in a spray of blood, bone and chunks of brain tissue.

Before the gunner hit the ground, Zhou heard the rattle of two machine guns opening up from the ranks of the Tibetans.

ALEX NANOS TRIED to match the pace of both the Chinese and the Tibetans on his way to join Nile Barrabas. Anyone moving conspicuously fast or slow on a battlefield caught the eye. Catching Chinese eyes would be fatal while catching Tibetan eyes wouldn't be entirely safe. The Tibetans were friendly but untrained; trigger-happiness was as common as blisters among untrained soldiers.

For the first couple of hundred yards, Nanos escaped detection. Both sides were too busy to notice one man moving independently. It helped that in the darkness Nanos's swarthy complexion was almost indistinguishable from either the Tibetans or the Chinese.

At the 250-yard mark, Nanos's immunity ran out. Bullets whipped past him, three short bursts from a Chinese assault rifle. Arriving late was better than not arriving at all. Nanos hit the dirt.

The rifleman went on shooting, two more bursts. Nanos realized that the rifleman was following some other target. He also realized that whoever it was, he was firing from the Tibetan position.

The Starlites let him scan the Tibetans until he saw a man lying behind two bodies. The man was pumping out short bursts, no longer even in the general direction of the Chinese.

The Starlites let you see where somebody was but not who they were. Nanos pulled them off, thought he saw a blonde head above the two bodies—then froze as a mortar flare burst overhead.

The Chinese, he suspected, were trying to give their men good targets now that they'd closed in. That, or maybe just keep them from hitting each other.

A second flare burst, and Nanos stopped worrying about what it would do for the Chinese. He had a clear look at McPherson rising from cover and squeezing off another burst from a borrowed Type 68 toward the Khampa. He didn't seem to care about filling Billy, Claude and Lee with lead in the process.

This, Nanos decided, was no way to win friends and influence SOBs. Actually, it would influence at least one SOB—to finish McPherson ASAP.

When Nanos had his FAL sighted on McPherson, things got even livelier than before. Another flare burst, a lot of Chinese came storming up from behind, and the SOBs McPherson was shooting at all went down. Nanos hoped they were taking cover instead of being hit, but he had to hit the ground himself too fast to be sure.

As the flare faded, the Chinese stormed past him and the Tibetans opened up. The Chinese didn't notice Nanos. To eyes still getting back their night vision, he probably looked like one of their own scouts.

Nanos had shielded his eyes and kept his night vision. Both Tibetans and Chinese were firing wildly. All the bullets were whistling overhead, and he had plenty of time to relocate McPherson.

The Chinese were experienced infantrymen. They decided to stop and regain fire superiority before closing with the Tibetans. Two of them went to ground right in front of Nanos. He squirmed forward until he was less than a yard behind them, then leaped.

Nanos's weight smashed down on the backs of the two Chinese. He heard spines and ribs crack. Being a tidy soul, he also smashed his massive fists into the backs of their heads. This added cracked skulls to the damage.

The Type 68 Nanos snatched up clicked empty after only six rounds. That was enough. McPherson had jumped up to rally his Tibetans, making himself an easy target. At less than three hundred yards, Nanos didn't need easy targets.

McPherson was dying before he struck the ground. He was dead before the first of his Tibetans could roll to his side and try to stop the bleeding. By the time McPherson had help, the bleeding was stopping by itself as the CIA man's bullet-shredded heart gave up.

Nanos was pulling one of the Chinese corpses over himself like a poncho when he heard the Tibetans crying out. The cries built up to a chorus of lamenting, and the Tibetan firing slackened off.

The Chinese got the message: something had happened to shake the Tibetans' morale. On either side of Nanos, Chinese who'd been lying flat rose and sprinted forward, firing from the hip. Nanos didn't need a Starlite to see the Tibetans rising and running from the Chinese charge, except for those who stopped Chinese bullets and didn't run very far.

"Oh, shit."

Nanos spoke too quietly to be overheard, but with great feeling. McPherson had been too dangerous to let live, but the Greek wondered whether there were better times to kill him. It began to look that way, if his death broke the morale of his Tibetans, and the SOBs were left all alone to fight off a PLA company....

If that happened, Alex Nanos had screwed up but good. Maybe there was a table in Valhalla for good fighters who screwed up in the end and got their friends killed. But it was probably down by the kitchen door, with fast-food hamburgers and light beer served once a day by sixty-year-old retired belly dancers. No mead, no pork, no Valkyries for Alex Nanos.

Since he had nothing to lose, Nanos jumped up. In one hand he held a Chinese grenade, in the other the second captured Type 68. He pulled the pin and pitched the grenade into the largest group of Chinese, then let fly with the rifle.

Firing an automatic weapon from the hip looks better in the movies than on the battlefield, most of the time. One of the other times is when you have an easy target at short range and have to hit it *fast*. This was one of those times.

Bullets and grenade fragments wiped out a dozen Chinese before the rest turned to face the new attack. Nanos moved far enough in that time to confuse their aim more than his.

He ran, dropping the Type 68 and unslinging his FAL without breaking stride. Bullets whistled too close to him, even closer to the Chinese. Realizing they might hit their friends, the Chinese ceased fire, right about the time Nanos would have been a safe and easy target.

He charged up from the rear, unloaded two more grenades to the left and half a magazine to the right. That left only three Chinese on their feet. A three-round burst nearly beheaded one and let Nanos close with the others. He kicked one in the groin, then slammed the rifle butt down on the back of his skull as he fell.

The last Chinese was nearly the same size and shape as Nanos. The hand-to-hand grapple lasted nearly thirty seconds before Nanos's training gave him the advantage. The Chinese found himself rising into the air, held by the neck and one leg. He had just time to scream before Nanos slammed him down head first. Skull and neck both cracked under the impact. Nanos dropped the corpse and sprinted toward the retreating Tibetans, shouting, "Friend! Friend!"

15

Company Commander Zhou resisted the urge to scratch his face. The machine gunner's drying blood was beginning to itch. He also resisted the urge to scream at the messenger from the right-flank platoon. Neither would accomplish anything, except to make those around him wonder if he had lost the courage a PLA commander had to show even if the imperialists might be storming Peking!

"You received no orders to bring this tale to me?" Zhou snapped at the messenger.

"No. I—I saw no one alive to give the order. I knew if we all died there, you would never know the truth."

"I do not know the truth now, I think."

For a moment Zhou was tempted to shoot the man on the spot. But that would tell the men that their commander thought the situation was desperate.

The man saw the thought in Zhou's eyes and cringed. "Comrade Commander. I beg you. I told you only what I saw."

"I am sure you did. But you are not the first fighter to see what was not there, or not see all that was. Return to the battle with me, and I will think you made a mistake instead of committing a crime."

"Oh yes, Comrade Commander. I shall come gladly. But be wary. There may be more imperialist advisers than we thought."

That was not impossible, Zhou realized. But he would not say so out loud, at least until he had arranged a solution for that problem.

That solution would be to man the first machine gun again and bring the second forward. Then the mortar would open up again, ending the Tibetans' rally and perhaps killing some of the advisers. The machine guns would move in close and support the attack of the second platoon against the demoralized Tibetans.

Zhou had considerable faith in riflemen and mortars. He had even more faith in a well-handled machine gun. His grandfather had commanded machine guns in Korea, and told many tales of how well they worked. Not just against Koreans or the American Army, either, but even against United States Marines, who were better than any Tibetans ever could be, even with imperialist advisers aiding them.

Zhou looked at the still-trembling messenger.

"On second thought, I want you to go with Fighter Gao to the mortar position. Return with the other machine gun. When you return, be once more a soldier of the Revolution."

"I shall do my best, Comrade Commander."

The two men vanished into the darkness. As they did, the enemy's machine guns opened fire again. Zhou listened, and realized that only one was firing. Perhaps the right-flank platoon had done more than he'd thought?

CLAUDE HAYES CEASED FIRE after only twenty rounds. Lee Hatton handed him a full magazine, and he inserted it into the Bren. Lee began slipping the last rounds from the discarded magazine into another, to make one full magazine out of two half-full ones.

As she finished, she realized that Billy Two was nowhere in sight. His Bren stood ready and aimed, set firmly on butt and bipod, with three spare magazines ready. But Billy himself was gone as completely as if Hawk Spirit had carried him off.

Lee crawled forward and tapped Claude on the heel. He turned, took one look at the untended Bren, and muttered something uncomplimentary about Billy.

"At least he took his FAL," Lee said. "Either he's done this on his own, or Hawk Spirit knows basic tactics."

"Yeah, and maybe the Chinese'll think he's a ghost when they see him in his undershorts. Just as long as the Tibetans don't think the same thing."

Lee conjured up a picture of both sides fleeing in panic from William Starfoot II, Osage warrior and evil spirit. She smiled, then a voice came from behind her that took away the smile.

"The spirits do walk with him," Ragpa Dapon said. His English was heavily accented and halting, but recognizable. He was still in lotus position, which must have put a considerable strain on battered limbs and sore muscles. Lee made mental notes to save a couple of painkillers for the Khampa, if the wounded Tibetans didn't clean her out.

"May they continue to do so," Lee said. At least that sounded better than "Hunh?" She saw Claude Hayes wrestle with the temptation to make some smart remark about spirits, then settle for a nod.

Silently Lee asked that whatever Billy believed in be something that could—no, not protect him, a warrior did not ask that, for herself or for a comrade.

Let him do his best. That was the warrior's wish. Not to mention that Billy Two's best had been too good for a lot of opponents and was quite likely to be too good for the Chinese.

BILLY TWO WALKED across ground whose chill might have frozen his feet, whose rough spots might have toppled him, through enemies who might have ended his life. None of these things happened, because Hawk Spirit was with him.

He had seldom been so aware of the god's presence. Yet he had seldom been so uncertain what was expected of him, either. Hawk Spirit often spoke in riddles, but with the years Billy Two had come to know how to puzzle out those riddles. Not quickly, perhaps, but soon enough, even when Hawk Spirit came in the middle of a battle.

Do you speak through my brother Ragpa Dapon, Hawk Spirit? Is that why I know you are present but not what you want? Or is it that what you want is so simple you think there is no need to explain it.

Neither is false, neither is true, came the god's voice. Remember that, remember that you have a warrior's wisdom, and remember that a warrior's wisdom can be very great.

It had better be very great, Hawk Spirit, because my comrades and I face a hard fight. These Chinese soldiers are warriors themselves.

This I know. I also know that they hate the spirits. This is a weakness, if you have the strength to take advantage of it.

Hawk Spirit left Billy then, but not as swiftly as usual. Billy had time to feel his normal senses returning, understand what they told him and respond.

That response was fatal to three Chinese who came out of the darkness carrying a machine gun and its ammunition. Billy flung his arms wide, then snapped them together. The two gunners were in between. Their skulls smashed together, each acting like a hammer on the other. The two gunners dropped. Billy plucked the machine gun out of the air with one hand. With the other he stopped the third man's bayoneted rifle in midlunge.

The man was a heartbeat too slow letting go of his rifle. Billy swept one leg in a circle, scything the man's feet out from under him. The Chinese lost his rifle as he went down. Billy tossed it, caught it by the butt, and rammed the bayonet into its former owner's chest. A scream was stillborn in a bubbling gasp.

Billy inspected the gun, more by touch than by eye. Hawk Spirit was no longer with him, but intimate knowledge of automatic weapons was. When he was satisfied that the Type 74 had survived its change of ownership, he collected the ammunition, winding the spare belt around his waist.

Then he began retracing the machine gunners' tracks. At the end of their tracks lay what Hawk Spirit wanted him to find.

That turned out to be an 82 mm mortar hidden behind a rise in the ground. Billy came in on the left flank, against a mortar crew concerned with the maximum rate of fire and not with self-defense. Their C.O. had probably told them that all the Tibetans were either dead or too demoralized to counterattack. Every army had that kind of officer, and in every battle where they commanded, the price their men paid was the same.

Sudden death first reached the mortar's observer. The 7.62 mm bullets smashed the lower part of his face and drove the binoculars back into his eyes. Bullets and binoculars together peeled off the top of the soldier's skull.

His comrades of the mortar crew were already reacting when his body landed among them. They didn't react quite fast enough. The security men with their assault rifles went down first, then the NCO with a submachine gun. The two men actually feeding the mortar died last, one of them after lifting a grenade.

Billy Two wished he'd shot the last man first when he saw the grenade arcing out of his failing hand. The grenade plunged into the mortar's barrel. The explosion knocked the mortar over, breaking the tripod and bulging the barrel. Billy Two didn't need a second look to know that the mortar was now as useless as a Ping-Pong paddle.

At least what was useless to one was useless to all. Billy was starting to strip the fallen Chinese soldiers of weapons and ammunition when a last enemy appeared on top of the rise.

He started to unsling his rifle, then took one look at the huge figure standing over the bodies of his comrades, dripping weapons. The Chinese was too scared to scream— Billy heard a faint squeak that might have come from a stepped-on mouse. He wasn't too scared to run. All the energy he hadn't put into screaming went into his feet. They carried him off into the darkness as if he'd been shot out of the mortar.

For the first time that night, Billy Two laughed. Then he shifted his load about until it rode almost comfortably and headed back for his own lines. He was carrying more than a hundred pounds, but it would still have taken a good runner to keep up with him.

THE TERRIFIED FIGHTER ran out of the darkness behind Company Commander Zhou. He appeared so swiftly and silently that for a moment the lieutenant was ready to believe in spirits.

Then he recognized Fighter Jiu of the mortar crew. Fear of spirits gave way to fear of what human enemies might have done. He remembered brief bursts of gunfire from the rear, almost lost in the firing from ahead.

"The mortar has ceased firing without my orders, Comrade Fighter. Return to it at once and—"

"They're all dead. All, all! The *miqu* took them! It killed them all and stole the weapons!"

If Zhou had not had a few seconds anticipating bad news, Fighter Jiu would have joined his comrades, shot down on the spot. A few more seconds and Zhou returned his pistol to the holster. His hands shook, but his voice was steady as he interrogated the man.

"That was no *miqu*," Zhou said finally. "It was only one of the imperialist advisers, or perhaps—" He broke off. The Khampa's flight had been concealed from the men, and they were told he had fallen down a cliff. Had the Ragpa Dapon not only reached the Tibetans but been believed and allowed to fight? Westerners grew larger than Chinese or Tibetans, but that large?

No answer came out of the night. Only the steady crackle of Tibetan rifles meeting the left-flank platoon, with an occasional burst from the Tibetan machine guns.

That was enough of an answer for Zhou. With both machine guns and the mortar apparently disabled or destroyed, he had no chance of victory. He had some chance of avoiding disaster if he ordered the remaining platoon to break contact at once.

Quickly he scribbled a message to the platoon's commander and handed it to Jiu. A mission seemed to steady his nerves. He saluted and ran off.

Zhou and his guards stripped all the bodies within reach of weapons and ammunition. Enough Tibetans were dead to weaken the guerrillas, if they could not rearm and reequip themselves from battlefield loot. One man was still alive. Zhou faced the mountains and put a bullet in the man's head.

Then he led the fighters toward the mortar position. Whatever or whoever had attacked there, it was about to learn that it was no match for a whole PLA platoon!

NILE BARRABAS silently watched Billy Two unloading his loot and pulling on his clothes.

What was that old medal awarded by the Austro-Hungarian Empire, the one that could only be won by successfully disobeying orders? The Order of Maria Theresa, that was it. Well, Billy had just put himself in line for that with his solo attack on the Chinese mortar. It wasn't the first time for him or for the rest of the SOBs, either.

Although come to think of it, Billy hadn't actually disobeyed any orders. Barrabas and Hayes hadn't thought to order him not to do something they had no idea he was going to do. That's what came of having Hawk Spirit around—he made the big Osage even more unpredictable than usual.

Of course, if Hawk Spirit could let Billy do things like this on a regular basis, maybe they all ought to talk to gods.

Lee Hatton came up, followed by Alex Nanos. He had a Bren gun under one arm and an antique-looking sword under the other.

"Casualty report," Lee said tonelessly. "Eighteen dead or too badly hurt to travel. Fifteen minor casualties or people who can be left in a village. I'm going over all of them. They should be okay unless the Chinese sweep the area in retaliation."

Barrabas didn't ask what had happened to the crippled. They were dead, with or without the help of friends. Was it the doctor in Lee that made it hard for her to take that? Or was it the same as for the rest of the SOBs, the reminder that the same fate might be waiting for them one day.

"Oh, yes," she added. "McPherson's dead. He was hit in one of the early Chinese attacks. Alex was overrun but played dead, then picked off enough Chinese to let the Tibetans rally. They seem to be getting over the shock of McPherson's death pretty well. Counting about fifty Chinese bodies hasn't hurt.''

"Yeah, Nile," Nanos said. "But you might want to sit down with Tsering and a couple of his buddies and—"

"When I want advice, soldier, I'll ask for it," Barrabas said. The aftermath of a battle never left him in a mood for unnecessary chatter.

He pointed at the sword. "What's that?"

"That is Ragpa Dapon's sword," Billy Two said. "Where did you find it, Alex?"

Nanos blinked. "About fifty feet from McPherson's body. I guess he had it on him when he got zapped. Then some Chinese must have tried to lift it, and *he* got zapped. Wonder if it's bad luck?"

"For others, perhaps," Billy said. "For my spirit brother, it is part of his soul." Nanos had no time to move back before one huge hand plucked the sword from under his arm.

"Just hold it right there, Billy," Barrabas said. He wanted to shout, but had the feeling that someone neither Tibetan nor Chinese nor American would hear him if he did. "What were you going to do with that sword?"

"I think we could unbind Ragpa and give him back his sword. If he behaves himself in the next battle, then we could be sure the spirits are guiding him truly, and he could have a rifle for the next battle."

"I suppose that makes sense. Go ahead."

"Thank you, Colonel."

The gratitude in Billy's voice was an unmistakable as the lie in Alex's. Billy was saying what he thought was true. Alex was saying what he knew Barrabas had to hear about McPherson's convenient death.

Both of them had earned the right not to have their C.O. asking awkward questions. Particularly when their C.O. had just inherited the command of a band of Tibetan guerillas five hundred miles from the nearest friendly force.

Barrabas squatted down and began to fieldstrip his FAL. The job would give him time, and that time might give him answers.

If it didn't, it would at least give him a clean rifle for the next fight. Nile Barrabas was too experienced an infantryman to ever doubt the value of a clean weapon.

16

"Coming up on our final turn," came Arthur Gordon's voice from the cockpit of the Troopship. "Cargo crew, to your stations."

Jessup grunted, heaved his bulk out of the jump seat and slogged aft. He moved slowly, to avoid disturbing the plane's balance.

The Troopship was droning along barely three hundred feet above the Tibetan plateau. It would climb slightly for the drop, to give the parachutes time to open. Right now it was so low that any unbalancing could send it into the ground in spite of Arthur's skill and the power of the two 2,800-horsepower turboprops.

Captain Thapa and Bajbir followed Jessup. Three men to slide out a two-ton drop was just enough. Arthur could make more than two passes over the drop zone, but every additional pass increased the chances of Chinese intervention. Of course, every load carried back to Nepal reduced the SOBs' survival chances....

The cargo deck tilted right, then left, then leveled out. Jessup managed to keep his balance without flailing wildly. The two Gurkhas stood as if they'd grown from the deck, legs slightly flexed, smiling faintly at Jessup's struggles.

"Climbing to drop altitude," Arthur said. The deck tilted again. This time Jessup had to clutch at the overhead rail.

The two Gurkhas had slid the first load into place when the rear door started swinging down. The roar of air passing at a hundred and twenty knots tore at Jessup's ears. Beyond the end of the door he saw the dark Tibetan pla-

teau whipping past. The moonlight left even the closest
mountains shapeless blurs. Jessup was suddenly glad he
hadn't seen the mountains they'd flown through on the
way.

He understood that Arthur Gordon knew these mountains like he did his own villa. He also realized that night
would hide them from Chinese eyes, while low altitude hid
them from Chinese radar. He would still be much happier
when his feet were on solid Nepalese ground again.

"Ground signal!" Arthur snapped. "First load!"

The two Gurkhas put their shoulders to the pallet of
crated ammunition. It slid out the door into the slip-
stream, popped its drogue chute and vanished. Two more
loads followed it. By the time the third was gone, Jessup
saw the first swaying down to the ground under its camouflage chute.

As they came around for the second pass, firefly glows
winked on the ground. Jessup read off the code for the safe
landing of all three loads and felt like dancing. To save both
the plane and his energy, he only whistled "The Eyes of
Texas."

They could have packed the ammunition to drop in one
pass or even one load. Jessup and the pilot both vetoed
that. They both recalled Dien Bien Phu, where ammunition and food came down in two-ton installments. The huge
loads caved in dugouts and crushed people if they landed
in French lines. If they landed outside the lines, they were
a gift to the Vietminh, too heavy to be moved by the hungry, exhausted defenders.

The signals vanished as the Troopship came back for the
second pass. Jessup blinked sweat out of his eyes and
stared. Captain Thapa was pulling on a parachute. As the
plane straightened out, Bajbir handed him a helmet and an
FAL. Thapa tightened his straps, then finally seemed to
notice Jessup's gape.

"Your friends will need help with the heavy weapons. I
knew machine guns as a soldier. I have not forgotten
them."

"But—"

"The other Gurkhas will obey you as they would me. They have eaten your salt. Besides, 'Rank hath its privileges.'" The grin widened. "One of them is going to be a last fight against the Chinese."

"But—from this altitude?"

Bajbir grinned and said something that made the captain laugh.

"He says maybe you do not have the soul of a Gurkha after all, to fear a parachute jump from this height.

"In World War Two, a British officer asked the men of his Gurkha regiment to volunteer to jump from airplanes at five hundred feet. None volunteered. Even the subadar-major said that three hundred feet was high enough.

"The officer begged them to remember the honor of the regiment and the reputation of the Gurkhas. He also assured them that parachutes seldom failed.

"Now the subadar-major smiled. 'Ah, we use parachutes, do we?' he said. 'That is very different.' And they all volunteered."

"Will you comedians finish your act and start pushing ammo?" came Arthur Gordon's voice. "Or do you really like stooging around in the middle of night in the middle of Tibet?"

Walker Jessup handed Thapa the coded message for Nile Barrabas. He wished he had time to add a line or two explaining that the captain joining the party wasn't *his* idea. Then they went to work.

The second three loads went out faster than the first. As the drogue for the last one blossomed, Thapa ran to the door, relaxed into a jumper's position and let himself fall out into the night.

NILE BARRABAS LOOKED up from Billy Two uncrating the Carl Gustav ammunition, to Captain Thapa folding up his parachute. The Gurkha looked quite unrepentant about crashing the SOBs' party, but seemed reluctant to meet Barrabas's eyes.

"Okay, Captain Thapa. You're here. There's not much point in trying to figure out ways of sending you back.

You're with us to the end of the mission—win, lose, or fall down a cliff. But you've just insulted my men by hinting that they needed help. Why?''

Barrabas didn't really expect any of his people to give a damn if six little green men with purple tentacles joined them. They were professionals. They took or refused help depending on whether they trusted the helper. They would certainly trust Thapa or any other Gurkha. But Barrabas was curious about the Gurkha's motives, and he needed an explanation for that curiosity that Thapa would accept.

"I mean nothing against your people. I knew they were as good as Gurkhas, and the fight proves it. But do they have more than two hands and two eyes? Can they be in more than one place at once?''

"Can they kill all the Chinese, or will there be some left for an old Gurkha who wants a few more?'' Barrabas asked. "That's what you really want to know, isn't it?''

Thapa laughed. "You see clearly, Colonel Barrabas. Yes there is that too. But do not call me 'old' if you do not want me asking why you insult me. Perhaps I cannot outrun the three boys I left with your Fixer, but otherwise I am all the soldier they are.''

The man was almost certainly right, Barrabas knew. Besides, there was something else he hadn't mentioned probably because he knew a professional like Barrabas would already have thought of it.

Thapa was another set of head and hands to train the Tibetans with the heavy weapons. Some of them understood English, more Nepalese. In a few days, when the SOBs and the rubies flew out, the Tibetans would be handy enough with the weapons they'd inherit.

"Okay, Captain,'' Barrabas said. "You're Director of Training. Anything you don't know about these pieces, one of my people can tell you. Right now, though, we're going to move out as fast as we line up the ammo bearers.''

The Gurkha saluted and turned away, leaving Barrabas to return to the Fixer's letter. He'd already read it twice. Now he returned to the account of the attack on the ammunition.

...don't know who was behind it. Probably won't find out soon, either.

With the ammo in to Tibet, the prime target for these bad guys is out of their reach. It'll take a while for them to find another place to squeeze us. Maybe it'll take them so long that you people will be back and the rubies out of our hands. That won't break my heart.

Other problem is getting cooperation from the Nepalese. The police do their best, which isn't too good. They've stopped worrying about us being drug barons. The military is kind of dragging their feet, though. Maybe they think they've done us enough favors, with all the looking the other way they've done. Maybe they think the Chinese will notice if they do any more.

Meanwhile we've got Gurkhas on the job, and the Gordons and I are all packing guns. Anybody who wants to live to be paid for offing us probably can't. We'll need a little luck, but we won't hog more than our share even if Weng can't do as much as he promised. There'll be plenty left over for you people who really need it.

Yours wearily,
Walker Jessup

Kind words from the Fixer, Barrabas thought. Will wonders never cease? Oh well, he's probably worried about his cut.

Not that there wasn't something to be worried about. It looked as though Weng's people might not be on the job, keeping the competition away from Dr. Gonpo and the Fixer until the rubies arrived.

Barrabas wondered if maybe the Senator had tipped off Taiwanese intelligence. If they were in the field, Weng might be backing off. The Triads valued good relations with Taipei, at least enough not to shoot Taiwanese agents wholesale.

The fact that this might get the SOBs killed wouldn't bother the Senator at all. He might not put out any termination orders on them again, but putting them in the way of "accidents" was another matter.

It was also one to be dealt with when the SOBs were out of Tibet, with or without the rubies. From the Maxims of Nile Barrabas: You can only worry about so many things at a time.

"Hey, Colonel," Billy Two said. "We got a couple of extra goodies packed in with the Carl Gustav. A bottle of Scotch and a gem assayer programmed by Nate Beck. Says he ran up the software on the advice of an old friend of his uncle who didn't ask any questions, and cannibalized a laptop computer for the hardware."

Nate Beck might no longer be an SOB, but they could still draw on his ability to make computers do everything but sing grand opera. Although he could probably make one do that, too, if the SOBs ever needed it.

They didn't need that now, but they did need the ability to tell rubies from rocks before packing them out of Tibet. Thanks to Nate, they now had that ability.

The bonds forged when Beck was an SOB hadn't frayed away. In the chill Tibetan night, the thought brought warmth to Barrabas as if he'd taken a slug of the Scotch.

"Pack them both, Billy. We'll save the Scotch for a celebration."

"The drop isn't worth celebrating?"

It was nice to know that the big Osage still had a normal thirst for good booze. That meant he wasn't completely gone on Hawk Spirit. Just gone far enough to do the impossible on a pretty regular basis.

"We celebrate when we get either the rubies or Colonel Yao. Right now, we start packing up to move out."

"Can do."

Billy started repacking the assayer. Barrabas headed for the Tibetans, who should have picked their ammo bearers by now. They'd need to hurry from now on, no matter how much they were carrying or how valuable it was.

You didn't hand somebody like Colonel Yao a free gift of time to cook up something nasty. Colonel Yao *and* his soldiers—those PLA people had known their business.

In many years of fighting, Nile Barrabas had seldom liked the people he ended up killing. After all, they were usually trying to kill him, sometimes just for the hell of it.

Sometimes he'd hated their guts and been glad to see their bodies sprawled in front of him. He reflected that he'd throw the party of the century if Karl Heiss ever turned up finally, completely and undoubtedly dead. There really were some people so evil that they ought to be disposed of, like sewage.

Nile Barrabas had never ignored the skill of even the most vicious opponent.

THE SCREAMS of the captured Tibetan villager faded into moans. Commander Yao contemplated the bloody face and torso for a moment, then drew his pistol and shot the man through the head.

"Throw that offal off the nearest cliff!" he snapped. Two fighters leaped to obey. No one failed in instant obedience to Yao these days.

As the men hauled the body out of the shepherds' hut, Yao holstered his pistol and turned to Company Commander Zhou.

"Well, Comrade Zhou? What would you have us do? Shall we comb the villages for the wounded the guerrillas have hidden?"

Zhou frowned. Even he was not immune from Yao's wrath these days. Nor could he pass down his own humiliation by abusing the platoon commanders. That was unworthy of a commander in the PLA at the best of times, and these were not the best of times.

Even minus a quarter of its strength, Column Yao was still a match for any band of Tibetans. But the men had come to doubt that, and besides, they were no longer fighting only Tibetans. They were fighting the Western advisers, and today it seemed they were even fighting their own superiors.

"I would hope we pursue our major objective, the rubies of Bandit Su," Zhou said. "We could not move into the villages quickly enough without the helicopters we have been refused. Even if we receive the helicopters, I would rather use them to move swiftly to the mountain. At least we know where it is at last."

"Yes, and so do the imperialists and their Tibetan running dogs!" Yao's voice was almost shrill. "We are racing them, and who knows if they have a lead? Their lead would not matter if we had the helicopters. As it is, it seems their airplanes fly freely over territory that should hold none but ours! Our air force not only cannot let us use the sky, it cannot even prevent the imperialists from using it!

"And this is what we have, after feeding money to the air force until we must make do with obsolete tanks and artillery and delay new weapons even for the infantry. We must beg on our knees for the imperialists' technology, which will be cut off the moment we are dependent upon it. Chairman Mao, what would you say to this corruption of the PLA?"

Chairman, Mao, being dead, said nothing. Zhou, being prudent, said the same. It was clear that Commander Yao would for some time be unable to vent his wrath on the imperialists and the Tibetans who'd threatened his mission and killed his fighters. Until then, he would sometimes need to rage at *somebody*. The air force was today's target.

Zhou hoped the next battle would come quickly and end in victory. It would be best for the Chinese People's Republic, for the People's Liberation Army, for Column Yao, for Regiment Commander Yao, and not least of all for Company Commander Zhou.

17

The stone must have rolled most of the way downhill in a gully that both hid and silenced it. It leaped out at the Tibetans like a Chinese ambush.

It didn't surprise Nile Barrabas that there were casualties. One Tibetan was nicked by a flying bit of rock. Lee Hatton cleaned and bandaged the cut in five minutes.

"He'll do fine," she added. "With the high altitude and dry climate here, wounds don't get infected nearly as easily."

The more serious casualty was Gendun Tsering. The stone had clipped his left ankle, laying it open to the bone. The bone itself wasn't broken, but torn muscles and bleeding made it impossible for him to walk.

"It won't even be safe for him to walk for a few days," Lee said, after debriding and disinfecting the wound. "I'd suggest we drop him off in the next village, with a supply of medicine and instructions on using it. With the resupply, we've got some to spare."

Tsering couldn't have been angrier if Lee had threatened to castrate him. His anger outran his command of English; all the names he called her and the SOBs were in Tibetan.

Finally Tsering ran out of breath. Barrabas was about to order him to follow Lee's instructions when Ragpa Dapon loomed over the leader. Barrabas stepped back to give himself room for either shooting or unarmed combat.

The Khampa only knelt beside Tsering, ignored the man's glare and ran a hand over him from forehead to belly. Then he rose.

"The spirits walk with this one," he said. "We leave him, they maybe leave us. I walk for him."

Tsering's glare turned into a frown. He spoke to the Khampa, who nodded, then to Barrabas. "He says he will carry me until my ankle is well."

Barrabas looked at the Khampa. If anyone in the band besides Billy Two and Alex Nanos was strong enough, it was the Khampa.

Then he admonished himself. Hurry up, Nile. The Tibetans won't like it if you stand around picking your nose for even ten extra seconds.

Billy Two saved him the trouble of making a snap decision. He also knelt beside the Tibetan, but only seemed to look at something beyond the farthest mountaintop. Then he rose and stood beside the Khampa.

"My brother in the spirits speaks the truth," Billy said. "If Tsering goes on with us, it will bring good fortune."

"That's a pretty hefty piece of carrying he's promising," Barrabas pointed out.

"If my brother weakens, I will bear his burden," Billy said.

Barrabas opened his mouth to order Billy to save his strength for his Bren gun, then shut it. Billy's strength and endurance were impressive even without the aid of Hawk Spirit. With the aid of Hawk Spirit, he might have been a robot.

"I will bear Tsering's rifle and Mr. Starfoot's Bren gun if necessary," Captain Thapa said. Barrabas hadn't seen him come up, and for a moment wished that the Gurkha would follow the stone off the cliff. Out from under Mc-Pherson's heavy-handed leadership, the Tibetans seemed to think this mission could be run by committee.

What the hell! As long as the notion didn't infect the SOBs, Barrabas was ready to roll with the punch. Besides, Tsering really was one of the people holding the band together. They'd need him all the way to the jeweled mountain, and even more afterward when the SOBs went home. Taking him with them made sense, even if the way they'd reached the decision didn't.

"Dapon, Billy. Take charge of Tsering. Just remember that if you drop him over a cliff, you'd damned well better jump after him!"

Dr. Gonpo raised a cup of butter tea. The expression on Walker Jessup's face stopped the cup in midair, then sent it back to the table.

"Thanks," Jessup growled.

"Enough tea can restore the balances within you," Gonpo insisted. "The more you foreswear your Western gluttony, the less tea will be needed."

"All the tea in Tibet couldn't do the job," Jessup said. "I wouldn't let it, anyway. Doctor, do you realize how much careful gluttony it took to unbalance my system? You want to destroy the work of half a lifetime?"

"If the work will otherwise destroy you, both my Western and Tibetan oaths oblige me to try."

"You can try until the cows come home," Jessup said. "I'm damned sure you won't succeed!"

The doctor refilled his own cup and seemed to contemplate the steam rising from it. Then he smiled. "I do have one way of persuading you to moderate your appetite."

"Yeah?"

"If you cease to devour everything in your path, I will consent to be guarded night and day by the Gurkhas."

Jessup's jaw dropped open. Fortunately he'd finished his dinner half an hour ago, and it hadn't been much of a dinner anyway. More chicken and *chapattis*, stretched by a big dish of *chick-peas*, for God's sake! He hadn't eaten chick-peas since an undercover assignment in Berkeley twenty-five years ago. He hadn't liked them then, and he didn't like them now.

He also didn't like being blackmailed. He was the Fixer. *He* was the one who put on the squeeze.

Or rather, he had been until he met Dr. Gonpo.

The Tibetan's smile widened. "You understand, I seriously doubt that anyone has designs against me. I think you see ghosts and demons where none exist."

"It wasn't any ghosts who tried to take out our ammo!"

"No, but they are certainly ghosts now. If they find another incarnation soon, it will hardly be as more than mice or cockroaches. Neither can harm us."

"What about their friends still incarnate as men with guns?"

"What about them? With the ammunition in Tibet being fired at Chinese, there is nothing those friends can do."

"Except strike at easy targets like you."

"Or like you. Perhaps you are better guarded, but you are *much* larger."

Jessup said a lot of things that would have got him thrown out of any respectable biker bar, about people who didn't have the brains to pour piss out of a boot. He said them under his breath, although it was a real temptation to say them out loud. It would have relieved his feelings, even if it didn't take the smile off Gonpo's face.

When Jessup stopped muttering, he realized that for once somebody besides Nile Barrabas had him over a barrel. If somebody tried anything against the doctor, the SOBs would be extensively pissed. He wasn't an SOB, but he was Lee Hatton's friend. By their code, he would be someone to be taken care of—or avenged.

This could get a lot of people killed, an unnecessary complication in the other wise simple business of getting Prince Su's rubies into the hands of the Triads. Keeping Gonpo safe might keep those people alive.

Jessup held his cup out for more tea. He even managed to get the tea down without gagging.

"Does this mean you agree to our bargain?"

"You write me up a diet and I'll stick to it. I'll cut orders for a Gurkha, and he'll stick to you. Fair enough?"

"Almost. You will also swear to keep the diet, by Aesculapius, Apollo the Physician, and any gods you may worship. Or have you made a god of your belly?"

"Doctor, I didn't swear to sit still for insults."

"I apologize."

The hell you do, Jessup thought. He also remembered that he hadn't *sworn* not to approach the Tibetan Youth

Congress for some of their muscle. He'd just said that under the circumstance he agreed it wasn't necessary.

Circumstances had changed, though. Maybe enough to persuade the Tibetan elders to hold still for him and the TYC.

Then there'd be some extra people guarding Dr. Gonpo. The Gurkhas could relax, and Jessup could drop this damned diet! He'd be dropping it as soon as this crazy mission was over anyway, but a man could lose twenty, thirty pounds in that time. It would take a solid month of pigging out to build up his waistline again after that kind of ordeal.

COMPANY COMMANDER ZHOU reflected that contour lines on a map lied like Intelligence officers. No, it was more than a simple lie. They told you part of the truth. The part they left out was always more important.

No map had told him what a tangled nightmare of valleys and ridges the last twenty kilometers were going to be. Slopes that would tax a fly, ridges normally looked at only by birds, and even snowfields certain to spawn avalanches met his eye at every turn.

The fighters of the column saw the same thing. They had proved that they were good men by the way they recovered from the battle with the guerrillas. They had worked hard to care for the walking wounded, unload the resupply of machine guns and ammunition, and cover a steady twenty kilometers a day.

Now they could see ahead that they would work harder yet. The distance to the mountain of the jewel cave was twenty kilometers in a straight line. In these mountains, no one but birds could travel in a straight line. To cover the twenty, the column might march fifty.

Zhou's legs and ankles had turned into hot iron on the last climb. The heat seemed to be spreading upward, giving him aches in his head and stomach. He sat down and waited for Commander Yao to come up.

Yao almost bounced up to Zhou, which annoyed the younger commander. A man nearly old enough to be his father should not be able to spring about these mountains like a goat.

"Is there any chance of air-landing a small security patrol on the mountain?" Zhou said. "It wouldn't need more than rifles and a radio. The mountain must be full of places where a dozen men could delay a hundred. I would like it to be our dozen men delaying the imperialists' hundred, not the other way around."

Yao looked at the mountains. The ones in sight certainly matched Zhou's description. Disgust twisted his face.

"In a perfect world there would be no problem. Even in this world I would offer the air force officers women, gold, opium, even tickets to Taiwan if I thought they would help us.

"They will not. Also, they might not be able to land a helicopter high enough with an adequate load."

"I would gladly jump."

"I would let you, in some other kind of terrain. These mountains are no place to begin one's career as a parachutist. You and your men would be lost or killed and accomplish nothing except to make yourself easier victims for the imperialists."

"The whole column will be easier victims for the imperialists if they get too far ahead of us!"

"We can make ourselves veritable turtles, I think, if we deploy our heavy weapons properly."

Zhou recognized Yao's tone as the one he used when presenting a younger commander with a problem to test his knowledge. He frowned.

"One machine gun up with the lead platoon. The RPGs with the second platoon. The recoilless rifle in the rear so it can deploy at leisure out of enemy range."

"One of the radios up with the scouts, too," Yao added. "Remember, a radio is also a weapon."

"I have not forgotten, Comrade Commander. I only wished to risk as little as possible."

"We can no longer afford to think too cautiously, Comrade Zhou," Yao said grimly. "We run a race against a swift opponent. The side whose last man carries away the rubies will be the winner.''

Zhou recognized that Yao did not care if he was not the last man, so long as the last man was Chinese. Such dedication might be hard on the column. It would be deadly to the imperialists.

"Commander Zhou! Look!"

A deputy platoon commander was shouting and pointing. Zhou raised his binoculars. He didn't know what he would see, but he did know that the man had been in the PLA for fifteen years.

The ridge came into focus, the black specks crossing the long trailing snowfield took shape, and Zhou laughed.

"Comrade Commander?"

"Mountain sheep. No danger to anything, except maybe our stomachs if we eat too much of their meat!"

Zhou handed the binoculars around and was happy to hear others join in the laughter.

His own laughter ended quickly. Today it had been sheep. Tomorrow it might be Tibetan guerrillas—and they would be wiser than the sheep. They might not cross a snowfield to warn of their presence.

THE SUN DIPPED behind the ridge. Lee Hatton turned and walked back downhill to where the SOBs and Tibetans were settling into camp. She was too seasoned to silhouette herself, but she'd wanted to see the sun go down.

Many thoughts were spinning through her mind. Am I getting afraid I won't live to see it rise? Probably, but why more so now than before? I've always known the risks I faced, and faced them with open eyes.

Did Geoff's going make me more aware of my mortality than a soldier ought to be? Is his monument going to be my doing a Nate Beck?

God, I hope not!

Meanwhile there were the wounded to examine. To her left, the click of dice on rocks floated out of the shadows. Curious, she approached the circle of kneeling men.

Ragpa Dapon rose from the circle with a roar of anger. She saw his hand gripping the hilt of his sword. Several of the Tibetans stepped back and looked ready to unsling their rifles or draw their knives.

Sitting by the dice, Gendun Tsering saw the uproar. He shifted his battered leg and grinned at Lee.

"Oh, it is nothing to fear. Only he is a Khampa. For him, a woman comes where he gambles—it is bad luck."

"Well, I don't want to make trouble. But if I don't examine your ankle I'll be bringing bad luck to you. Ask him if he wants that."

Dapon muttered a short reply to Tsering's question. The leader laughed. "He says you do it tonight. If he loses, you not come where he gambles again."

Lee knelt by Tsering's ankle and began her examination. Prodding and smelling were about the best she could do without taking off the dressing. They were too short of medical supplies to risk, that unless the wound showed signs of infection.

It seemed to be healing cleanly. Circumstances didn't encourage hygiene, but Tsering was certainly tough. Also, high altitude really did make normally rugged bacteria lie down and twitch feebly.

"Tomorrow or the day after, you can begin walking again. Only a short time, and on level ground at first."

"Where we find level ground?" Tsering waved at the mountaintops fading into the twilight.

Lee nodded. If this country was spread out, it would cover more area than Texas.

"We'll think of something."

"I know it, Doctor. In last incarnation you very brave, to be like you are now. Both warrior and healer—this very good."

"I do my best."

"Your best save lives." Tsering bent forward and put his lips close to Lee's ear. "I think I not gamble with Khampa any more."

"Why? If he wins—"

"He lose. You see, I use my own dice. And how he pay me if lose? I not want to bring him or you bad luck."

"Thank you."

That was as much as Lee could get out with a straight face.

18

The view in front of Nile Barrabas matched all the intelligence he had. There were the two peaks, in the right directions and at the right distance. He began studying it with an eye to tactics.

The ridge ahead of him dipped toward the west, ending in a thousand yards of nearly open, nearly level ground. Holding that would give the Antonov a safe landing strip. At the end of the strip, a glacier spilled down from another mountain. It fed a small stream that meandered along the edge of the strip. A flock of wild sheep drank from the stream. From this height, their rough fleeces made them look like unpruned bushes.

Barrabas looked at Gendun Tsering, standing with the aid of his rifle. The man had said he would need only two days to be back on his feet, instead of Lee Hatton's prediction of three. From the drawn look on Tsering's face, Barrabas suspected Lee had been right. She usually was.

It didn't matter. Tsering nodded, and Barrabas unfolded his map. The SOBs and Tibetan leaders gathered around him.

"Either these mountains have two identical landscapes, or we're where we want to be," Barrabas said. "The cave should be about two thousand feet up that way."

He pointed toward the summit pyramid of the mountain they stood on. "I want to get it located before dark. We've won the race, but I don't know by how much. I also don't know what shape the cave is in. We may have to do some digging, and I want a team ready to start work tonight."

Nobody argued or even spoke. The SOBs were avoiding any suggestions in order not to undercut Barrabas's authority with the Tibetans. The Tibetans had come to trust Barrabas over the past two days. Not that they had much choice, with the Chinese certainly in the neighborhood, but it moved things along a lot faster.

It wasn't going to be easy, Barrabas realized, pulling out and leaving these people to the nonexistent mercy of some thoroughly pissed-off Chinese. It was necessary, but necessary things weren't easier or more pleasant because of that.

He considered that maybe the Fixer could put in one more fix, with the Company this time. Pull these people out of Tibet, maybe all the way to India. Claim that it was needed, now that McPherson was dead—and hope nobody would ask too many questions about why McPherson was dead.

"I'll go up, Colonel," Billy Two said. "Me and Ragpa are probably the best climbers."

"What about all the toting your brother's done these past two days?" Barrabas asked.

The Khampa grunted. "When I was boy, I carry yak calf. He heavier than Tsering. Wiser, too."

Tsering laughed. "Yes, yaks wise. They not help Chinese."

The Khampa started to glare, then laughed. "Maybe Khampa not wise as yak. Chinese most stupid of all. They spit at spirits. Fools!" He said a couple of impolite things about the Chinese in his native tongue, then turned to Billy.

"We go, brother?"

Barrabas watched the two big men start their climb. Billy Two carried his FAL slung across his back, the Khampa his sword in the same place. The Khampa didn't carry a rifle, only because there hadn't been a second fight with the Chinese to prove his loyalty.

That would change soon enough. Even if it didn't, Barrabas was going to give the Khampa a rifle. He'd been a tower of strength on the march, and most of the Tibetans tolerated him. He'd need to defend himself against the ones who didn't, as well as against the Chinese.

"Captain Thapa, take one of the Brens and set up an observation post on the south face. Take Starlites, a flare pistol, a radio and enough Tibetans to have two men on watch at all times. I want complete radio silence until we find the rubies. Use flares to warn us if the Chinese try coming up the far side of the mountain. We can reinforce you from the people around the cave."

Their main job would be defending the cave and keeping the Chinese out of range of the landing strip. Not that the SOBs couldn't walk out if they had to, rubies and all. But the An-2 was definitely "appropriate technology" for hauling ass when the time came for that.

As the Gurkha saluted, a distant, echoing crack floated across the mountains. Barrabas turned, searching each patch of landscape until he was satisfied nothing moved except the sheep.

"Probably an avalanche."

"Probably," the Gurkha agreed. "But . . . it might also have been a mortar or rocket launcher." He spoke so quietly that only Barrabas heard him.

Only the Gurkha was close enough to see Barrabas jerk his head in a quick, grim nod.

BEFORE THE SMOKE from the 75 mm shells had cleared away, the lead platoon was on its way toward the Tibetan position.

The platoon had lost its commander and a third of its strength in the fight with the guerrillas. At Yao's suggestion, Zhou was using it today to restore its confidence and test its skill. Yao watched through his binoculars until the platoon disappeared into a ravine. For as long as he could see them, the men seemed to be moving steadily and in good order.

Yao let the binoculars fall and looked at the 75 mm recoilless rifle, the latest addition to the column's heavy weapons. It was not as pleasant a sight.

It wasn't the weapon's back-blast that concerned Yao. That highly visible back-blast hardly mattered here in the mountains, which offered little concealment anyway. Nor did it matter against an opponent with no weapon that could match the 75 mm's range.

Yao's discontent was with the ammunition. They had used six of the thirty rounds to blast the suspected Tibetan position. Three had been duds. This slowed the firing rate dangerously. Against a stronger force, such a rate of fire would have allowed the enemy to disperse, even counter-attack.

Like flies or rats, the Tibetans had to be destroyed the moment they were in reach. Otherwise they had too many hiding places in these cursed mountains.

"I thought it was only the air force that had abandoned us," Yao said sharply. "Now it seems that the ordnance officers have made an alliance with them."

"The ordnance officers are victims of the air force, too," Zhou replied sturdily. "What are they to do when they can only send out ammunition as old as some of the column's fighters."

Too late, Yao remembered that Zhou had once commanded an antitank platoon of just such recoilless rifles. He reproached himself for this lapse of memory. Would he be able to bear his burden these last few days before victory? He would certainly do a better job if he asked himself no useless questions and instead answered Zhou's useful one.

"Doubtless they have done their best. It may well be good enough. Our men will do the rest. But I want an armorer to examine those failed rounds. If they cannot be repaired, I want their explosives salvaged. Reaching the cave does not mean reaching the rubies. We have some demolition charges, but we may need more."

"Very surely, Comrade Commander."

Zhou's look of surprise and respect warmed Yao. The excellent young commander did not know everything, and the weary old one was still not past teaching him what he did not know.

With the two of them leading the column, victory might be even closer than Yao had allowed himself to believe.

BARRABAS CLIMBED the fifteen hundred feet to the cave within half an hour after receiving Billy Two's signal. Three Tibetans climbed with him, as well as Alex Nanos with a Bren gun and Nate Beck's gem assayer. Barrabas wanted enough firepower at the cave itself to delay any party crashers until reinforcements could come uphill.

With an IR lamp, Barrabas illuminated the cave mouth, then examined it through his Starlites. The check showed a cave that matched the description exactly, except for one minor problem.

Thirty feet inside the mouth, the passage was completely blocked by a rockfall. It looked as if a section of the entrance tunnel's wall had toppled across it. A well-fed cat couldn't have crawled through the remaining gap.

"Shit!" Barrabas said. It was more of a clinical description of the situation than a curse. He handed the Starlite to Nanos.

"Double shit!" Nanos said. "We shoulda stood in bed, or maybe brought some pickaxes. Wait a minute, the Tibetans have some, don't they?"

"Yeah. But it'll take forever to chop that hunk down to size."

"Maybe, maybe not. Wanna bet if we cut it so that Billy, Brother Ragpa and I can all get handholds, we can *roll* the sucker out of the way?"

"How about far enough so that we can hitch a rope to it and a bunch of Tibetans to the rope? No need for you guys to hog all the glory."

"Come on, Colonel. I don't take people up on sucker bets. Only thing is, we're gonna need some more light, and I don't mean IR. How about spreading a couple of tents over the cave mouth?"

"Any light will only end up painting a big bull's-eye on our asses."

"Staying around here is hanging our asses out so far they'll be hit, bull's-eye or not."

Barrabas didn't disagree. He'd been making sure Nanos had everything thought out. As usual, the hefty SOB had it all together. Off duty, Nanos spent all his time chasing what might loosely be called women. On a mission, he was as cool as Lee Hatton.

"We'll get you the picks," Barrabas said. "But I'm also going to bring up Liam O'Toole and a few charges. I don't want to risk explosives until we're sure how solid the rest of the cave is. But if it looks like it can stand it, we may be able to save you guys a bit of sweat."

"No problem, Colonel. I want to save a little strength for a couple of nice girls back in Kathmandu."

"Alex, if they're waiting for *you*, 'nice' isn't the adjective I'd apply to them."

Nanos saluted with an upthrust finger. "With all due respect, Colonel Sir, bugger off and give us 'real men' the tools for the job."

"On the way."

"SO WE USED SIX ROUNDS and wasted the last of daylight killing half a dozen Tibetan yak herders?"

Commander Yao was shaking with rage, frustration and fatigue. He knew he should have gone to sleep while the platoon explored the ridge. It would have strengthened not only his body and will, but his reputation for invincible calm in the face of trouble.

He wondered how much trouble they had brought on themselves. Some, certainly, but perhaps no more than they could cure—and without the help of anyone outside the column, neither. Yao was beginning to wonder if some of those he had counted on to help him were in alliance with his enemies. Or did they merely lack the wits to open their trousers when they wished to piss?

Zhou frowned. "Do we know that they were not scouts for the imperialists and guerrillas? Even if they were not that they were bandits, or they would not have been where they were. They were enemies, certainly."

Yao managed to smile. He had been prepared to criticize Zhou harshly if he had said anything remotely defeatist. Instead Zhou was trying to turn a mistake into a victory.

Zhou went on. "Comrade Commander, I suggest that I go on ahead with a band of the best and strongest soldiers. We shall take the RPGs and several sniper rifles.

"We are now so close that there is no danger of such a vanguard being isolated and destroyed. If we reach the cave first, we can hold it until you strike the enemy's rear. If they reach it first, we can pin them down until you arrive. Either way, they will find their lives shorter and harder than they have expected."

"Very likely. But I think you can be trusted to command the greater part of the column. I will lead the vanguard myself."

Zhou's face was so blank that it spoke louder than a mask of rage. *I am younger, fitter and need to regain my reputation in the eyes of the men! Why are you going to be greedy for glory as well as the rubies?*

Yao shrugged. "Commander Zhou, that is my order. Also, remember that you will have many more opportunities to fight in the field. I will not."

Also, the scouting party will be first to lay eyes on the rubies. I have not sought them for three years to give that honor to someone else.

ALEX NANOS STEPPED BACK from the rock slab. His massive torso was armored in muscle. The muscle was now coated with rock dust and sweat. He wiped his forehead with the back of one hand and thrust out the other for a canteen.

Barrabas stuck the canteen in Nanos's hand. One rule for commanding people like the SOBs: When you can't do the job yourself, stand back and don't bug the people who can.

"Liam," Nanos said, as he kicked the underside of the rock, "take a look under here. What would you say to a small charge down here to save us time?"

Liam O'Toole knelt while Nanos held a flashlight, then dusted off his hands and stood up. "I think a little chemical-explosive therapy might do the patient a whole lot of good. Not to mention everybody's backs.''

"Risk factor?"

Liam wiggled a hand. "Low to negligible. There's a couple of what look like fractures to play with. Split even one of them, and we've got more manageable pieces. If the slab doesn't crack, it'll tamp the charge and localize the concussion. I'd recommend going ahead. We don't want to use up all our time or Tibetans on this one. There may be more rockfalls farther in."

There were also certainly Chinese on the way, if not already in the neighborhood. Did they want to attract unfriendly attention?

They didn't, but if they saved time it might not matter. No matter how unfriendly your neighbors got, if you'd moved out of town before they came calling, there wasn't a hell of a lot they could do.

Also, every Tibetan not tied up on the rockfall was one more rifle on the firing line. If the neighbors couldn't be avoided, it still might be enough to shoot them.

"Okay, Dr. O'Toole," Barrabas said. "Get out your scalpel and forceps and start operating."

"WHAT WAS THAT?" several men muttered.

"Silence!" Yao hissed. He not only wanted the scouting party to maintain silence, he wanted to hear the echoes of the distant sound as they rolled around the mountains.

"An avalanche starting, I think," he said at last.

"It sounded like an explosion, Comrade Commander," one bold fighter said.

Even in the darkness, the fury on Yao's face made the man flinch. "You fool! Have you never learned that the beginning of an avalanche sounds just like an explosion? You were there in the Uluk Pass. Is it hearing you lack or wits? If you lack either, perhaps someone else should take your place in the ranks of the PLA."

"I beg your pardon, Comrade Commander." The man sounded far more frightened of Yao than of all the Tibetans ahead.

"You will have it if you hold your tongue. It is your work as well as mine you make harder if you frighten your comrades."

"Certainly, Comrade Commander."

The vanguard resumed its march. Yao dropped back to the rear where he could reassure any other men uneasy at the mysterious sound.

Mysterious to them, at least. To Yao, it was either what he had said it was, or the imperialists already at work in the cave.

As long as the men did not think of the second possibility and lose heart, it hardly mattered. The more work the imperialists did, the less for Column Yao.

Besides, Yao found himself almost hoping the imperialists would be at the cave. For once they could not run. They would have to fight against the courage and strength of his column, and they would lose.

That would be far more satisfactory than simply snatching the rubies from the dead hands of a decadent Imperial aristocrat!

THE EXPLOSION BLEW the weighted tent over the cave mouth to shreds. Fortunately it also put out the lamp in the tunnel. In the darkness, rock dust and smoke poured out in a choking cloud.

Nanos and O'Toole plunged into the cave without waiting for the smoke to clear. A moment later Billy Two followed them, and a moment after that an Osage war whoop echoed around the mountainside.

"Good news, gentlemen?" Barrabas asked.

"Pretty good," O'Toole replied. "We busted the slab right in two and pretty much crumbled one piece. We might not even need the Tibetans if we can have a little light on the subject."

Barrabas signaled the Tibetans to rig another tent over the cave mouth. The moment they had it in place, a mighty crashing and clattering floated out of the cave. Barrabas thought of warning the rock-pile gang not to knock themselves out, then locked his jaw. All that would do was prove the C.O. *didn't* have nerves of steel—which he really didn't, but that was Top Secret.

By the time Nanos poked his head out of the cave, Lee Hatton had joined the party. "Mind if I take a look?"

"Be our guest."

Lee vanished inside the tunnel only to pop out a moment later. She handed her FAL and medical kit to Barrabas.

"What the—?"

"Nile, they've cleared away enough rock to let me through. Nobody else, and even I'm going to have to strip down a bit. If you can hand me in some tools and the Nate Beck Handy Dandy Gem Tester, I can get a head start on the jewels."

Barrabas managed to state only legitimate objections. "What if there's another rockfall beyond? Or if the rock falls again behind you?"

"The sooner we find out about any more rockfalls, the sooner we can start on them. I'll trust the guys not to let me be cut off."

There might not be much the rock-pile gang could do, but Lee Hatton was a woman with her mind made up. She was already taking off her jacket, then kneeling to unzip her boots.

When Lee was down to her underwear, Nanos grinned. "Now I know why I lost track of Billy in that last fight. When he's in his undershorts, he doesn't draw the eye the way you do."

"That's every woman's dream, to be the center of attention in a firefight. Flashlight, please."

Nanos slapped one into Lee's hand, and she vanished into the cave.

DAWN SILHOUETTED the summit ridge of the mountain. Through Yao's binoculars, it also silhouetted the tiny figures perched on the ridge like sparrows on a housetop.

His pencil danced across the message pad. The faint *skritt* as he tore off the paper and handed it to the radio operator sounded like a shell burst in the silent dawn. Those fighters not already asleep jumped.

"We shall have another chance to avenge our comrades after all," Yao said. "Zhou will hold their attention on his side of the mountain while we slip up on them from behind. I want every man to be ready to fight as though the fate of the People's Republic depended on him alone."

The People's Republic might or might not survive Prince Su's rubies falling into the hands of barbarians allied with the imperialists. It probably would. The Republic had many strengths. More than Regiment Commander Yao, who also had nearly as many enemies.

The radio operator began tapping out the message to Zhou. By the time he received a reply, most of the vanguard was asleep. Rather to his surprise, Yao found that he could join them. This close to the end of his long hunt, he had expected to be as restless as a hungry tiger.

Perhaps what made the difference was knowing that the hunt would be over within a few hours.

THE SUN LIFTED over the peaks to the east. Under the flashlight, the rubies had seemed to glow. In the light of day, they seemed to pulse with a life of their own, like a gigantic heart.

Lee Hatton finished binding up the last of the teak boxes. They were heavy, actually weighing more than their contents, but no other wood could have survived so many years in the damp chill cave. The gilded Imperial dragons on the hinges and latches were scarred and tarnished, and the silk bags had rotted into smelly rags.

From inside the cave came more rattles and crashes. On Barrabas's orders, Billy Two and the Khampa were blocking up the cave again. There was a fortune in Chinese and Tibetan treasures still down there, but the SOBs had no way to haul it out. They could at least see that the Chinese didn't loot it for one of their museums or for sale to greedy antique dealers.

At last the din faded. Billy Two and Ragpa Dapon climbed out of the cave. They wore only their undershorts and boots, and looked not just like brothers but like twins. The Khampa looked out at the mountainside as if he expected to find something that wasn't there, then shrugged.

Lee was handing the two men a canteen when a shout came from the summit ridge.

"Chinese! On west face."

Barrabas hooked one of the radios to his flak jacket and counted the magazines in his bandolier. He'd barely taken two steps uphill when they all saw a Tibetan scrambling toward them from below.

Barrabas waited until the man was almost up to him, then said, "Let me guess. Captain O'Toole sent you to tell me that the Chinese are in sight on the plateau."

The Tibetan gaped, made a gesture against the evil eye and nodded. "How you know?"

Barrabas was tempted to say that the spirits told him, but something in Billy Two's look made him think again. Billy Two was looking at the Khampa and frowning.

"So you were right after all, brother. Forgive me," Billy said at last. "Sorry, Colonel. He kept saying that the mountain spirits sensed an enemy and wanted him to tell his brother. I thought it was just the bad air in the cave. I guess we owe him a rifle. He really sweated on the rocks, too."

Barrabas picked up one of the captured Type 68s. "On one condition, Mr. Starfoot."

"What's that, Colonel?"

"Why didn't you believe *his* spirits?"

"Hawk Spirit is the only one who speaks to me. Not all the gods and spirits are good. Even some of the ones who speak to Hawk Spirit are ones he's warned me against. I couldn't be sure who was talking to my brother."

Ask a silly question...

No, that wasn't fair. Billy's answer made as much sense as anything else about Hawk Spirit and his fellow gods. The world was a lot simpler when the only kind of spirits Nile Barrabas had to worry about was good or bad whiskey.

Barrabas snapped the safety on the rifle, seated a magazine, picked up a bandolier and handed both rifle and ammunition to the Khampa. The big man looked as if he wanted to go down on his knees, but stopped with a jerk of his head.

"You fight for the spirits," he said. "They reward you."

"Lee," Barrabas said. "Get on the horn to our friends and stay on until they acknowledge. Let's hope the spirits' reward is Art Gordon showing up before the Chinese chase us away from the landing strip!"

19

"Tighten that nut!" Randall Gordon yelled.

"Which way?" Walker Jessup grunted, shaking sweat out of his eyes.

"Christ, didn't they teach you how to tie your shoes?"

"Save the insults, old man."

Jessup felt the nut giving; he had his answer. By the time the nut stopped turning, the sweat was running into his eyes again. He leaned on the wrench a couple more times, then stepped back.

"Well, don't just stand there playing with yourself—ask what's next!" Randall snapped.

"Easy, Dad," Arthur Gordon said, leaning out of the cockpit. "We're almost done. Dad, check the wiring on the RATOs. Walker, how about you relieve Gaje on sentry and send him around?"

"You're not going to take him, are you?" Jessup asked.

"Nervous in the service?" Randall asked with a wicked grin.

"No," Jessup lied. "Just thinking the way you are. The belt-and-suspenders approach, you know." He waved a hand at the An-2.

If Oleg Antonov had seen his plane now, he'd have sent his bootlegger to the gulag. Under one wing hung a pod of two-inch air-to-ground rockets; under the other hung something shaped like a skinny dill pickle—a three-barreled 7.62 mm minigun. Governed down so that it wouldn't shake the wings off, the gun could still put out two thousand rounds a minute. If Colonel Yao's men were caught in the open, one good pass with either weapon could put half of them out of action.

Inside the fuselage, half of the space the SOBs would use coming out was taken up by an inflatable fuel tank. With a couple of tons of extra fuel aboard, the An-2 would be able to loiter until the SOBs secured its landing strip, or even divert to another.

To get the whole load out of Nepal, four Rocket-Assisted Takeoff units on each side would help blast the An-2 off the runway. A second set rode in the cabin, in case the Tibetan takeoff run was shorter than they'd allowed for.

To put the chocolate sprinkles on the sundae, Randall Gordon was flying into Tibet with his son. Randall seemed to be the only one not surprised at this.

"Remember, boys, I go back a ways," he said. "When I learned to fly, a pilot had to be a pretty good jackleg chemist, mechanic and electrician. I left the chemistry to Mary, but I never let a piece of wiring or machinery go past without giving it the eye."

After Randall installed all the wiring for the gun, rocket pod and RATOs, nobody was arguing. Least of all Walker Jessup, who suspected that Tibet might actually be safer than Kathmandu these next few days.

Thinking of a sundae—even a butterscotch sundae—made Jessup's mouth water. Thinking of Dr. Weng coming to Kathmandu to take the rubies personally made Jessup's mouth dry up.

He couldn't be *sure* that the middle-aged man who'd landed in Kathmandu four days ago was Dr. Weng. The Nepalese police hadn't been able to give him a photograph, and they certainly had no way of knowing for sure.

Jessup wasn't going to wait to be sure, either. Worst-case planning was the only way to go in a situation like this. He was going to plan for Dr. Weng's being in town and whistling up all his boys. Not just the Chinese the Triads would surely have planted anywhere there was drug business, but their non-Chinese hangers-on, Nepalese and others.

Dr. Weng could whistle up a small army to protect Walker Jessup. He could also use it to make sure Walker Jessup kept his bargain.

Problem was, Walker Jessup had every intention of keeping that bargain. What bothered him was the danger of Dr. Weng's not knowing it and pulling something that would truly annoy the SOBs. Then Walker Jessup would really be between a rock and a hard place—or rather, between a rocky Triad and six hard people.

Dr. Weng would be no better off, of course. A small army wouldn't save the Triads, not from people who'd beaten large ones. But a real stomping match between Weng and the SOBs would probably give the Nepalese an excuse to butt in and grab the rubies for themselves.

Which would leave Walker Jessup with not a goddamn thing to do. No, there was one thing he'd *have* to do. He'd be so short of money he'd have to stay on Dr. Gonpo's diet until he could find another fix!

Given the choice between that and being dead, Jessup knew that he'd have to think twice.

Meanwhile the SOBs were a long ways off with their own problems. They were on the jeweled mountain, and they had firm possession of the rubies. *Not* undisputed possession, however—Colonel Yao was prepared to dispute it with about a rifle company of Chinese, all as determined as he was.

That was pretty determined. Maybe even determined enough to give Nile Barrabas and all his people real grief. Determined enough to beat them? Jessup wasn't going to worry about that. Dr. Weng, the Nepalese authorities, earthquakes, dysentery—those were real threats.

Colonel Yao beating Nile Barrabas wasn't.

Arthur jumped down from the cockpit and led his father in a thorough preflight. Once the Gordons were done and on board again, things happened fast.

The big radial roared to life. Arthur let off the brakes, and the plane lumbered onto the runway. The throttle opened wide as the plane turned for takeoff, the loaded wings rocking drunkenly. Then the Antonov gathered speed, a fine mist of spray shooting from under its wheels.

Halfway down the runway Arthur fired the RATOs. White smoke and steam almost hid the Antonov. When it reappeared it was airborne, climbing like a fighter under the four tons of solid-fuel thrust.

As the Antonov vanished into the clouds, Arthur jettisoned the burnout RATOs. They came smoking down from the grayness, plummeting into the forest at the end of the runway. When the roar of the engine died away, the smoke from the forest was the only trace of the Antonov.

That was the way Jessup wanted it. The Nepalese authorities might look the other way for an unarmed plane even if it was carrying some mighty funny people or cargo. An unmarked plane armed for close air support was something else.

Jessup walked back to the truck parked at the edge of the airstrip, Gaje following with his Sterling ready for action. As he slogged through the mud, Jessup toted up his assets for dealing with Weng if the man really did start playing games.

They weren't going to be much until the SOBs got out of Tibet. They'd have been a whole bunch better if Captain Thapa hadn't decided to fly off to fight Chinese. At least Thapa was shooting at Chinese who needed shooting at, instead of guarding against Chinese who might not.

LIAM O'TOOLE LIKELY would have agreed with Walker Jessup that Colonel Yao's Chinese needed shooting at. He might have differed, though, with the opinion that the Chinese were nothing for Nile Barrabas and his people to worry about.

In fact he might have wondered if the Fixer was playing with a full deck.

O'Toole shifted position to scan the northern slope with his binoculars. The act drew several bullets. One clipped his heel. Another chewed up rock dust and stung his cheek with enough chips to draw blood.

O'Toole wiped the blood out of a stubble of beard, so filthy it was hard to tell that it was red. He slipped back under cover, movement that drew more fire, fortunately none of it close.

Captain Thapa grinned. "I thought we'd proved they had excellent observation and good marksmanship."

"Well, they might have all lit up joints and stopped caring."

"Yes, and then they will invite us to a feast with roast pork and rice wine."

"What, no dancing girls?

"Have you ever seen the women of the Chinese army? I would pay them *not* to dance for me."

O'Toole gave the Chinese a chance to turn their attention elsewhere and start reloading. Then he and Thapa scrambled fifty feet to the left to settle in behind the Bren gun. Its Tibetan caretakers moved to make room for them.

One Tibetan moved a little too far. Four hundred yards downhill a squad of Chinese was alert for targets. Their rifles put five rounds into the Tibetan, spattering the machine-gun position with his blood and brains.

O'Toole cursed and started cleaning the Bren. From the ridge a Tibetan howled in rage and anguish. Another one beside O'Toole shrugged.

"Ngan's brother, Captain," he said. "How long we wait?"

"As long as the colonel wants us to."

"Maybe he wait too long."

Maybe he would, O'Toole realized. Nile Barrabas wouldn't make an unsound tactical decision, but he might stretch the nerves of the Tibetans too far.

"McPherson always say we fight Chinese in place where we go away when they come too strong. Colonel think same?"

"Colonel Barrabas has fought the Chinese and many other people," O'Toole reassured the Tibetan. "He's forgotten more about war than the rest of us ever knew."

O'Toole could read skepticism on the Tibetan's dirty brown face. Well, he didn't blame the man. A stand-up firefight against the Chinese usually meant a death sentence for the guerrillas.

It helped that they'd beaten off Yao's first attack, in spite of heavy casualties. It didn't help that here were Yao's men all over again, big as life, just about as feisty, and nearly as well-armed.

The redhead shook his head in response to his train of thought. *I get the feeling that Yao's cut from the same cloth as the Colonel. Too bad. I might get a few more poems written if Nile was unique.*

Downhill something went *prrffump* irritably. A smoke trail climbed the mountain with a flaming *something* at its end. O'Toole stared for two heartbeats, then yelled, "Hit the dirt!"

Everyone who didn't understand his words understood the gesture. The whole outpost was as flat as the rocks would let them when the RPG round burst just below them.

"Shit!"

An armor-pierced, shaped-charge warhead would have expended itself harmlessly that far from the men. Instead fragments screamed uphill, seeking exposed flesh and sometimes finding it.

Now it wasn't only fragments screaming. Without moving, O'Toole saw a Tibetan clawing at a bloody hole where one eye had been, another fingering the stump of an ear.

Not moving seemed like a really good idea right now. He'd heard rumors of a fragmentation warhead for the Chinese RPGs, and they made sense. Why lug around something that heavy just to wait until the other guys turned up with tanks? Why not waste a few of the other side's grunts while you waited for big game?

His instincts to counterattack aroused, O'Toole jumped up, aiming the Bren as he did. The moment the sights came on the distant figures wrestling with the RPG, he let fly. He kept the trigger down until the Bren clicked empty, and by some miracle the gun stayed under control.

The Chinese shot back, but the Tibetans who'd seen O'Toole's defiance of odds were also firing. The air above the slope acquired a high lead content, with men going down on both sides.

One by one the Tibetans dropped under cover to reload. Most of them stayed there. The Chinese went on shooting well after they ran out of easy targets. One of their officers finally screamed orders loud enough for O'Toole to hear, and they ceased fire.

O'Toole looked around. From RPG and small arms put together, the Tibetans had one dead and five wounded. Three of the wounded were still in shape to fight.

Could be better, could be worse, he summed up for himself. At least you convinced the lads the RPG isn't an invincible superweapon, and you didn't get your arse shot off in the process.

COMMANDER YAO STOPPED cursing the RPG crew, even under his breath. They were dead and his curses could not affect them. Besides, he had other and more important things to do.

"Casualty report, and quickly, you turtles' bastards!"

The answers came as quickly as Yao could have wished. They were not entirely encouraging. Shooting downhill, the Tibetans had an advantage. A bullet that fell short could ricochet the rest of the distance to a human target. From the number of casualties, quite a few must have done so. Either that, or the madman with the machine gun had aimed very well indeed.

Certainly Yao now had ten casualties out of his forty men. The three RPGs were all operational, but he now had no spare crews for them. He had also lost his deputy platoon leader, down with a bullet in the thigh.

The urge to curse the dead RPG crew filled Yao's throat until he had to swallow it like bile. If the fools had not been so eager to shoot the moment they saw the machine gun, four rounds might have struck instead of just one. It was hard to believe that the machine gun, the imperialists, or the Tibetans' fighting spirit could have survived such an attack.

Well, one failure did not mean defeat. How to contrive success the next time? Yao studied the hillside, searching for any piece of ground that might conceal his men as they closed.

He found none closer than a hundred yards from the enemy. At that range they could pound his men with thrown stones, never mind rifles! Beyond that, the hill was as bare of cover as a barracks floor.

Yao had many times lectured on the need to take and hold the high ground. Now he was getting his own lecture back, with bullets thrown in! How to make sure his defeat was not the subject for the lectures of the imperialist advisers?

Simple. He was exposed, but Zhou was not. Could Zhou find a safe place from which his 75 mm could reach over the crest? With its fire directed by Yao, the recoilless could break Yao's opponents before turning to the Tibetans facing it.

No doubt the Tibetans would counterattack. But as they launched their attack, Yao would be smashing their rearguard. Caught between two Chinese forces on an open slope, the Tibetans and their advisers would be crushed swiftly. Their only refuge would be the ruby cave itself!

If the rubies were out of the cave, Yao rather hoped the enemy would flee into it. Then he would have the pleasure of the simplest and swiftest end to the fight.

He would seal the cave and let the enemy die gasping in the dark.

THE BACK-BLAST of a recoilless rifle was unmistakable. The burst of its shell was less distinctive, but a lot more worrying to Nile Barrabas. Twisting his neck, he saw the smoke rising from beyond the ridge.,

Beside him, Lee Hatton didn't take her eyes from the binoculars. "Colonel, I don't know what kind of recoilless that is. But for anything the Chinese have, they've brought it in a lot closer than they need to."

"If we're the target, maybe," Barrabas said. "But I don't think we are. Look." He tapped her on the shoulder. She looked.

"Damn." By now, Lee's swearing attracted no comment. Her hair might have attracted some, if any of the SOBs had been a hairdresser. It looked like dark auburn barbed wire, and any urge Barrabas might have felt to run his hands through it wouldn't have got to first base.

Barrabas pulled out his radio. "Chief to Brave Four, Chief to Brave Four. This is an authorization to move at your discretion. Acknowledge."

"Acknowledging, Chief, but I don't think that's too cool," O'Toole's voice came through the static. "That recoilless is being spotted by the boys downhill. We gotta do something about them before we can move safely. Any bright ideas? We've already done a good bit with the Bren."

"We'll send a second Bren with Billy Two and Dapon." O'Toole wouldn't need an explanations of basic small-unit tactics: one Bren keeping the Chinese observers' heads down while the other moved.

"What if they can't rejoin you, Colonel. Your turn's going to come, and the bloody Bren won't do much good if it's swanning—"

"Mr. O'Toole, I take your point. I'm also giving the orders. Over." He called up Billy Two's position.

"Chief to Brave Two. You and your brother move to Brave Four with all your war gear."

Again, no need to explain that he thought that the main Chinese pressure now was on O'Toole.

"On the way, Chief. My brother is carrying his sword as well as a rifle."

"Tell him that I hope it will drink well," Barrabas said. He didn't know what Khampas believed about their swords, but he figured Billy's affinity would provide the inspiration to translate it.

ZHOU SAW THE SMOKE from the 75 mm shellbursts swirling up from beyond the ridge. Every explosion came over the radio as a particularly fierce burst of static. After every shellburst came Colonel Yao's corrections. Sometimes they also came through as wordless static. Yao always put his message through sooner or later, but the poor reception was slowing the rate of fire.

While it merely annoyed Zhou, it might do worse to the column's chances of victory. The recoilless was an easy target if the enemy counterattacked. Its back-blast stood out like a neon sign on top of a Shanghai theater. It could be moved, but not quickly, and not without breaking off the bombardment of the ridge position.

Zhou ordered half a platoon to get ready to move uphill, using a ravine speckled with man-size boulders and child-size bushes. The machine gun would suppress any Tibetans at the head of the ravine until the fighters were well up it. Then they could reach the head of the gully and the flank of the ridge position in a rush. Move the machine gun up to join them, and the rush might end the battle.

The recoilless flung another shell over the ridge. This time Yao's voice was clear and so happy he sounded drunk.

"Right in the middle of the barbarians! More, more! Hit them before they can run!"

Zhou signaled "Rapid fire" to the recoilless crew without canceling the orders he'd already given. In theory, the two sides of the Tibetan position should be attacked together. But theories had killed too many good fighters. Zhou was not about to add to the number.

The recoilless fired six rounds before Yao ordered the cease fire. Zhou waited for word to either open fire or launch a general attack. He hoped it would be word to attack. The assault fighters had already vanished into the gully, and the recoilless was down to five rounds.

That news came just as Zhou noticed a Fong Shou-2 circling over the ridge. The markings were so faded that he couldn't make them out. It did seem to have loads ready for air-dropping slung under either wing.

Zhou moved toward the radio. If the pilot was no wiser than his superiors, he probably wouldn't recognize an infantry battle when he flew over it. Then one of those machine guns might have an easy target.

The pilot hadn't given the orders that kept the air force from cutting the imperialists' supply lines. An innocent man didn't deserve to die.

Zhou pulled the radio toward him and tried to read the plane's number as it vanished behind the ridge.

20

Liam O'Toole had lost most of his clothes and some of his hearing to enemy shells quite a few times. This was the first time it had happened at high altitude. He felt his acclimatization deserting him, his limbs moving as if he was hauling concrete blocks, his head throbbing.

So it wasn't surprising that he didn't recognize the An-2 when it first swept low over the ridge. His first thought was that the Chinese had finally whistled up some air support. Then as the plane began to bank, O'Toole finally recognized the mismatched left aileron.

O'Toole let out an Irish war cry, followed by an Osage war whoop, and slammed a magazine of tracers into his Bren. He rolled to the left, ignoring a spatter of bullets, until he had the cover of three dead Tibetans.

One of them wasn't quite dead, but groaning with head and chest wounds. O'Toole murmured things that he hoped were soothing, because they were all in Gaelic. He murmured them until the An-2 had finished turning and was coming back toward the ridge.

Then a callused, smoke-blackened finger tightened on the Bren trigger and a stream of tracers lashed the Chinese RPG gunners.

"FIGHTERS, against the machine gun!" Yao shouted. To reach those out of hearing, he leaped to his feet. His rifle on full automatic, he hurled bullets toward the enemy machine gun.

All around him the surviving fighters joined him. Even the RPG crews slung their weapons and used their rifles.

"Use the Type Ks, you drinkers of tiger piss!"

The RPG fighters' rifles fell silent. So did the enemy machine gun. The RPG gunners shouldered their weapons and took position in a ragged line, their loaders beside them. Yao shouted to a couple of fighters too close to the backblast for safety. They moved, as the drone of the Fong Shou's engine swelled behind Yao.

The first Type Ks were slamming into the launchers when the tearing-canvas sound of a multibarreled machine gun tore at Yao's ears.

The bullets missed Yao. He felt the hot breath of bullet-torn air above him, but nothing more. He saw dust and rock chips fly into the air. The dust could not hide the fighters falling like puppets with their strings cut.

All three RPG crews went down, and so did a dozen other fighters. Yao stared at the still bodies and the writhing ones, listened to the groans and the screams, saw the spreading blood and the gaping chests and bellies. He wished desperately that there was some quotation from Mao Tse-Tung that would make all this go away, bring his men to their feet, send them forward against an enemy already half-defeated.

That had not changed. The enemy was still half-defeated. What had changed was Yao's men. In a single burst from the sky, they had lost the power to turn half a defeat into a whole one.

Yao hardly noticed the plane climbing to bank over the ridge, where it would be safest from Chinese fire. He only began screaming curses when he saw the Tibetans rise from among their dead comrades and charge downhill.

LIAM O'TOOLE JUMPED a foot when Billy Two and Ragpa Dapon loomed up behind him. Billy carried a second Bren gun and a bandolier of magazines, as well as his own FAL. The Khampas had his Type 68 slung and carried his sword.

A wiry figure popped up from behind a boulder, binoculars in hand. Captain Thapa studied the Chinese positions, then shouted.

"Captain O'Toole! They are shaken. Their rocket launchers are destroyed. If we press them now, they will be finished!"

O'Toole hesitated for all of ten seconds. He realized later that was about nine seconds too long if he wanted to argue with a Gurkha determined to attack.

"Ayo Gurkhali!"

Thapa plunged down the slope. His legs turned into a blur as they carried him over the roughest patches as smoothly as if he'd been on skis. O'Toole felt strength flowing back into his own legs.

"Follow me!"

Billy Two and the Khampa didn't need an order. They were already on their way downhill when O'Toole stepped off. The sight of the four leaders charging pulled even wounded Tibetans to their feet.

Leaving their dead behind, the defenders of the north face charged downhill at the Chinese.

COLONEL YAO DID NOT USE the word "impossible." He knew that his senses were not deceiving him. What he saw and heard was really happening.

Now it was his men who were half-defeated, with the enemy pressing home their advantage. Yao slammed a fresh magazine into his rifle and noted as he shot it off that it was his last.

A few meters ahead lay three of his men, two wounded, one dead. That was all he saw; he did not dare ask himself where the rest might be. He could only run forward and try to strip the dead man's bandolier from his body.

The enemy came downhill on the run, firing as they moved. In the lead moved two men with machine guns, one of them a giant, another giant with a sword that somehow looked familiar, and a Gurkha.

The Gurkha reached Yao first. Yao aimed at the little man, as one of the wounded Chinese staggered to his feet. The Gurkha's *kukri* swung high, then fell like an axe. The wounded Chinese's head leaped from his shoulders, falling to the left as the spouting body toppled to the right.

Yao realized he had a clear shot at the Gurkha. Before he could fire, he sensed one of the giants approaching. He swung back to face the man, flinched at a demonic war cry and fired wildly.

A moment later it seemed that a mountain fell on Yao's right shoulder. His rifle swung drunkenly in his left hand, then clattered to the ground. Yao went to his knees, tried to stop himself from falling with his right arm and discovered that it was as weak as rice straw.

He rolled as he fell, now seeing clearly the man who had struck him. It was the Khampa interpreter. It occurred to Yao that there should be some appropriate curse for such a traitor. That was his last thought before his blood-starved brain stopped working.

The Khampa's sword had cut through Yao's shoulder blade and ribs, deep into the chest cavity. As his blood poured out of severed arteries, his brain came to the end of its career. A moment later his heart twitched for the last time.

Yao's blank eyes never saw the Tibetans charge past him, some dripping blood, all following their leaders like a pack of wolves. Yao's surviving soldiers fled like deer, but the wolves were faster.

"CHIEF TO BRAVE FOUR! Come in, Brave Four! O'Toole, get on the horn or you'd better join the Chinese!"

Barrabas broke off trying to raise Liam O'Toole as the Chinese attack burst out of the ravine. They were exposed targets but moving fast and shooting.

The Tibetans shot back, but most of them were short of ammunition. Barrabas heard them cursing as they ran dry and fumbled for their last few magazines. Some shouted war cries. A grenade exploded among them, and curses turned into screams. Barrabas slapped his cheek where a fragment gouged it and did some cursing of his own.

Come on, Alex. Move your ass and your Bren and get shooting.

Barrabas had spotted the Chinese flank attack early on. He'd waited until the last moment to move Alex and the remaining Bren gun. Maybe he'd waited too long.

The Bren stuttered. Half a dozen Chinese fell as if their legs had been kicked out from under them. One of them was holding a grenade with the pin out. It blew, finishing the job Alex began.

Whoomp! With his usual fondness for bringing the heaviest firepower to bear on any problem, Claude Hayes had unlimbered the Carl Gustav. He couldn't reach the Chinese recoilless, but he and his Tibetan loader did a nice job of fumigating the ravine. Any Chinese on the wrong end of those 84 mm rounds would have to rethink their retirement plans.

The Bren and the Carl Gustav took care of the middle of the Chinese attack and any reinforcements. The soldiers in the rear took cover. The Tibetan riflemen made sure they stayed that way.

The Chinese in front got in too close for Alex, Claude or the Tibetans. Nile Barrabas's training told him there couldn't be more than half a dozen. His guts told him there were fifty. Not for the first time, he understood clearly how people came to believe in the "human wave" attack.

The Chinese were too close to use their own fragmentation grenades. Two concussion grenades burst on either side of the SOBs position. Claude Hayes's loader screamed clapping both hands to blast-ruptured ears. The blast also slammed Lee Hatton against a boulder, hard enough to knock her rifle from her hands.

She was reaching for it when three Chinese dropped into her position. She promptly dove under the thrust of the first bayonet and speared a hand into the soldier's groin. He screamed even louder than the Tibetan loader and toppled back against the man behind him.

The third Chinese fired wildly. The muzzle-blast of his rifle must have nearly deafened Lee. It didn't keep her from wheeling, crushing his ribs with a leaping side-kick and crushing his larynx with a *shoto* strike.

By the time the second Chinese got up from under his writhing comrade, both Barrabas and Claude Hayes had their pistols out. Barrabas put the crippled man out of his misery, while Claude shot the second in the head. The 9 mm slug hit the Chinese in the nose, making both the entry and the exit wounds spectacularly messy.

How the other two Chinese of the point squad wound up dead, Barrabas never found out. He had just time to note that they were dead when the An-2 came over the ridge. It was already banking into a turn that would take it down over the Chinese in the open.

That pretty much told Barrabas what had happened on the other side of the ridge. At least what had happened to the Chinese. He *still* didn't know diddlysquat about what was going on with Liam, Billy, Captain Thapa, the Khampa and any Tibetans still on their feet.

Some Chinese must have had the smarts to shut down the recoilless as soon as the plane turned out to be hostile. They didn't have time for the next steps—moving it or at least dispersing the ammo.

Barrabas figured that the secondary explosion when Arthur Gordon salvoed his rockets was the recoilless ammo. He couldn't think what else could make such a fireworks display.

When the smoke cleared away, Barrabas saw the recoilless barrel rolling downhill, muzzle almost at right angles to the breech. He saw a few bits and pieces that might have been the tripod. He saw even more bits and pieces that had certainly been the crew. He didn't see any living, or at least fighting, Chinese.

The next five minutes trimmed Chinese strength even more. Arthur made two firing passes with the minigun, breaking up any visible groups of Chinese. That must have used up the last of his ammo, because on the third pass he jettisoned both the minigun and the rocket pod.

Through his binoculars, Barrabas saw them hit, then roll after the fleeing Chinese. The soldiers must have thought the jettisoned pods were delayed-action bombs, because some of them ran faster, others threw themselves down.

As the Antonov banked at the end of the last run, a mob of ragged figures burst into sight from the right. Barrabas studied them through his binoculars and decided that his lost sheep had turned up.

At least he didn't think the Chinese would have two giants, one with a sword, and a Gurkha with a *kukri* leading them.

He switched the radio to the day's air-to-ground frequency.

"Chief to Gull Alpha. Thanks a bunch. Land where you think it's safe. We'll conform to your movements."

"Gull Alpha to Chief. If that mob on the plateau is your people, tell them to police up any stray Chinese. I've got some loiter time still on the cabin tank. Then I can bring her down and we can haul ass."

"That's a roger, Gull Alpha. See you around. Chief out."

Barrabas slung the radio and stood up—cautiously, in case there were any live Chinese still in range. After thirty seconds of silence, he signaled the other SOBs and Tsering to gather around.

"Tsering, send a squad up to guard the wounded on the ridge and leave another squad with the wounded here. Bring the rest of your people with you. We'll leave all the weapons except our rifles, and the plane brings more medicine for your wounded. I wish we could do more."

Tsering spread his hands. "No man who has killed so many Chinese should feel shame. In three years, McPherson did not lead us to bring death to half so many."

"Thanks. Lee, line up your bearers with the rubies. Alex, you're on point. Claude, turn the Carl Gustav over to the Tibetans and be the rearguard. Let's move, people. We're still in a race, even if we've scrubbed Colonel Yao."

THE RAIN WAS GROWING steadily heavier. Dr. Gonpo had just stepped back under the awning at the hotel entrance when a taxi lurched around the corner. It was an elderly yellow Fiat, and if it had been human, Gonpo would have said its spleen and kidneys troubled it.

Bajbir stepped up beside Gonpo as the taxi pulled to a stop just short of a puddle. He studied the Fiat's driver, then stepped around the puddle and opened the back door.

The shotgun blast from the back seat nearly cut Bajbir in two. He still had the strength to stay on his feet long enough to draw his H&K P-7 and fire one wild shot. The right rear window shattered, but the Chinese who leaped out of the back seat was unharmed.

So was the one who popped out of the trunk like a demon in a temple play. He sprang behind Gonpo, kicking him in the back to hurl him forward against the taxi. The front door opened, and driver and back seat man grabbed the doctor. He bit one of the hands grabbing him, drawing a gasp without loosening the iron grip.

The third man was covering the hotel entrance with a drawn pistol. The doorman was gaping, holding his empty hands out well in front of him. The puddle had turned red from Bajbir's blood.

That was all Gonpo saw before the door slammed behind him. The taxi shot away from the hotel, with Gonpo draped over the front passenger seat.

"Very good, Dr. Gonpo," a voice said in fluent English. "My name is Lo, and I work for Dr. Weng. My orders are not to harm you unless you resist. We do not wish you dead, only as a hostage until the rubies are delivered."

That wasn't as surprising or as terrifying as it would have been a few months ago. Perhaps emanations from the soul of Walker Jessup and the SOBs gave anyone around them knowledge of the way of violence?

It needed no teaching by Walker Jessup for Gonpo to know that he was in some danger of passing to his next incarnation. The fate awaited all men, of course, and Gonpo knew that fearing the moment of it was futile. Also, no man could be sure how what he had done in one incarnation would affect his next. Men were poor judges of their own virtues and vices, although Gonpo knew he had done his best to do no harm when he could not do good.

What annoyed him a trifle was the fate of Walker Jessup. The fat man was still nearly a hundred pounds short of restoring all the balance he would need. At a hundred kilos—two hundred twenty pounds—he might have a long life.

No, Gonpo corrected himself, not unless he gave up his present profession. It was not one that allowed a man to hope for long life. But another hundred pounds of fat gone, and Walker Jessup's body would no longer be his own worst enemy.

COMMANDER ZHOU did not know what had happened to Yao and his vanguard. He feared the worst after losing radio contact, but had little time to taste that fear.

The traitor Fong Shou came over the ridge, and his men died swiftly. They died torn to shreds by direct hits, pulped by concussion, riddled by fragments of rocket or rock, torn and gutted by bullets. They died like fish in a net, and the only fear that Zhou felt was that he would live to remember seeing them die.

It was almost a relief to feel the bullets tear into him. One tore a thigh, bringing him to his knees. A second opened his belly. He lay down until the pain struck, twisting him so that he rolled on his side.

As he rolled, he saw his fallen rifle, almost within reach. It took more pain than he had imagined anyone could suffer before he reached and gripped it. As he did, the pain seemed to ease.

With a new clarity of mind, Zhou saw that he was dead but not finally defeated. The enemy would be within range sooner or later. Perhaps the traitor Fong Shou would actually land where the Type 68 could hit it. A few bullets into some vital spots, and the imperialists and the rubies would be stranded. Doubtless they would flee on foot, but the PLA would be at their heels.

Zhou was almost grateful for the wounds and their pain. The wounds would make him look dead or at least helpless unless someone came very close. The pain would not drive him into unconsciousness. Rather, it would keep him awake and vengeful until he could do his last duty as a fighter of the People's Liberation Army.

BARRABAS AND THE RUBIES reached the level ground just as the Antonov touched down. The prop wash blew dust over several bloody Chinese corpses.

Barrabas couldn't see any surviving Chinese close by. A few live ones were running off downhill, looking ready to run all the way to Lhasa. Some of the Tibetans who'd come round the mountain with Liam and Captain Thapa dashed off to make sure the Chinese didn't change their minds.

Barrabas turned to Tsering, as Lee Hatton came up with the rubies and Claude Hayes came up with the rearguard. The Tibetan was covered with dust and spotted with blood, none of it his own, and his clothes looked ready to stand by themselves. He was still grinning.

"This is where we return to our separate paths, is it not?" Tsering said.

"So it must be. If I and my people do not fly the rubies to safety, the Chinese may yet take them back. Then all the bloodshed would be wasted."

"Much blood has been Chinese. We not forget that. But you speak truth. We walk farther toward free Tibet if rubies are safe from Chinese."

At least the Peking Chinese, Barrabas thought. And if the Triads wind up selling the rubies to the mainland, I am not even going to waste time strangling Walker Jessup. Dr. Weng and company are going to be explaining matters to their ancestors.

Randall Gordon popped the Antonov's cabin door and started tossing out bundles marked with a red cross. "Soon's we dump the fuel tank, we can take off, Nile," he shouted. "Your people ready?"

"Damned straight." Barrabas turned back to the Tibetan. "We have brought more medicine for your wounded. In time, we may be able to fly out some of those who are no longer fit to fight. If that happens, the plane will also bring in more ammunition and weapons. McPherson's death does not mean that those who sent him will turn against you."

"I never think so, Colonel Barrabas. Some of my men maybe, at first. Even they stop when they see you and your people fight. What you want us to do, you do first."

Brrrpppp!

Bursts from two automatic weapons made both men spin as if they'd been hit. Dust sprayed up around the Antonov's tail wheel. It also sprayed up around a Chinese corpse. The corpse jerked and twisted in the dust cloud until the magazine of Alex Nanos's Bren ran dry.

"What the—?" Barrabas yelled.

"Sorry, Colonel. One of those Chinese was playing possum. I forgot to order our Tibetans to police up all the stray weapons. But I got on to him before he hit the plane." Nanos put down the Bren and pressed a hand to his thigh. "Don't think I was so lucky, though."

Lee Hatton signaled her beaters to start loading the rubies and headed for Nanos. A minute later she turned away from examining his thigh.

"Just a through-and-through flesh wound. Better plan to fight sitting down for a couple weeks, Alex." She popped open her first-aid kit and laid out antiseptics and dressings.

The empty inflatable fuel tank hit the ground with a slimy noise. It looked like something out of a horror movie. Barrabas slung his FAL.

"May you live to see your land free, Tsering."

"May you live to return for the last fights, Colonel. We have many more Chinese to kill. Enough to share with men like you and Ragpa Dapon." Tsering's grin nearly reached his ears. "I honor Dapon. When I gamble with him, he use his own dice now."

"Hey, Nile," Randall shouted. "If you want a blessing, ring up the Pope. If you want a lift, get your ass in gear."

Nanos gave the Gordons the finger, but tottered to his feet, using the Bren as a cane. A last box of ammunition clattered on the dusty ground as Lee Hatton swung herself into the plane.

In two minutes the last of the SOBs was aboard. In five minutes more, the only sign of the plane was the wheel ruts in the dust and a fading drone beyond the mountains.

Some of the dust settled on Company Commander Zhou's staring eyes and the out-flung hand still gripping the rifle. More settled on the blood, already drying quickly in the thin dry air. At this altitude, there were no flies to feed on the blood.

21

The Gordons' living room would have been roomy for the people in it—without the tension. The tension was a tangible presence, taking up as much space as all the SOBs put together. The grim look on Captain Thapa's face didn't help things.

Walker Jessup popped the top on a bottle of Indian beer and swung his feet down off the coffee table. The floor creaked as he stood up. Barrabas noted that Jessup didn't need a grip on the back of the sofa to stand. Maybe it just wasn't imagination that the Fixer wasn't so fat anymore.

"Okay, people. Not much point in arguing over who pissed in the beer. Not much point in arguing over what we're going to do about it, either."

"And what's that?" Barrabas decided that maybe a rhetorical question would dispel some of the tension.

"We go and get Dr. Gonpo back, then turn the rubies over to the Tibetans."

"I'll be damned," Nanos said.

"Your leg bothering you, friend?" Jessup asked.

Barrabas decided to be quiet until he could pull his foot out of his mouth. He'd expected Jessup to honor the agreement with Weng, even though the man had started screwing around. That had been misjudging the Fixer—so big a misjudgment that Barrabas hoped Jessup would quietly ignore it.

But Barrabas wondered about himself. Am I just tired from too much Tibet, or am I really slipping in judging people? If it's the second, maybe it's time to pull the pin.

Maybe. But after you and your people are done taking some Triad names.

"No argument," Billy Two said. "But in the words of that great native American, Tonto, 'What mean *we*, white man?'"

"Gather round, oh ye of little faith," Jessup said, pulling a map out of his bush jacket. The man definitely *had* lost weight, Barrabas realized. The bush jacket actually hung in places, instead of being filled like the skin of a grape.

Jessup finished his beer, used the empty to weight down the map, then reached for another. It fell off the table. Jessup picked it up and popped the top.

The beer didn't spray all over Jessup. It sprayed all over Ganparsing Thapa. His grim expression broke into a ghost of his usual grin. He wiped his face with a grimy handkerchief and looked at Jessup.

"And what, oh one pubic hair, are we to do once we have gathered around, besides be drowned in beer?"

"Not a bad way to go," Jessup said. "But what we're really going to do is plan how to kick some Triad ass." He ran a thick finger along the middle of the map.

"I got the stuff on about a dozen houses in this area. Weng's holed up in this one here. I couldn't get a plan without risking a leak, but that's not critical. Thing is, it's got real stiff slopes above and below and only one road down.

"Now, Colonel, I don't want to tell you how to run a mission. But to this ol' Texas boy, it looks like somebody could drop on top of the ridge and rappel down. Somebody else blocks the road, and the Chinese aren't going anywhere you don't want them to go."

"How many?" That was Claude Hayes.

"Maybe as many as thirty."

"Poor bastards. They're outnumbered.," Nanos said.

Barrabas tried not to grin like an idiot. He could feel it himself, in the others, and even in Jessup—relief bubbling like a a pot of hot coffee. Relief that the rubies wouldn't have to go to the Chinese Mafia to be turned into drugs or bribes or hitmen's fees. Relief that a particularly dirty mission might finally wind up just about as clean as this business allowed.

"I think you may have something, Fixer," Barrabas said. "In military circles, it might even be called a good idea. I'll let you know when you're cleared to get praised."

"A man could just shit, waiting for your praise," Jessup said. "But how about we knock off the grab-ass and start planning? Weng's message was that either he gets the rubies, or we start getting pieces of Dr. Gonpo inside of twenty-four hours."

The high spirits deflated like a popped balloon. Just walking in on Weng's men and cleaning them out wouldn't even be a healthy workout for the SOBs. Keeping Gonpo alive in the process made the whole thing slightly more complicated—like about six or seven times more.

"Okay," Barrabas said. "For starters, what's on top of that ridge above the villa . . . ?"

THE CAMOUFLAGED PARACHUTE popped open above Nile Barrabas. It barely had time to slow him when the ground seemed to leap out of the darkness below. He started to swing left, banged into something that felt like a branch and dropped the last ten feet. A five-point roll broke his fall without breaking anything else.

His chute floated down and snagged on the branch before it fell on top of him. Trying to free it, Barrabas discovered that what he'd taken to be a branch was the ridgepole of an abandoned house. There'd been a village on the ridge until a few years ago, when the villagers' croplands in the valley were washed out by a flood. Most of them moved in with relatives elsewhere or moved to Kathmandu.

Thumps, cracking wood, and muffled curses told Barrabas that the rest of the SOBs were landing more or less safely. From the sky, the drone of the Antonov's throttled-back engine faded into the damp clouds. Another twenty miles, and Arthur Gordon would set the automatic pilot and a fuse, then hit the silk himself.

Fifty miles farther on, the ten pounds of C-4 in the gas tank would blow. The Antonov would come down as a rain of untraceable pieces. Anybody who wanted to figure out what happened to Weng's people would have one more piece that wouldn't fit easily into the puzzle.

By Barrabas's watch it took a minute less than the planned ten for everyone to gather. The team was only dim shapes in the darkness, but Barrabas didn't need to see anything to know what he had with him.

Everybody carried Sterling SMGs with plenty of extra magazines, climbing ropes and a smorgasbord of grenades. Liam, Claude, and Billy carried demolition charges, Lee carried a medical kit. Everyone wore black coveralls and black camouflage cream—even Claude, whose skin could get a little shiny when he worked up a good sweat.

They were all going to do that tonight. They might not be up against professionals of their own quality. They were up against twenty to thirty people who knew one end of a gun from another, fighting on their own ground. Surprise wouldn't hurt, but it might not be enough.

Barrabas keyed a single code word on his radio. That would let Alex Nanos know the airdrop was in place. Unable to drop with his wounded leg, Alex was guarding the front door to the villa with two Gurkhas and the Ashok Leyland five-tonner.

Barrabas wished he could reach the third party in tonight's mission. But Walker Jessup and Captain Thapa were already inside the villa, if they were on schedule. Barrabas wished even more devoutly that they weren't even on the mission, but there'd been no stopping either man.

Jessup had led off. "Seems to me I recall an old teacher of mine. Man said, 'The best diversion is to make the other guy think he's got it in the bag.' So how about I go in and give them the rubies, just as you people are coming down to kick ass?"

"Yes," Thapa said. "If I go with Mr. Jessup, it will also give us another chance of rescuing the doctor. No, please, I do not wish to spend time arguing.

"I do not know what my fate is. I know that it is not to sit by and let others pay the price of my mistakes. Dr. Gonpo has eaten the salt of my battle comrades. That is nearly the same as his eating mine."

When a Gurkha argued along those lines, Barrabas knew, you could kill him but you couldn't argue with him. So Thapa and Walker Jessup were both walking into the dragon's den, hoping that things wouldn't turn into a flame-breathing contest!

Time for the good dragons to get a move on. Barrabas slipped downhill past the last house to the edge of the cliff. Far below, the lights of the villa shone yellow and steady.

"No sign of an alert," he whispered. "Billy, use that tree for the belay. We want to be fast, not fancy."

"On the way, Colonel."

THE HALLWAY TO THE LEFT, Captain Thapa decided, must lead toward the rear of the house. If you followed it far enough, it would probably lead to a back door. Would that back door be close to the big propane tank that supplied heat and cooking for the house?

Thapa turned his attention back to Walker Jessup, Dr. Weng and the four teak chests sitting on the rug between them. It would not do to miss any of the subtleties passing between the Fixer and the Chinese. It would be even more foolish to be seen studying the house. The four Chinese in the room stood in pairs, two behind Weng, two behind the visitors. All looked ready to kill at a word from Weng, and Weng looked ready to give that word at the slightest suspicion.

It was, Thapa realized, a time for him to look harmless. Assuming that a Gurkha ever could look harmless, that is.

With an effort, Thapa kept from reassuring himself by touching the hilt of his *kukri*.

Dr. Weng raised his voice to what would in a Westerner have been an angry shout.

"You are expecting me to believe that you came here armed and with a bodyguard, without planning any treachery?"

Jessup sighed. It may not have been an act. If it was an act, it was a good one. His entire bulk seemed to quiver in sympathy with the sigh.

"Dr. Weng, I don't want to insult you. But you're trying to scare me by pretending to be a damned fool. You can't bring it off. I know too much about you.

"You're not so dumb you don't know that other people are after the rubies. You think I'm so dumb I don't know it, too? Or that I wouldn't make sure they weren't hijacked on the way to you? Come on, Doctor!

"Besides, if I am planning something—well, I used to be good, and Captain Thapa still is. But neither of us is Superman. We can't try anything with four guns aimed at us.

"It's got to be outside people. Every minute we stand here jawing, they might be getting closer and closer. Do you feel their breath on your neck? Do you feel them crawling through your guards?" Jessup hunched his shoulders in mock terror until Weng finally laughed.

"Very well, Mr. Jessup. I take your point. We have an experienced jewel assayer with us to test the rubies. I do not question your colleagues' competence, but they might not be wholly disinterested.

"Once the rubies pass the appropriate tests, we have no further business in Nepal. Our operation will only continue for the purpose of guarding Dr. Gonpo until the rubies are safely in Hong Kong. After that, I give you my word of honor that he will be released unharmed."

Thapa found it harder than ever not to touch his *kukri*. He also found more respect for Jessup, who didn't even blink.

Rescuing Gonpo was the most important mission tonight. Keeping the rubies out of the Triads' hands could be sacrificed, if necessary. Everyone hoped it wouldn't be necessary. The victory would lack style.

Thapa remembered his company commander in Borneo, a British captain who wore his battle dress to rags during a month in the jungle. Coming out, he found himself invited to the High Commissioner's office with nothing but that battle dress to wear. So he washed and ironed those rags, and walked into the office as if he was wearing full-dress uniform.

Ganparsing Thapa wanted to end his career on a similar note.

THE LAST OF THE TEAM came off the rope onto the patch of level ground behind the villa. It was Billy Two who coiled up the end of the rope and hid it under a rhododendron. The camouflaged rope should be invisible to anyone not looking for it.

Besides, anyone looking for it was going to have other things on his mind in about two minutes.

Barrabas covered the last ten feet to the villa wall in cat-footed silence. The Chinese hadn't completely ignored security. Two strands of barbed wire ran around the top of the nine-foot brick wall.

Barrabas pulled out a pair of insulated wire cutters, while Nanos and Billy Two knelt, making a step of their shoulders. Barrabas climbed onto that step and went to work.

The cutters *kllnnkkked* three times, and the wires fell clear. Barrabas dropped the cutters, flexed his knees and soared up onto the top of the wall.

Looking over the wall, he looked directly into the eyes of a Nepalese girl. She was lying on the muddy ground, bare from the waist down, while one of the Triad gunmen applied himself to her. The girl's eyes widened and she started to scream.

This lack of attention to him offended her partner. He slapped her hard, then cursed, and only then thought to look up. By then Barrabas had launched himself down the inside of the wall. He landed, wheeled and kicked the gunman in the head so hard he not only popped out of the girl but rolled over three times before he stopped. His head was at an impossible angle to his shoulders.

A shadow loomed—a second gunman ready for his share of the fun. The girl jumped up, screamed and ran for her life without bothering about dressing. The scream seemed to paralyze the second man. Barrabas used the time to unlimber his Sterling, toss a flash-bang grenade and turn his head so the grenade wouldn't destroy his night vision.

Lee Hatton came soaring over the wall, landed rolling and came up as the grenade went off. Her Sterling joined Barrabas's in chopping the second gunman apart.

Billy Two and Claude followed, using a knotted rope with a hook at one end. As they landed, Lee and Barrabas heaved more flash-bangs through nearby windows. Bits of glass peppered Barrabas, making him feel as if his exposed skin had been massaged with a rose bush.

Liam O'Toole joined the rest of the team with the climbing rope coiled around his waist. As he landed, all the lights in the villa went out.

"That's no way to treat guests," Billy said. "Colonel, let's find our host and complain."

22

Dr. Gonpo heard the scream, then the SMG fire and the explosions. He quickly looked around his narrow room for something to use as a weapon.

He found nothing. Perhaps one of the mercenaries could have turned something like the window shade into a deadly weapon. Gonpo thought of the story of the man in the Bible, who slew a whole army with the jawbone of a donkey.

Well, he was no mercenary, but he did have his own jawbone to use as a weapon. That was probably the best he had, in fact. He could use it as long as he was not drugged or stunned. If he seemed dangerous, he would doubtless be made so at once. Otherwise he might keep the use of his wits and limbs until the Chinese were ready to leave for Hong Kong.

He thumped on the door, loud enough to be heard over the sudden din of voices all over the villa.

"Ha! Guards! Let me out!" He could not hide his excitement. He could only hope it would be taken for fear of capture by his enemies.

"Silence! You are to stay there!"

Gonpo switched to Chinese. "Be reasonable. I know those are your orders. But the situation has changed. Do you know who is attacking?"

"Nobody is attacking!"

Gonpo's laugh was no act. "Then you must be holding a fine party. I suggest you put the guns away before everyone gets so drunk that they shoot each other."

Two more explosions interrupted the doctor and prevented any reply from outside. Falling plaster and running feet followed the explosions. Someone was shouting either orders or warnings.

"Fools!" Gonpo shouted. "Someone is attacking, and they might be my enemies as much as yours. Do you think Peking or Taipei will leave me alive any more than they will you? Do you think it is honorable to leave me here to die like a trapped rat when you have the rubies? Your ancestors will not smile on you nor your superiors if you live!"

Most men among the Triads probably had no more honor than a rat. If the guards were among the other kind, the appeal might be worth the effort.

Another appeal made even more sense. "Remember also that I am a doctor."

"Tibetan witchery!" one guard growled.

"You sound like a Communist," Gonpo replied, with a laugh. This silenced the guard. The doctor raised his voice.

"I have a Western medical degree as well. I am the only doctor around if you are wounded."

"Why should you treat us?" the other guard asked.

"I have sworn the Hippocratic oath, and other oaths in my Tibetan training. I have a conscience. Finally, you may be wounded by those who would kill me. Only a fool will not heal those who protect him."

The two guards were talking now, so quietly that all Gonpo could understand was that they were both uneasy. He shouted now, with real impatience.

"Curse you! Do you want to die of a belly wound or have your manhood shot off because you locked up the only doctor around!"

Another explosion. The next sound after that was a key turning in the lock. The door opened. One of the guards motioned with his pistol.

"Come with us. We will take you to Dr. Weng."

Gonpo nearly had to run to keep up with his guards. The gunfire and explosions now seemed to come from all around the villa, and the hallway was filling with smoke.

As he hurried around a corner, an unpleasant thought struck Gonpo. Suppose he was actually telling the truth about the attackers coming to kill him as well as the Triad men?

WALKER JESSUP had noted down the four Triad men as professionals. He now revised the note to "Not quite professional enough." They were getting jumpier as the uproar of the SOBs' assault on the villa swelled. They had their guns drawn—three Colt Pythons and a Browning Hi-Power—but not aimed. They also didn't keep their eyes on Jessup and Captain Thapa.

That might give Jessup and the Gurkha a useful few seconds if Weng finally made up his mind to order them killed. Jessup wasn't planning on doing anything, unless and until that order came.

He wasn't even sure it would come. Maybe Weng had been in firefights thirty years ago, but not lately. Any fighter's reflexes he'd ever had were long since gone. That could make him dangerously unpredictable when he moved, but slow his moving in the first place.

"Dr. Weng," Jessup said, as if trying to gentle a nervous horse. "I think we ought to talk."

"About what?" The voice was shrill, tight, nervous.

"About releasing Dr. Gonpo right now." He lightly kicked one of the teak chests. The assayer, bent over another one, glared at him.

"You have the rubies. That's as far as our agreement went. It said nothing about hostages. If you don't release Dr. Gonpo immediately, I can't be responsible for the consequences.

"Consequences!" Weng practically shrieked, leaving the impression he was definitely out of his depth. "Consequences?" he repeated, more quietly. "You are bringing the consequences on me, on your friend the doctor and on yourself. Or rather, your friends are bringing them."

Jessup opened his mouth to say "Why do you say 'my friends'?" then saw Weng's hand rise in a signal to his gunmen.

No point to any more delaying tactics, Jessup decided. Time to move.

He stepped forward until he was in the line of fire between the gunmen and Weng, then bent, lifted a chest of rubies and hurled it. Walker Jessup's muscles still had something left over from propelling his fat from place to place. They now propelled two hundred pounds of teak, metal and rubies squarely into Dr. Weng's face before the Triad chief could blink. He crashed to the floor, his ruined head mercifully hidden under the chest.

The chest was still in midair as Thapa moved. He ducked under the sandalwood table and flipped it like a playing card. It crashed into one gunman, taking him down to the floor with it. Jessup stamped hard on the man's wrist, grabbed his Colt Python and emptied it into a second gunman.

That left three Triad men in the room, two gunmen and the assayer. The assayer tried to get out the front door without opening it. The effort flattened him on the mat and left the gunmen with clear shots at Jessup and Thapa.

"*Ayo Gurkhali!*" Thapa screamed.

Kukris aren't thrown. The captain's blade still couldn't have reached its target faster if it had been. The Browning Hi-Power fired three times, but twice it was a dead hand on the trigger. The dead hand of a Triad gunman with his skull split down to his upper jaw at a single blow.

Whatever the fourth gunman's plans, they changed abruptly as all the lights went out. Jessup had a better idea of the man's location than the man had of his. He swung wide, came in on the man's gun-hand side and grabbed. Hands like steel pincers closed on the man's arm. He didn't have a chance to use his martial-arts training before he found himself in midair. Jessup was half as fast but twice as heavy and considerably stronger, lending the Chinese a terminal velocity enough to break both his neck and his skull when he hit the wall.

"Thanks, Captain," Jessup said.

The answer was slow in coming, and strained and breathless when it did.

"You're welcome, I'm sure."

"You hit?"

"Probably. I had better... sit down, I think."

"Here."

Jessup handed the Gurkha the last gunman's Python and started rummaging around the floor for another weapon for himself. His fingers finally touched the Hi-Power.

"Good. We'd better sit tight. I don't know if this is Nile's line of retreat. I'm damn sure it's the way Alex and his people are coming in."

The firefight seemed to be in a lull now, but the smoke was rolling thicker every minute from the back of the house.

IF THE SOBS CURSED when the lights went out, they did it quietly. Their opponents weren't so disciplined. Four of them died silently for not being silent, two at Barrabas's own hands. Lee Hatton broke the neck of a third, and Billy Two stabbed the last one.

"Spread out, people," Barrabas whispered. Hand signals, although quieter, were useless in the sudden darkness.

It was the old dilemma of room-to-room fighting. Concentrate, know where your friends are and be an easy target for grenades; or spread out, be less vulnerable to the enemy and risk fatal cases of mistaken identity.

Right now spreading out had one more virtue than usual. It cast a wider net for Dr. Gonpo.

"Only a fool fights in a burning house," was a line Nile Barrabas remembered seeing in a *Star Trek* rerun. Not bad as far as it went, but it didn't go far enough. Sometime fighting in a burning house was the only way to get somebody out of it.

Low voices sounded ahead. Barrabas rammed the folding stock of his Sterling against his torso and drew his combat knife. At this range, one-handed fire with an SMC was accurate enough, even with the Sterling, and he didn't want to risk a noise by changing magazines.

The Chinese came on. Barrabas heard the faint click of someone pulling the pin on a flash-bang, then a fainter grunt as the grenade flew.

"Fire in the hole!"

The shout and the grenade explosion came almost together. The blast lit up eight Chinese crossing the room at the end of the hall. All had pistols, and two carried H&K MP-5K SMGs.

The H&Ks hosed the air above the SOBs with 9 mm slugs. The return fire was more accurate. One H&K spun out of its owner's hands as Barrabas smashed both gun and gunner with his last eight rounds. Three other Chinese went down as darkness returned. The others fired wildly, not hitting each other, but not hitting the rapidly-closing SOBs, either.

Barrabas rammed his knife up under one Chinese throat, to hear a gurgling scream and a sulfurous expletive from Lee Hatton.

"Niles, that was my finger you nearly took off!"

"Sorry 'bout that."

As the Chinese thumped to the floor, Barrabas realized that he'd fallen into a patch of orange flames. The grenade had ignited the floor mats.

The radio beeped three times, then twice, then three times again. Alex Nanos's signal—his truck and Gurkhas were in position to block the enemy's escape. If all else failed, the SOBs would have Triad hostages to hold for Gonpo's return.

The radio beeped again—four times, then two. *That* was the signal for reinforcements. *Friendly* reinforcements, joining Nanos and his Gurkhas.

Barrabas looked at the team. They looked back. Barrabas hoped he didn't look as confused as he felt. Who the hell else could be joining in on their side?

They could ask for explanations later. Right now there were still too many live Triad men. Probably enough to go around, even if six new Gurkhas *had* shown up.

Barrabas slipped a fresh magazine into his Sterling, then waved it to give the move-out signal.

CAPTAIN THAPA had been hit. In fact he was dying. Walker Jessup bent over the Gurkha, so busy trying to seal a sucking chest wound that he barely saw two figures loom above him.

The first one was already raising a gun when Jessup looked up. Then the figure behind him swung something large and black. It struck the first man's head, and he toppled on top of the Gurkha.

Jessup stared. "Dr. Gonpo, I presume?"

"Yes. I talked my guards into letting me out. I said the Triad men might need a doctor. One of the guards left to find friends. The other was so alert for dangers coming from elsewhere that he did not notice when I picked up this table."

Gonpo dropped the ebony side table and knelt beside Thapa. As he did, the captain's eyes drifted shut and his breathing stopped.

"You did your best, Mr. Jessup. In your next incarnation you may well be a doctor."

"And you may be a mercenary in your next. But let's not be in too much of a hurry to find out."

In the following moment, though, Jessup was sure he was on his way to his next incarnation. A powerful flashlight lighted up the room, and the sound of tramping feet almost drowned out the crackling flames from the back of the house.

Then a familiar voice called, "Cavalry's here, Fixer."

"Okay, Alex. We've got the doctor, and—"

A babble of excited Tibetan made Jessup look up. Six solid-looking Orientals stood behind Nanos, all with drawn pistols. One of the pistols was an antique broomstick Mauser, but all six looked as if they could use what they were holding.

"Tibetan Youth Congress," Nanos said with a wave of his hand. "Gonpo had made contact without telling us. These guys showed up about ten minutes after I did. They were going to make Weng-baby an offer he couldn't refuse. I persuaded them it would be a better offer it we made it together."

Jessup felt light-headed with relief. That saved him the trouble of searching for somebody to guard the rubies while they were being transferred. The TYC men looked ready to eat Triad squads for breakfast, without even a side dish of *chapattis*. Jessup felt relieved all over again at the thought of never having to eat a *chapatti* again.

Nanos was now looking around. "Christ, Fixer. Remind me never to stand between you and a good dinner."

Nanos's flashlight revealed the man Gonpo had killed. It was Mr. Lo, a professional who'd taken his eyes off a non-professional for just a bit too long.

Jessup was savoring the thought of his first steak, when a giant boot seemed to kick the house. Orange light poured into the room and a wave of heat followed. The concussion squeezed Jessup until he felt his skull, ears, ribs and everything else would collapse. All around him, walls, ceiling, doors, floor matting and furniture seemed to jump into the air. At the top of their jump they rearranged themselves and came down every which way. Jessup found himself on the floor, covered with plaster dust and with Dr. Gonpo's ebony table poking a splintered leg into his ringing ear.

He rolled away from it and lurched to his feet, ignoring the pain in his ears and other places. "The team! They're back there, closer to the blast, and the house is going to go up like a haystack!"

Everyone except Nanos looked blankly at him. Then the light dawned on Gonpo. He spoke quickly to the TYC people. They looked down at the rubies.

"For God's sake, move it!" Jessup bellowed. "Those rubies can't die of smoke inhalation!"

"Calm down, Mr. Jessup," Gonpo said. "These men have a plan of the house. We'll have your friends out in—a jiffy?"

A "jiffy" in this case wasn't more than five minutes. None of the SOBs except Lee Hatton were conscious, and she had a greenstick fracture of one ankle. She also had the spirit to glare at Nanos through a mask of camouflage cream, plaster dust and smoke.

"What are you doing on your feet?"

"Physician, heal thyself," Nanos said with a grin. A sharper wave of heat from the rear of the house ended the banter. The Tibetans started hauling the prostrate SOBs out to the truck.

Jessup picked up the chest of rubies he'd thrown at Weng. Hardened as he was, he didn't care to look at the man's face. The Triad chief would be hard to identify even if the fire left anything of his corpse.

Another five minutes and they were rolling downhill toward the highway. Riding shotgun in the rear while Gonpo tended the wounded, Jessup looked back at the burning house.

It was a mass of flames now, and anyone still inside wasn't going to get out. Anyone who did get out would probably be too busy evading the Nepalese police to worry about who'd snatched the rubies.

And after that? Weng had a good many rivals in the Triads who wouldn't think that his demise called for vengeance. He'd also had enough would-be successors in his own organization so that the infighting would tie it up for quite a while.

Jessup had a feeling that he and the SOBs could spend their money in peace. Almost as important, he could warn his people in Hong Kong—and once he'd caught up on good dinners, he could even send them traveling expenses for relocating.

NILE BARRABAS WOKE UP to a splitting headache and the thought that he'd been captured by the Triads. The face bending over him was not Caucasian.

Then he recognized Dr. Gonpo. He also recognized his bed as a blanket in the back of a truck going downhill fast. It swayed, lurched and ground its gears with an occasional screech that did nothing for Barrabas's headache.

"Where's Lee?"

"Dr. Hatton has a broken ankle. In fact all of you were hurt when the gas tank exploded. Mr. Nanos is now the fittest of you."

"Gas tank?" Something about that didn't quite track.

"Yep," came Walker Jessup's voice. "The mighty SOBs smote the enemy as usual, then damned near got wasted by an exploding propane tank." Jessup went on to summarize the action in the same cheerful tone.

Barrabas must have muttered something impolite, because the doctor grinned.

"I would suggest you relax for a day or two, Colonel. A falling beam struck you on the head. The opposite side of the head from where you were wounded, fortunately. Your doctor's advice is still to lie down and take it easy."

Since he really didn't feel like doing anything else, Barrabas decided to follow doctor's orders. By the time the truck hit the level, he realized he actually *wanted* to relax.

It wasn't the way he usually felt this soon after a mission, with the bodies not even cold yet. It usually took him days, even weeks, to come down—although the more help from Erika, the less time.

This mission was different. Somehow they'd waltzed through every possible obstacle and come out with the job done. Not just done, but done so that the rubies were in the right hands.

Barrabas knew that he and his people were the best, but skill wasn't quite enough to account for this victory. They'd been lucky. Which wasn't that bad, come to think of it—hadn't Napoleon always asked if a man was lucky, before promoting him to general?

Maybe the SOBs were all going to be generals someday.

And that would be one hell of an army.

A secret consortium conspires to terrorize the world

DON PENDLETON's
MACK BOLAN

Tightrope

One by one, the top officials of international intelligence agencies are murdered, spearheading a new wave of terrorist atrocities throughout Western Europe. Mack Bolan's mission is compromised from the start. The line between good and evil is a tightrope no man should walk. Unless that man is the Executioner.

Out of the ruins of civilization emerges...

DEATHLANDS

The Deathlands saga—edge-of-the-seat adventure not to be missed!

TAKE 'EM NOW

FOLDING SUNGLASSES FROM GOLD EAGLE

Mean up your act with these tough, street-smart shades. Practical, too, because they fold 3 times into a handy, zip-up polyurethane pouch that fits neatly into your pocket. Rugged metal frame. Scratch-resistant acrylic lenses. Best of all, they can be yours for only $6.99.

MAIL YOUR ORDER TODAY.

Send your name, address, and zip code, along with a check or money order for just $6.99 + .75¢ for postage and handling (for a total of $7.74) payable to Gold Eagle Reader Service. (New York and Iowa residents please add applicable sales tax.)

Remove from pouch...

unfold once...

unfold twice...

and they're ready to wear.

GOLD EAGLE

Gold Eagle Reader Service
901 Fuhrmann Blvd.
P.O. Box 1396
Buffalo, N.Y. 14240-1396

GES-1A

Offer not available in Canada.